TEMPT

TERRAWAY
BOOK FOUR

MARY E. TWOMEY

MARY E. TWOMEY, LLC

TEMPT

BOOK FOUR IN THE TERRAWAY SERIES

By

Mary E. Twomey

COPYRIGHT

DEDICATION

For my brother, Brian.

I don't totally understand how you haven't murdered me yet after all the times I've annoyed you by accident (just kidding. We all know it's on purpose), but kudos to you for the epic self-control.

You keep me organized, quell my insanity, and listen when I rant and babble. Or at least you pretend to listen, which is sometimes just as good.

Not many girls are lucky enough to have their brother turn out to be one of their best friends.

Also, I totally stole your brown jersey, and you're never getting it back. Bwa-ha-ha!

1

BIG, SCARY MAN

I was grateful when Finn let companionable silence fall between us to replace our bickering. When I looked back in the direction we'd come, I couldn't even see the circle we'd entered in on anymore. Everything was brown, brown and more brown, so landmarks that stood out were hard to come by. The famine had struck Silo in the usual way, scorching the *buhay* shoots so there was precious little for the inhabitants to eat. It also hit them in the form of a drought, drying up most of their rivers and leaving the landscape dull, dusty and bare.

The suns were setting, and we'd put a fair amount of distance between us and the entrance to Silo. With my backpack stuffed with half a dozen *baga* roots Finn had unearthed not two minutes after he'd ported us to Terraway, I was ready to get a piece of the sagrado stone to its rightful place. If we dropped a portion of the rock into the well in the main city, the suns wouldn't burn so hot, and nature would have a chance to right itself again.

I'd left my two Reapers, my brother, Ezra and a bucket full of baggage Topside when I'd made the decision to go rogue and start the mission to deliver the sagrado stone without the crew. I needed space, and they needed to breathe. A whole new world of breathing room seemed like the right move. Since Captain Finn didn't care much for rules or waiting around while the nations continued to wither away, I brought him along to be my guide.

We passed a few houses here and there that looked like thatched-roof barns, but mostly we kept to the woods, so we would go unnoticed as long as we could. The trees were dry with only crusty, shriveled leaves that held on for dear life. I looked around at the nothing all around us. There weren't even any houses anymore after we'd travelled by those first few. Just brown, dusty mountains spread out, and cavernous craters where I'm guessing water used to be. It was like walking by mini Grand Canyons everywhere.

Maybe I could deliver the stone before the guys even noticed I was gone. Hopefully they'd think I wanted to be alone at home, and would go back to the mansion for a few days. Von wouldn't look for me; he'd slung some mud in a nasty fight I knew he wouldn't take back. And Mason? Well, we were actually doing alright, but hopefully he'd have his hands full cleaning out Bev's trailer with Ollie.

Bev. I couldn't go there in my mind. Her lost expression

when we'd found her in a state of shock in her trailer haunted me, and made me feel like a shell of who I was supposed to be. I'd always firmly believed in taking care of your family, but I was left spinning on this one. I needed more information, but knew I couldn't handle another word, be it apology or raging blame.

"It's quiet," Finn observed, scratching his gills. He'd discarded his scarf and dress clothes into his backpack, changing into the black soldier-wear that was common in Terraway. He'd chuckled at me when I'd turned around so I didn't have to see him half naked. He craned his neck to look down at me while we walked. "You're quiet."

"You're tall," I offered back my own observation. "Talk away, if that helps you."

"You want to tell me why you ran from your Pullers and Ezra?"

"Nope." A bat flew overhead, its wonky flight path catching my eye.

Finn studied me curiously. The growing darkness was starting to fall around us as the horizon began to swallow up the setting suns. "You're usually annoyingly chatty."

I shrugged in response, unsure how to tell him to butt out, other than the obvious obnoxious way. "I guess it's your turn for that now. Don't know what to tell you. It's your lucky day. No annoying chatter from October. Santa Claus does exist."

Finn squinted in warning at the bat that came back to circle us. The creature responded to his silent threat, flying in the opposite direction. "Sylvia. She sends out bats to be her eyes and ears."

"Did she make us?"

Finn quirked his eyebrow at me. "She's probably looking for her own people, to make sure they're not lurking where they shouldn't. This is Kabayo's land, and there've been too many skirmishes for them to be welcome here right now."

"Should we be out in the open like this? Is she going to report back to Ezra that she saw us?"

"Her spy doesn't know to look for us, I'm guessing, so there's nothing to report. You're awfully skittish about Ezra finding out. Tell me, what did you do that you're running from him?"

"Nothing at all." My eyes tracked the bat who flew off into the distance. "How worried do we need to be about monsters trying to ambush us?" I voiced the concern I'd felt for a while.

Finn quickened our pace. It took two of my steps to equal one of his long strides. "Not very. The Ekeks and Manas will be expecting you to travel in an entourage. Smart thinking to keep it just us."

"I daresay that sounded almost like a compliment."

"Well, it almost was." Though Finn had been a little harsh, in control and kind of sleazy when we were Topside, he seemed to be taking his post seriously. It was just the two of us on this mission, and we were both determined not to screw it up.

Finn cleared his throat next to me. "I don't spend much time Topside. What do you think of our world so far?"

My thumbs looped in the straps on my backpack, pulling them like suspenders. "I don't think I can judge it just yet. The only times I've been in Terraway have been with the suns all wonky and the government trying to abduct me. So, I guess that's a thumb's down so far."

He chuckled at my assessment. "Silo has been suffering a drought for too many years. Occasionally the morning brings enough dew to keep things going, but they've had to borrow more water from us than they can ever afford to pay back."

"Yikes. How do they buy it? Like, do you all have the same currency? I can't tell how separate the different countries are."

"Gold is the universal language we all speak. Goods, women. The usual."

"Not for nothing, but don't let anyone trade me for a cup of water." I shivered, despite the heat that made my clothes cling to my skin. "Let's just do this and get back home."

"You wouldn't be attractive to Tikbalangs." Then to clarify, he added, "Horse on top, person on the bottom half. And I can promise you that my king has all the women he could ever possibly need." His eyes flickered to me. "Though if you ever meet King Banak, you may want to keep your head down. He has a thing for mouthy women with legs."

My eyebrows furrowed as I tried to keep Finn's pace. "Your king likes women who have legs and mouths? I can't imagine I'd be all that rare if he's casting that wide a net."

"You forget the women in Dagat are Mermaids. No legs. And they know better than to talk back. Something tells me you wouldn't fall in line so easily. Everyone has a healthy fear of our king because he has me to carry out his dirty work. They all know I'm bewitched to carry out his will," he said bitterly. King Banak wanted Finn to watch me to make sure I was performing up to par, which was why he'd been Topside in the first place.

Finn informed me that he had also been instructed to keep an eye on me to make sure I wasn't some giant walking danger. I'd kind of accidentally murdered off an entire species – taking Goblins clear off the map in a single terrifying blow. I couldn't really blame this Banak guy for wanting me observed. "No, we don't get many mouthy ones anymore in Dagat. They know better than to cross me."

"Because you're a big, scary man?" I teased with half a grin.

"Oh, *kendi*. I love when you toy with me in that sexy, coy way you do. It'll make your fear that much sweeter when you see me in my element and off Ezra's leash. I bet you're a beauty when you're terrified."

"You know, I think you try to sound sleazy out of habit. I don't think you really care all that much about hooking anyone, least of all me. But it's nice of you to pretend, I guess."

Finn quirked an eyebrow at me, confused that I wasn't shirking away from his fat mouth. "Nice? I think that's the first time I've been called that. Perhaps I should be offended."

"Oh, sweetie. My nickname was Jailbait. I treated men in a prison for a paycheck. If I cared about intimidation tactics or sex jokes, I wouldn't have a leg to stand on. Fire away. I really don't care. If you need to be big and scary, I'll play along once the stone's delivered. Until then, I've got too much on my mind to pretend I'm afraid of you."

Finn looked down at me as if I was the strangest animal. "I don't know what to say to that."

"Well, that's good. I'm not really paying attention anyway."

Finn let out a loud, guttural laugh that looked so foreign on him, it confused us both. We walked along the forest's edge toward the village in the distance with decidedly less tension between us. I kept looking over my shoulder to make sure my Reapers hadn't found us. They were probably still on regular earth and hadn't even noticed I'd split.

Finn followed my gaze back toward the direction where we'd entered. "They're not here yet. We've got a decent head start," Finn informed me. "You're running from them, aren't you? That can't be good. Ezra's got a mean streak he doesn't often use, but it's there."

"He's preoccupied. And I don't much care if Ezra's mad at me, no more than he cares when I'm pissed at him. But yeah, I'm running. Needed a break. Having two Reapers is intense. Going from living alone to sharing my house with two grown men who don't know how to wash a dish? It's not the easiest thing for me to adjust to."

"It's more than that. You're not stupid enough to defy Ezra over dirty dishes."

I tilted my head up at him. "Do you care why? I thought you wanted the stone delivered. This is the quickest way. I'm not doing any reaping down here, so I don't need them to do any pulling. They could use some time off from the job." *And I am the job*, I reminded myself of Von's harsh parting words.

"Fine by me. Just know that I'm not Duwende. I can't pull from you, so if you see a dead body that might have a lick of human in it, stay away."

"Roger that. I only need you as a guide. If I had a map, I could've done this on my own just fine."

"You say that now. Wait until we get nearer to the town."

My shoulders sank. "Awesome. What are we about to get into?"

"It's nothing I can't handle."

2

CAMPING WITH FINN

We walked for twenty more minutes until the dark engulfed us, threatening our steps as our feet became harder to see. "We should set up camp. There's no use ambling through the night."

"Don't you have the light-up hands, like Lang?" I asked.

"I do, but that's a dead giveaway that we're here, and I think it's best we make it through Silo unseen, if possible. Besides, it's a three-day hike to the main well. We have to sleep sometime. Might as well be with the rest of the country. Let's go further into the woods. I don't like being so visible on the edge like this the closer we get to civilization."

"You're the boss." I turned into the forest with Finn, but immediately was unsure of my footing. The trees were easy enough to spot, but the knee-high brown crackly bushes and bramble were not. The roots proved problematic and made me trip a few times before Finn reached out and held my hand to steady me and keep us together. I hated when people touched my hands. The thought of all the germs crawling on me gave me the icks, but I tried to keep my cool through it. It was a land of horse people. I guessed hygiene wouldn't be all that accessible on this trip. I breathed through it, hoping my OCD wasn't too noticeable, and dropped his hand three seconds later. "You need help with the tent?" I asked when we reached a small clearing several stones' throws into the woods that Finn seemed pleased with.

He took off his pack and unhooked the two rolls beneath the sack. One was a tent, and the other a blanket, and he shook them both out with a hearty crack. "I've got it. You don't look like you do much camping."

I chuckled lightly. "Are you kidding? Ollie, Allie and I lived in a tent for half a year once. It was a little bigger than this one, though."

"You're kidding. I didn't think Topsiders lived outdoors. You all seem to have homes."

"We were between homes for a while," I said evasively. It seemed a more sophisticated way to say that we'd been homeless. I grabbed one of the tent poles and worked it through the loops while Finn anchored the corners to the ground. I could barely see what I was doing, but somehow we managed to get the thing constructed without bickering.

I crawled inside and laid out the blanket, wishing I

didn't have to share a tent with a grown man who helped acquire women for his king's harem. Finn wasn't my favorite person in the world, but he was a good guide, so I took what I could get. "Okay. It's all set up. Take your shoes off and come on in."

Finn handed me the gear so it would stay in the tent with us. Then he crawled inside, kneeling on my hand and nearly knocking me over as we fought for space in the tent that could really only fit one of us comfortably. "Oof! That's my face," Finn informed me when I felt around in the dark for the zipper to close the tent.

"Sorry. Just lay down. That'll get you out of the way while I close up the tent." I leaned over what I assumed were his legs to secure the bottom flap, but I couldn't quite get it to shut all the way. I stretched further, slipping on my knees and Heimliching myself on his hip as he turned on his side. "Sorry!"

Finn took a chance with his life and slapped me square on the butt. He had the nerve to chuckle at my fist swinging in the dark, swooshing through the air to announce my indignation. "Come lay down, *kendi*. It's been a while since you've slept with only one man."

"Shut up. Let's just get through this, then we never have to see each other again. Be cool, Finn. I'm serious. I've got no problem laying you out."

If it wasn't for the gear, we might've been able to both lay on our backs, but as it was, we had to get cozier than I was happy with. I was nervous as I reclined in Finn's outstretched arms, holding my breath as if I was being dunked underwater. My body was rigid, as if it knew I shouldn't be here. "Relax, little Omen. I know the wrath would come for me if I bedded you against your will. Ezra isn't the pacifist he imagines himself to be. I'm already facing his fury having escaped with you."

"Keep that in mind then, and be a gentleman."

"Yes, ma'am." He was quiet a few minutes while I situated myself in his arms, unsure if it was worse if he spooned me or if we were face to face. I could feel his breath on my nose, and decided to just close my eyes and pray for daylight. "Are you thirsty?" he asked.

The second he mentioned it, my throat was parched. "Sure, but I wouldn't want to drink the water here even if we could find some. If it killed a man-horse guy, I don't think I'd stand much of a chance." I shuddered at the memory of the severed horse's head Kabayo had set on the dining table, green foam crusted at the maw.

Finn chuckled and sat us both up with no effort on my part. "You forget what I am."

"You forget I know nothing about your world or what you are. I know you can breathe underwater and above. I know you're a violent tool who helps imprison women, but that's about it."

"I love that you're not afraid of me." His voice had a note of reverence to it that I didn't understand. "It'll be a sweet sight when you see me in my element. There's something satisfying about watching a fighter cower."

I rolled my eyes and huffed. "Yeah, yeah. You're a badass. Good for you. I'm super scared."

Finn's thick arm wrapped around my back, bracing me so I leaned into him, despite our antagonistic back and forth. He smelled like the faintest bit of sand and ocean, mixed with a light puff of dust and man sweat from walking all day in the hot sun with me. He curled his arm around me so my head rested back against his shoulder. "Drink. My water's always safe." He cupped his free hand and tipped it to my lips, tsking me when I jerked my head an inch to the left out of distrust. "I'm thinking Ezra would have something to say if I let his daughter dehydrate."

A tiny smile brushed my lips at the mention of Ezra being my dad. I knew it couldn't last, but I was enjoying the ride all the same. "You take a sip first, so I know you're not poisoning me."

Finn huffed, but obliged me. My eyes were adjusting to the dark, so I could see the faint outline of his gilled throat constricting as he swallowed a gulp from his own hand. "There. See? Not poison."

"Alright. Thanks." When he tipped his hand to my lips again, I pressed my palms to the back of his hand to angle it like a cup I had some sort of control over. The water felt cool running down my throat, and I was surprised at how thirsty I was. I drank the well in his hand and sucked in more. His palm refilled itself as often as I wished. It was a pretty cool magic trick.

Finn's face was close to mine, and I shivered when he

spoke, his breath tickling my ear. "If you drink much more, you're going to make yourself sick." He pulled his hand away a few inches. "Here. Let me cool you off." With a minimal amount of water, Finn rubbed his hand over my sweaty face, lowering my body temperature and calming me as much as a bath might've.

"Thanks, Finn. That feels amazing."

I thought he would stop there, but he laved water over my arms and hands, too, calming my stress at not being able to wash my hands before bed. His fingers rubbed between mine, washing away the dust of the trail and a lot of my neurosis. "You missing your Duwendes?" he asked politely.

It wasn't in his nature to be kind for no reason, but I played along for the sake of not being antagonistic. "A little. But it's good we're getting some space. Mason needs time to deal with his strength being taken away, and Von needs time to go catch up on all the debauchery he's been missing, thanks to playing the dutiful boy by my side."

"Sounds like you needed a break, too." Finn gently tugged at the rubber band in my hair.

"What're you doing back there, chief?"

"Hold still." Finn was tender as he took my hair out of its messy ponytail. He ran his fingers through the tangles, dampening them and giving me the most luxurious scalp massage ever.

"Are you... Are you washing my hair?"

"Is this your first time bathing?"

"Why are you being nice to me?" I asked without preamble as my eyes closed. My head lolled forward while he washed and massaged the back of my neck. Rivulets of water rolled down my body, cooling me and making my shoulders slump.

"I'm not allowed to be nice?" He took off his dirty shirt, washed his chest, and then picked up my hair, guiding my head back to lean against his firm chest. He draped my hair over his solid shoulder so my auburn curls hung down across his back, cooling us both. I sighed contentedly as his thick fingers started at my forehead and massaged backwards, washing and relaxing as they went. "I've known Mariang a long time. She goes half a day without Danny pulling for her, and she's a wreck. You have two Reapers, so you're used to being at zero every night. I don't want you to fall to pieces before we save Kabayo's people. I need you on your game."

"I didn't peg you as the type to care so much about a country you're not responsible for. I thought your curse forced you to make decisions based on what was best for your king's people, not all of Terraway. What gives?"

Finn was silent a few beats, his voice quiet when he finally spoke. "Kabayo answered first when the call came that you were locked in Geon's prison. He would've gone in after you even if no other countries showed up. I feel like I owe him for those few hours he doubted whether or not I could come." His tone shifted back to his usual antagonism. "And I care a great deal for the state of Terraway. I do what I can for the countries we're not at war with. It keeps relations strong during dark times. It's as much for the benefit of my country as it is for the others. That's not something my king cares much about, but I do. So while he's elbow deep in the harem, I trade in favors. I put a few of my men on a rotation in Kabayo's central city once I learned about the poisoned wells. They're doling out fresh water as often as they can. It's the only thing keeping much of his land alive."

"Mm," I moaned as he tugged on a particularly delicious spot that had me almost drooling. I felt him sucking the water from my hair and my clothes so I wouldn't be uncomfortable. "That's right decent of you. Didn't know you were such a philanthropist."

He scoffed as if the compliment offended him. "It's got nothing to do with that. It's all about public relations. I do favors, I get favors, which benefit Dagat. Some kings don't realize that when they go to war, it affects the rest of the countries eventually in some way. The favors are preemptive help to make sure our land stays strong and my king's rule is secure. No one bothers to go up against King Banak because we're usually the first responders when help is needed. Taking you down here ahead of schedule? It'll get me far with Kabayo. You, too."

I frowned. "Will it look bad on Ezra?"

"If he's smart, he'll yell at me privately, so it looks like he sent me with you. Ezra's always played the politics game well." His hand drifted from my hair down my cheek, stroking the flesh there tenderly. It made my body relax in his arms, which caused alarms to ring in my mind. I'd never been a huge cuddler, but Von and Mason had gone above and beyond to break me of my prickly nature. I sat up and stretched. "You tired enough to sleep without your Reapers?"

"It's how I was doing it every day before I met them. I'm really not as delicate as you're all thinking. Mariang's been at this a lot longer than I have, so she's more worn down from it. I'm fine. I'm always fine."

Finn laid back, looking up at the ceiling of the tent and extending his arm for me to lay on. "Come on, little Omen. Tell me how tough you are. I could use a good bedtime story."

I rolled my eyes at him as I reclined in his arms, snuggling to his side reluctantly. The cooling effect his water had on me gave me a shiver. I studied his gills that were staring me in the face, wondering at the many twisted and stumbled steps I had taken to land myself here with Finn, of all people. His hand lay across his toned and naked stomach as he wound down for the evening with me in his arms.

3

BANAK, BEL, AND FINN'S CURSE

It was the eighth time I'd switched from laying on one side to choosing the other. "Are you usually this restless?" Finn asked, mildly annoyed.

"No. I don't know what my deal is. I'm sorry. I think it's the sleeping on the ground part."

"Sure. That must be it. It couldn't be because you're without your Reapers."

I scoffed. "I'm not four years old. I can sleep without a chaperone, no problem. I just can't seem to..." I tossed again, frustrated that nothing was comfortable, and my mind was racing a mile a minute. For no reason at all, I kept picturing the babies I'd reaped, looking up at me with their tiny, confused eyes as I absorbed their souls into my body.

I'd had innocent little babies' souls floating around in me. I'd reaped teenagers, the elderly, terminal patients, and people who thought they had all the time in the world to choose a better last meal than a carnival hot dog.

I turned onto my other side again.

I can't believe it took him that long to throw out his hands in frustration, but his huff informed me that I was keeping him awake. "I can feel every move you make, you know. Pick a side and close your eyes."

I finally gave up and sat upright, hugging my knees. "I'll go out and keep watch. I can't relax."

"Just admit that Omen work is hard, and that your Reapers serve a purpose."

I scratched a line down my forearm, sighing contentedly at the sting that centered me. "I didn't used to have such a hard time falling asleep. This isn't me." I closed my eyes and burrowed my head into my knees. "No offense, but your world's slowly tearing me up. Reaping babies? That wasn't in the welcome packet when I signed on."

Finn's hand on my arm was gentle, with a steady pressure that told me there wouldn't be a point in fighting him on this. He pulled me slowly down until I was lying on my side facing him. His light green eyes were clear and seemed endless, like his own portable ocean. "It's three days, and I'll take you back home. Three days, and you can sleep in your bed with your guardians." He surprised me when his arm around me started lightly scratching my back. "Until then, I'm your guard, and no offense to your Pullers, but I'm the best there is."

I closed my mouth and chewed on my words, lest they

come out in a tumble of worry. I didn't want to be a Death Omen. I was a healer. I was a nurse. Everything about the job felt counterintuitive, especially now that I had time to examine it all without the constant opiates from my Pullers. When I finally opened my mouth, my whisper boiled it down to the crux of my current dysfunction. "I don't like being death."

Finn mulled over my words, considering them before flat out arguing. "Close your eyes."

"I'm too keyed up for sleep."

"Close your eyes." He waited for my lashes to sweep shut, and then continued in a quiet voice that held a steady strength to it. "Last year, Prince Langgam called me to Sakuna for help. There were too many dead bodies, and he was having a hard time burying them all before they reanimated, mutated into Amalanhigs and made the undead pilgrimage to Sombi." Finn's fingers moved from softly scratching my back to dragging along the tips of my eyelashes. "I buried a fair amount of civilians that week. My men were put to work digging graves because King Geon couldn't be bothered to respect his own people with a proper burial." I sucked in my breath when his full lips placed soft kisses on my closed eyelids. "Trust me, *kendi*. You're not death. You didn't kill the children I had to bury, the babies with their mothers." He brought me closer in his arms so I was flush against him, his cheek on my forehead. "You brought us the chance to live. Terraway hasn't had a golden chance like this in a very long time."

I let that simmer for a few minutes before I spoke. "Finn?"

"Yeah?"

I didn't know how to ask for what I wanted, but knew this might be my only chance. "Can I touch your gills?"

"My gills?" Finn laughed like I'd told a good joke about tap dancing garden gnomes. "Sure. Whatever turns your crank."

"It doesn't turn my crank in the dirty way you're suggesting. I'm a nurse. It's only natural for me to be curious."

Finn lifted my hand and touched my fingers to his neck, stroking downward so I could examine the ridges. They felt like thin skin, and I was afraid to poke too hard. "Whoa! Totally bizarre. If I rub it up instead of down, does it hurt?"

"No," Finn replied, amused. He watched me observe his neck, smirking at my fascination. His eyes catalogued the details of my face as I studied him. "It feels a little like this." He moved his fingers to my arm and brushed the thin hairs upward, giving me the chills. He pulled me closer, using the hand that wrapped beneath me and rested at the base of my spine.

My eyelids were heavy, and despite Finn's usually antagonistic ways, I was actually not too uncomfortable in his arms. "What if I put my hands around your gills so you couldn't get any air through them?" I gently choked him, making sure not to put any pressure into the restraint.

"You forget I breathe through my nose and mouth, too. If you covered all of those, then I'd suffocate, sure. But we can hold our breath upwards of a few hours. The chances of you restraining me that long? Pretty slim."

"I didn't mean *me* choking you. I just meant in general."

"Of course you did." He watched me closely as I turned one of his gills upward so I could see it from every angle. I thought there would be raw skin or openings I could stick my finger through, but it was just skin with tiny slits I couldn't play with. "Are you quite finished inspecting me? I've got plenty more you can examine, Doctor," he said churlishly, bumping his pelvis to mine just to gross me out.

"It's like you want me to punch you. But actually, speaking of that, how does sex work? I mean, the Mermaids don't have legs."

"Mermaids lay eggs and the Mermen fertilize them. Like fish."

"Doesn't seem like a harem's needed for that."

"Banak's a Kataw, like me. He's got legs and all the other necessary equipment for Topsider sex."

"Then why does he have Mermaids in his harem? It makes no sense."

Finn's voice took on a darker note as he played with one of my curls, poking his finger through from the bottom and winding the strands like a telephone cord around his finger. "There's a shell King Banak owns. It was a gift from the Kapre to our people centuries ago, passed down from king to king. Banak has the shell on a necklace that he makes his concubines wear. It gives Mermaids legs, but not ones like yours. Theirs are misshapen, green and scaly. They're useless, too. The Mermaids can't use them for walking. It's only for the king's pleasure."

I shuddered. "Your king is straight up barfalicious."

"It's how things like this are done. You're a child, or you'd understand the ways of the world."

"And you're a useless old man, or you would understand you still have power to change the world when it's broken like it is."

The mood shifted in a breath, and I could feel the tension building, making me nervous. Finn grew cross, holding my wrist and squeezing, his words coming at me through gritted teeth. "What would you have me do? Give up my position in protest? Even if I could, then there would be no one to protect the women."

"Protect them? Is that what you think you're doing?"

"I'm the only one who feeds them. Their husbands can't even do that. Aside from Banak's affections, they're safe in my harem."

"Hello, you're helping them sign away their lives for food."

"You don't know what you're talking about. You run your mouth and expect me to jump. You forget I *can't* disobey the king. Even if I thought the whole thing was foolish and wrong, I couldn't act any differently. I don't have the luxury of a conscience."

My face fell. "Right. I forgot about your curse."

"You're just like the Mermaids with their singing." When I responded only with a confused expression, he explained, "You're trying to bewitch me to do your bidding and go up against Banak. The Mermaids can persuade men with their songs. Only a few have the strength of will to resist them. That's how I got to be King Banak's right hand."

I waited a few beats, hoping the anger flaring in his eyes would cool. "For what it's worth, I'm sorry you got bewitched. I wouldn't want anyone pulling my strings, even if it's for the greater good. I think it sucks Banak uses you like that."

"Banak needs someone he can trust, and he can only get that through the magic of a curse. Banak trusts me with his women, and I won't turn on him just because I don't like the way he does things occasionally. I *can't* turn on him."

"Occasionally?" I looked into his eyes to seek out the real motivation. "What's in it for you? Does he let you use the shell or something?"

"Of course not. Banak doesn't share. I get what I need out of doing what Banak asks. I get to run Dagat. He's so deep in his harem that he doesn't care what I do, what allies I make. He cares if he's satisfied. Like giving candy to a baby to make him shut up." Finn's eyes widened, catching himself in his scandalous confession. "I didn't mean that."

"You're stepping on who knows how many of your own countrymen to further your career."

"I don't do it to make myself greater. I do it to keep our land from going to war over the famine. How many more would die if I didn't keep Dagat from war? Sama's always on the edge of something dark. If it was up to Banak, he'd take Sama's rations and be done with it to shut up his people. We owe Sama nothing because of me." He shifted on his side, his face filled with stubborn pride I wanted to examine more closely. "I'll step on as many Mermaids as it takes to make sure my country doesn't go to war."

I turned away from him on my side, moving the backpack with the sagrado stone to my chest so I could hug it like a teddy bear. "You're disgusting."

"I'm in charge. I'm second only to the king."

"Your mother would be ashamed of you, treating women like that. What if your sister was in the harem? What then?"

"I don't have a sister." He was quiet a few beats before his hand cupped my hip. I don't know why he was being nice to me, or what he expected to happen by trying to soften my indignation. "I don't have family, but I had a Mermaid I'd promised to marry." His voice lowered so that I had to be very still if I wanted to hear him. "Dyesebel had long, red hair that went down to here," he said, marking a line at the base of my spine. "She had a voice that could make even me turn and wait for her commands, but she rarely used her magic to compel people. Bel was too nice, too beautiful, too gentle, and that's how she got swept up in the harem."

"Why didn't you just tell your BFF King Banak that she was already engaged to you? Maybe he would've stepped aside if he knew she was already spoken for."

"You overestimate the generosity of the monarch. Clearly you've been under Ezra's rule for too long. Banak knew my attention was divided, so he took her to teach me a lesson. To let me know that he was in charge. That was just before he cursed me." His thumb stroked the slope of my hip absentmindedly. "I learned my lesson, alright."

"Why the crack would I bring the stone to him, then? What's he done for his people? What a jag. Seriously. I'm sorry, Finn. Banak shouldn't have done that."

Finn's fingers coiled my hair into his fist, slowly pulling my head back to lean against his chest. He was angry, though this time it wasn't at me. "Do it because then the women will have options. They won't have to join his harem. They need food, and the stone can bring that to them."

"Maybe then Bel can leave the harem and go be with you again."

Finn quieted, his voice matter of fact. "Bel died her first week in the harem. Not everyone can take that kind of... Banak killed her a few days after he had his fill of her, just to show me he could take away anything I wanted. That my focus should be his kingdom, and nothing else. He used her to bewitch me an hour before he snapped her neck. She's the one who was used to curse me to obey Banak."

My sharp intake of breath and softened heart were unexpected, but I went with it. "That's awful."

"Banak promised her who knows what if she would make me more loyal to my job. She bewitched me to obey him, and then he killed her so the curse would stick, so she couldn't undo it." He cleared his throat. "That was years ago, though. I hardly ever think about it all."

I don't know at what point my mouth dropped open, but the horror on my face was plain. I finally reached my hand up behind me and rested it on his cheek, stroking the flesh that was starting to grow stubble. "I'll pretend to believe that you don't think about Bel if you need me to."

"I think I might."

"I'm so sorry, Finn."

He forced a chuckle. "Now, don't start all that. I don't want you being nice to me all of a sudden. Half your appeal is that you mouth off without thinking of the consequences." He turned his chin into my hand and kissed my palm.

I longed for my hand sanitizer.

"Well, anything I can do to be more appealing to you. It's what I live for, clearly." I tried to regain some of our back and forth. "No offense, but I can't really picture you with someone who's nice and gentle. Bel sounds light-years out of your league."

He chuckled at this. "That's my girl." He released my

hair and brushed his hand down my body to pull me closer to him, making sure not to touch the backpack that held the sagrado stone. "Who can you picture me with?"

"I dunno. Maybe a hunchbacked gremlin? A hairy troll? A woman who can light a mouthy man on fire if he presses his luck?"

"Oh, little Omen. You are entertaining. We'll see how your mouth fares in my land."

"Goodnight, Finn."

"Goodnight, *kendi*."

4

DREAM GUY

I didn't mean to dream about Philip, but there he was when the field of wildflowers materialized in my dream. I'd been planning some deep, contemplative thought time to process it all while I sat in the grass, but Philip was a welcome distraction, coming up from behind me. "Hello, sweetheart."

I shook my head up at him. "Boy, do you have some explaining to do."

Philip motioned to the patch of lush grass next to me, silently asking for permission to sit. I shrugged, moderately pissed that I was about to get in a fight with my fake boyfriend. "Are you very upset with me?" he asked as he blinked apologetically, brushing his shoulder to mine.

"Only a lot." I thought back to the suggestion my imaginary boyfriend had made that sent me to a carnival to reap to my heart's content just before a terrorist attack wiped out who knows how many civilians. "Why'd you tell me to go to Pemberton Elementary? How'd you know there'd be so many bodies to reap there?"

"How many were you able to reap?"

"I lost count. So many were an inch away from death. We only just made it out before a terrorist's bomb went off. A friggin' bomb! What gives, Philip? Seriously, how did you know? How can you give me insider information like that? And if you knew someone was going to bomb an elementary school carnival, why didn't you stop it?" I pulled my knees up to my chest and rested my arms on them, pissed that Philip was here in my happy escape place.

"How many did you reap?" he repeated.

"I dunno. More than forty, that's for sure. I lost count and almost died. You get that, right? I almost died. If Von and Mason hadn't gotten to me in time and gotten me out... I mean, they could barely keep up! I was in agony for the rest of the day. How could you send me straight into that? Headfirst into danger."

He wrapped his arm around my shoulders, but I shrugged him off. "You're mad at me."

"It's a good thing you're pretty. Of course I'm mad! I was out of my mind with pain. Do you think I enjoy being completely helpless like that? And Mason and Von had a rough time, too. How could you do that to me?"

"I honestly thought you'd tap out after a dozen or so

reapings. I didn't even know it was possible to reap forty in a single day."

"Try less than an hour, and it was more than forty. That's just when I started to lose count. I didn't mean to do that many. I couldn't get out! Every time someone would brush up against me, I'd reap them whether or not I was ready. For some of them, I didn't even have my Pullers with me. It was terrifying!"

Philip was less concerned and more fascinated. "Incredible!"

I was so pissed, I wound up and clocked Philip across his perfect jawline. "You suck! You're an awful imaginary boyfriend. You're not supposed to say 'incredible' when I'm in pain. You're supposed to be there for me, slay dragons and whatnot in my name. You don't send me into the pit, and when I manage to come out alive say, 'Oo! Incredible!'"

Philip rubbed his jaw and summoned the grace to look ashamed. "I'm sorry. You're right. I just had no idea it could be done. What you did? You amaze me."

"How'd you do it? How'd you know to send me there?"

Philip shrugged. "You must've had some subconscious knowledge of the bombing and acted on it. I'm only here because you imagine it so. I only know what you know."

"But I didn't know! And if I did, no way would I have let the guys go into a situation where a bomb was about to go off."

Philip picked me a white daisy, handing it to me as if

that would make up for all the things it would never make up for. "You're beautiful tonight. Where are you?"

"I'm sleeping in the dirt, and I don't care about being beautiful. I'm mad at you."

He leaned in and nibbled on my earlobe, ramping up my anger and somehow morphing it to the brink of breathlessness. "Tell me. I want to picture you there."

"In Silo. Sleeping in the dirt. I'm cuddling the sagrado stone, if that gets you going at all."

He smiled against my neck as he sewed kisses into my skin. "It does. What are you wearing?"

I didn't answer. I knew where this was headed, and I was still angry. "You should go." I carefully extracted myself from his advance. "I mean it. Get out."

Philip shot me an indignant look, put off that I wasn't in the mood to neck after talking about how he sent me to almost die. "If that's what you wish, fine. I'll be missing you, though." He looked around at the lush nature that surrounded us. We were in the middle of miles and miles of fields, filled with every color of flower imaginable. "Your dreams are beautiful." He leaned in and kissed my lips. "The time I spend with you? It's the only time I ever stop. I'm always going, always doing, always working. Only with you do I get beautiful things." His voice lowered to a whisper. "I didn't know about the bombing. How could I? I'm not real. I would never send you off to get hurt like that."

I kissed him again for the words that moved me an inch away from my resentment. Then again for the flower.

Then again for the way he murmured my name under his breath like a prayer. As if I could save him. As if *I* was the beautiful thing he came back time and again to see.

I let go of my grudge, since Philip was imaginary, and with my grudge I cast aside a little of my inhibition as we rolled around in the field together.

5

GOING FOR A RUN ON THE RUN

I awoke to a stiff neck, a heat that was dry and overwhelming, and Finn's hand cupping the underside of my breast. He was still asleep, so I decided against a punch across the face to serve as his human alarm clock. I cleared my throat and shifted against him to wake Finn up.

"Is it morning already?" he murmured, not moving his hand from where it surely did not belong. My makeout with Philip was still wringing through my overstimulated body, and Finn's unintentional fondling didn't help matters.

"Finn?"

"Yeah, *kendi*?"

"You've got about five seconds to move your hand before my fist rearranges your face."

"I've got five seconds, then?" Finn took a chance with

his life and gave my breast a light squeeze. "Go ahead and count nice and slow. Let me enjoy as much as I can. So soft."

Five seconds might've been misleading. I made it to one before I twisted around and socked him across the face. It hurt like punching concrete, but I wouldn't let Finn know he'd gotten me with his thick skull. "You think that's funny, groping me in my sleep?"

"Ow!" He released me and pressed his hand to his cheekbone. "You didn't have to hit me. I didn't mean to do it. It happened while I was sleeping." He opened his mouth wide to make sure nothing cracked. "How do I know you didn't put my hand there just to have a good excuse to pop me one? You that lonely without your Duwendes?"

I never had the patience for being groped. The second my fist launched out again, I knew it was a bad move. Finn was ready this time. He easily deflected my assault with a bat of his hand, grabbing onto my wrist and jerking me down across his torso so my butt stuck up awkwardly. Finn gave my backside a swat, and I think we both knew he was going to get it for that little treat. He thought I would eventually submit, but he didn't know much about me. I twisted in his grip, furious. My knee flew up and out, aiming for his jaw. It was a sweet victory when I made contact with him, forcing him to bite his tongue and clanking his teeth together enough to make his head spin. "You think it's funny to mess with me, fish boy?"

"Okay, that's it!" I wasn't sure how it happened, but Finn had me on the floor of the tent, pinned facedown beneath his hard body in the next breath. He was so much bigger than me, which wouldn't have been a huge problem if I'd been granted a little space to move. The tent kept us confined to short-range assaults, leaving me to thrash around beneath him to no avail.

Finn shoved my head to the ground, trapping it there so he could be sure I was listening. He wanted to make it clear that he was the alpha dog. "Now listen up, *kendi*. I wasn't trying to feel you up."

"Ha!"

"Okay, not at first. I was sleeping. Sorry if I scared you. I know better than to mess with Ezra's daughter. But you better believe that I won't hesitate to tan your sweet little backside if you try to hit me again. I've killed soldiers for far less. Understood?"

I tried my hand at squirming free again, but couldn't gain an inch. "Yeah, fine," I surrendered with a huff. "But next time, we're sleeping head to foot or something. I'm not part of your harem. Remember that little gem and tuck it in your pocket for when you get cold at night."

A rhythmic sound in the far distance reached our ears, causing both of us to stiffen. "Do you hear that?" he asked, still atop me.

"Yeah. What is it?"

The pounding went on a few more beats before Finn

answered with dread. "It's an army. Hurry! Let's pack this up and run."

We went from fighting to working in perfect synchronization. I folded up the blanket and latched it to his pack while he tore down and packaged up the tent. His shirt flew over his head, boots laced, and we were on our feet with our backpacks in place in no more than three minutes. "I can't see anyone coming. Are they invisible or something?"

Finn started off at a brisk trot. "No. It's Sama's army. Hear the steady drumming of the feet? Even my army's not as together as they are. They're coming, kid. We've got to get to the well before they do, or we won't stand a chance."

I shoved a piece of the *baga* root in my mouth and downed a pill from my prescription bottle in my pack. "Faster, then. I can keep up."

Finn eyed the backpack that held the sagrado stone I had cradled in my arms. "I can carry that. It's double bagged, right?"

"Double bagged and wrapped in plastic. I can carry it, but we'll get farther if I can run, which I can't do for long holding this thing."

"I can do it." He took the backpack from my arms as if it was a bomb. It took a few beats, but eventually his internal struggle died down. His legs picked up and ran forward, with me tagging along at his side. The steady drumming of the feet of who knows how many soldiers pounded the earth, driving us to run faster and longer than I would've thought possible. The woods gave way to a mountain on our right, and though we were still far from civilization, we felt exposed, so we picked up our pace.

When we finally came to a roadblock made up of a thick felled tree from our left and a small avalanche from our right, we stopped for a much needed breath. I leaned over, my hands on my knees, and panted as I fought to control my heartrate. Finn shifted the stone so he could shake out his arms, washing the sweat off his face with water from his hands.

We walked around the roadblock, still catching our breath. "How much farther?" I asked as we rounded the fallen tree.

"It's another day's journey, at least. But the closer we get to the city, the more we can travel at night. Sama's army won't stop for sleep. They don't need it. So we can't stop, either."

"You know, I felt bad for voting that Mariang should stay on the surface, but now I don't. No way would she be able to keep up. I feel better knowing that she's safe in her home Topside."

Finn nodded once. "Agreed. You're not bad to travel with, I admit. I thought we'd be doomed if anything chal-lenging came up on our trek, or if you broke a nail or something, but you haven't let me down yet."

"Oh, you and your precious compliments. You sure know how to make a girl blush. Water?" I requested, wishing it didn't come from his hands. We were both filthy from the dust of the road, and from wearing the same clothes two days in a row. How I longed for a shower, and then a really hot scented bath without Von. Though as I thought of this, I realized how much I was actually starting to miss him. Mason, not so much. We'd been through too much crap for me to really lean on him as I would've liked to. But Von had been there before he'd shown his true colors and been a complete jackhole. I remembered how it felt to be cradled in his arms, completely helpless due to my reaping exhaustion, but somehow I still felt safe. Von had been sweet to me, and despite everyone touting what a screw-up he was, he'd taken care of me when I couldn't take care of myself.

Finn let me drink from his hands just enough to wet my mouth. Then he washed my face off, cooling me down. "You ready to pick up the pace again? They're marching and we're running, so we're staying ahead of the army, but I don't want to lose our advantage."

"Fair enough. Give me one more minute of walking, then I'm ready for another run."

"You're keeping up pretty well."

"Thanks. Your legs are super long, so it's a stretch for me to keep your pace. But don't slow down. I'd rather be tired and sore than dead." I wiped some of the water from my chin. "Finn? What's the deal with Sama's army? Why don't they sleep? Is it that Sama drives them so hard they're not allowed to sleep until they reach their destination?"

"No. The soldiers don't require sleep at all. They're

undead. Amalanhigs. They follow Sama's orders blindly. Understand, they're not people anymore. They have no souls and no wills left from when they were alive. All they want is blood, organs and to fulfill Sama's orders."

"But I thought Mason took care of the zombies who migrated to Sombi. How come so many are with Sama? How does he control them?"

Finn chuckled at my simplistic phrasing. "Zombies? You mean the undead? Amalanhigs?"

"Whatever. I don't know all the magical words. We call them zombies."

"Okay, well first off, Mason's been with you for the past few months, so it's anyone's guess how many bodies Sama's bewitched. If Sama's got rations for us, you can believe he's got blood and organ rations for the zombies, keeping them active and loyal. Second, not everyone makes it to Sombi. Some bodies come from farther away, so Sama bewitches them en route and takes them into his army."

"I don't understand what the flip Sama wants with the stone. Why can't he just let me do my thing and let it go? Everyone's dying in Terraway without the stone. What's the point of an army if everyone else is dead?"

"You're forgetting that his whole army's made up of the dead. The more that die, the more bodies he controls." His tone switched to a conversational one as we walked at a brisk pace. "Do you know much about Silo?"

"Just that there's been a drought for a few years, and everyone here looks like Kabayo."

"But that wasn't always the case. There used to be centaurs here, too."

"Centaurs? Like, legit centaurs? Cool. What happened to them?"

"They only come with the rainclouds, so they've been extinct far too long. They're fierce – the original protectors of Silo. All the lore traces back to the centaurs holding the borders and making sure Silo never saw war. Now that the centaurs are gone because of the drought? Silo is wide open. Quite the advantage for Sama, don't you think? You can bet he won't let you bring the stone to Silo without a fight. If the stone gets delivered, then the rain will come. That means the centaurs will come back, and Sama won't stand a chance at taking over Silo."

"Awesome. So we're really racing an army of zombies?" *Bruce Campbell would so know what to do right now.*

"Amalanhigs," Finn corrected me. "If there's a battle that needs fighting, the centaurs are relentless. They come down from the clouds when they're needed. It's why we've only done battle with Silo when there's not a cloud in the sky. And yeah, it's why Sama's no doubt going to do every-thing he can to stop us. I don't know how he figured out we were here. Someone on the council must've talked."

"Wish it was raining right now, then. I don't like the feeling of an army breathing down my neck all the livelong day. I like to think we're helping make things better, but if Sama's marching on Silo anyway because he's chasing us, what chance do they have?"

Finn reached out and brushed the outside of his fingers against mine. "Oh, little Omen. Don't you know? Sometimes all we have is the promise of a chance. We can sit back and do nothing about it, then spend the rest of our days in regret that maybe we could've done something, or we can fight for change." He looked sideways at me. "Something tells me you love the fight, even when the chance comes with a deadly risk."

"Yeah, that sounds like me. And you just like winning." I looked up at his hard expression, taking in his stern jaw and thick lips that were set in a tight line. "Must be hard to obey King Banak when he took advantage and twisted your sense of duty like that. Taking Bel from you? Not cool."

He brushed his fingers against mine again. I couldn't tell if it was by accident or on purpose. "Yes, well, I've moved on. I'm fine."

"I know that 'I'm fine', and I'm sorry you have to fake it. I wish you had a safe place."

He reached out and held onto my hand, like we were close and did things like this all the time. My OCD did its usual flare-up, but I suppressed it. I was a champ at hand-holding now, thanks to Mason and Von. "Sometimes I wish that, too."

I blinked up at him, searching his face for lies. "Are you a safe place?"

Finn lifted my hand to his chest so I could feel his

heartbeat. "You get to decide that. It depends on who you're asking, I guess."

I shook my head slowly. "Not good enough. Be better. If you want better, you have to *be* better." I smirked as Ollie's lessons flowed out of my mouth without me stopping to examine who was really speaking – Ollie or me.

"Are you actually scolding me?" He sounded torn between affronted and amused. "No one scolds me."

"I'm not no one. I'm the girl who's going to smoke you on our next run. You ready, old man?"

"Old man? I'm only a year older than Mason, and he was your boyfriend."

I cringed at the label. "Mason was never my boyfriend. I'm not a fan of that word. We were figuring things out. Don't make it weirder than it was." I stretched out my legs in anticipation of speeding up our journey. "Quit stalling, gray hair. Let's go!"

Finn's grin was wide, his full lips stretching across his face to reveal his perfect teeth and a streak of glee he rarely got. This wasn't being *on the* run; this was going *for a* run, which made a big difference. We weren't being chased; we were doing the chasing, gunning down the well as we tried to outrun each other like children on a race to the swing set. Though the world was a grim place, for a small slice of time we were free from the constraints of it all. We weren't a soldier and a nurse. In the laughter of the moment, we were young.

6

SLAVE GIRL AND HAREM BOY

Finn laughed as I shoved him when he tried to run in front of me to block my path and keep me in second place. "You're cheating!" I cried, though that was about all I could eke out. We'd been running much too long, though neither of us would be the first to admit it. We were equally stubborn, which meant that we were making excellent time.

When the suns finally fell and we couldn't race anymore without fear of tripping, we made our way inland toward the village. The barns were close together and made up a commune of quaint rural buildings grouped in clusters of twenty or so. "It's not long until we reach the main city. If we keep on, we'll make it there in only another half a night or so."

I wanted to groan obnoxiously, but knew that would seriously hurt my street cred. I didn't want to knock us off the equal footing I'd tried so hard to get us on by keeping pace with a soldier. "Sounds good."

"You're such a liar. I can see you're almost ready to fall over. Why won't you just admit it?"

I scoffed. "I could do this all night. I was holding back for your sake. You look a little tired, old timer."

"Tired and hungry," he admitted. "I'm thinking we should see if we can't borrow a couple of the horses to ride the rest of the way."

"Um, that would be great, except I don't know how to ride a horse. And I can't really picture hopping on Kabayo's shoulders."

"No, no. An actual horse," Finn laughed. He'd been doing that a lot around me, and looked surprised each time it happened, as if he wasn't used to enjoying any part of his life. "The horses you have Topside are safest in Terraway. They're well-cared for by the Tikbalangs. Since they share common traits, most horses count themselves grateful to land themselves here in Silo."

"Okay. Just don't let me make some big political statement without knowing it. If I'm not supposed to ride a horse here because they're beloved, don't let me do it. I don't want to embarrass Ezra. He's likely to be pissed enough as it is."

"A little worried about hearing it from dear old dad, are we?" Finn tsked me as if I was a disobedient child, which I guess I was. I mean, I did run away from Ezra without telling him where I was going. "That's alright. Though it might be easier if no one knew who you were. Then Sama's soldiers can't torture it out of anyone."

"That can seriously happen? I don't want that. I couldn't live with myself if more people got hurt because of me."

He jerked his thumb over his shoulder. "Walk behind me. Pretend to be a slave I'm taking through Silo. Slaves aren't allowed to speak without permission, so no one will ask you questions you don't have the answers to."

I shot him a dubious look. "You can guess how I feel about being your slave girl, harem boy."

Finn looked down on me with partially lidded eyes and half a smirk that needed slapping. "Say it again. Say you're my slave girl."

"I'm not your slave girl, Finn."

He faked a shiver. "Just as sexy as I pictured it. Let me bind your hands behind your back."

I grimaced, punching his arm and holding up my fists to deflect his in case he retaliated. "I'll straight up lay you flat out if you don't get ahold of yourself. I'm just a friend you're traveling with. It doesn't need to be more complicated than that."

He put his hand over my fist, lifted it to his mouth and kissed it just to patronize me. "What'd I tell you about punching me? Don't make me take a switch to your sweet little backside."

"I barely chucked your shoulder, you baby. And don't talk about my butt."

"I won't talk about it, but I'll spend the next few minutes thinking about it. Why do you guess I let you run ahead of me those few times? Great view. That's the one thing missing from Dagat – girls who run."

"You're a dirty old man!"

I shoved him, breaking my indignation with a much-needed laugh when he grabbed his side in feigned agony and cried, "Oh, my hip! Take it easy on me; I'm so old!" Then he mussed my hair and permitted me to bump my hip to his to knock him off his path.

After a few beats of silence, Finn sobered marginally. "Seriously though, you don't know this world, and it's best you remain forgettable as long as possible. Sama can't know where you are. Slaves aren't allowed to speak, so that's your best bet."

My shoulders slumped. "I don't like it."

"Do you like getting captured and tortured by an undead army? How expensive is your pride?"

I hung my head. "Oh, fine. But don't make cracks about my body, and don't push me around."

"I won't. You have to walk behind me with your head down. You can't look up at me. No talking at all, or I have to shut you up, and you won't like how I do it."

I chewed on my lower lip, wishing for another way out. "Seriously? I don't want to be your slave, Finn. This is gross. All of this is like, the lowest common denominator." I started raking at the skin on the backs of my hands, scratching deep wells that felt good as they stung. I didn't like someone owning the deed to my life, even if it was all for show. It was a bad show, and I wanted no part of it.

Finn reached out and held my hand, not bothering to wipe his palm off first. "Hey, putting the sagrado stone where it belongs is more important than your pride. Let's get through this, and when we go Topside to take a break, I'll let you boss me around for a day to make up for it." He shivered again with a teasing smile. "Yes, that's definitely happening."

"Quit being gross. I'm psyching myself up here."

Finn stopped when we reached a fence post that wrapped around one of the clusters of barns. He turned to face me, and dropped the backpack with the stone off his shoulder onto the hard ground. Then he cupped my cheeks with his filthy hands, tipping my face to look up at him. My breath caught in my lungs, uncertain if it was safe to exhale my anxiety, or inhale his masculine scent. "It's time to walk behind me now. And remember, no talking, and keep your eyes on the ground. And you should carry the stone. I'm an official. I don't carry bags. That way there's an excuse for me not to bind your hands."

"Yes, Master," I whispered, hating the words.

"That's my girl." Finn kissed both my cheeks and released me to go stand behind him.

"When did we get on terms where you're the guy who kisses my cheeks?"

I expected something sarcastic, but was surprised when he eked out a wary, "I'm not sure myself. Mason and

Von do it all the time. You've just got one of those faces, I guess. I don't have to, if it makes you uncomfortable."

"You don't have to stop," I blurted out. I instantly regretted the words that gave birth to the curved smile he shot me over his shoulder. "I mean, I don't care one way or the other. Whatever keeps us from a fistfight." When he started sniggering, I glared at him. "Shut up about it."

"You want me," he said, strutting like the cocky son-of-a he was.

"Yes, that's exactly right. I've got a thing for arrogant jackfishes who don't have the first clue of how to speak to women."

"I knew it." I don't know why this made us both chuckle, but we shared a smile before work-mode descended on our shoulders, weighting the mood with our sense of duty to get the job done.

I slid the backpack on as I burned with all the things that were wrong in the world. I walked steadily behind Finn, keeping his regal pace as he made his way to the biggest stable in the cluster. Everything smelled like hay and manure. There were flies that swarmed around me, yelling at me that they knew I was filthy. They knew I'd been born in trash, for they sensed their own. I fought against whipping my arms around like a madwoman and kept my head down, letting the flies buzz around me and crawl on my skin when I moved too slowly. The whole thing made me want to scream, but I remembered I wasn't allowed to speak.

Finn knocked on the door, and when the brown half-horse, half-woman answered, she immediately gasped and fell to her knees. "Captain Finn, how can we serve you?"

Finn's voice was grand, but there was always that sliver of cruelty that sharpened his words enough to cut, if one wasn't careful to obey him. "I need horses to ride to the palace. I've got a slave with me, and have to bring her to King Kabayo as a gift from King Banak. I'm supposed to be there before the suns rise, but I'm afraid she's too weak for the journey."

The woman looked past Finn to take a peek at me with her bulging black glassy horse eyes. "Oh my, she's a little thing."

I gritted my teeth and tried to play the part of the weak little girl, slumping my shoulders and letting my squared gait go lax, though everything in me wanted to scratch my arms until they bled. I hated being called both "little" and "thing".

The woman wore dirt-crusted knee-length jean overalls I could tell she made by hand. Her horse head dipped down as she bowed again and again to Finn. Her horse tail swished at the flies that swarmed inside her house and at the entrance of the red barn. "Of course, Captain. We know it's you who sent Dagat soldiers to bring us fresh water. We owe you a great debt for your kindness. You can take whatever you need from my home. My horses would be happy to take you wherever you wish to go."

"Good to hear. I also need a bucket."

She ran back into the house and brought him a large basin that was at least two feet deep and two feet wide. Her big, glassy black eyes were bugged and hopeful as she offered the empty bucket for him. Finn spread out his fingers and shot water down into the steel basin until it was filled, much to the Tikbalang woman's elation. She stammered her thanks, her servitude, and her lasting praise for the Merpeople. "The horses who stay with us are in the back. You're welcome to take your pick. They can find their way back here on their own when you've finished with them. Thank you, Captain. May you live forever on a thousand hills and a thousand oceans with your magnanimous king. The city will hear of your generosity."

"Actually, if you could keep our visit quiet, I'd be grateful. The king wishes for me to travel in secret."

"Oh, of course. Then no one will hear a word of your visit, your grace."

7

ALL THE THINGS WRONG IN THE WORLD

Finn snapped his fingers at me. "Come along, slave."

I obeyed, swallowing my pride and everything Ollie and Allie had instilled in me to ensure that I never went running when a man snapped his fingers. I followed behind Finn, my eyes on the ground and my mouth shut as we walked behind the house to the barren grazing area. The horses munched on hay and a sparse mixture of oats and corn, which, judging from their slow, uninterested chewing, they didn't like. The dust was everywhere, and so were the flies. Horse tails flicked from side to side, and I could tell they were all a little irritable.

Finn motioned to two tall animals that were horses as I knew them, though I guessed these were more sentient than the average Topside horse with the way they held my downturned gaze. "We'll take these two."

"Yes, sir. If you have water to offer, I'm sure they'll have the strength to take you wherever you like."

The woman drew two horses over to us in the moonlight that was helped only by the torches posted on a few of the barns. One was positioned in front of me, and I wasn't sure what I was supposed to do. There wasn't even a stirrup to hoist myself up with, or a saddle to grab onto. I couldn't really picture myself John Wayne-ing myself up there. The midsection was taller than my shoulders. I didn't know how the guys in *The Princess Bride* made it look so easy. I looked up toward Finn, at a loss.

That was my first mistake.

"I don't know how to ride," I said quietly.

That was my second mistake.

Maybe I should've anticipated Finn's solid backhand across the face that knocked me down to my hands and knees, but it caught me completely by surprise. Judging by the woman of the house's squeak, she hadn't been ready for the violence, either. "Slaves don't have a voice unless their master grants it. Don't make me tear out your tongue before King Kabayo even meets you."

I couldn't process anything beyond the shock of the unmerciful violence. I'd socked him that morning because his hand needed to learn a few manners and stay off of my breasts. That was an obvious offense. Telling him I didn't know how to get up on the horse? What else was I supposed to do? It started to dawn on me afresh that I knew nothing about this world or the rules I was subject to.

My cheekbone was ringing, but I refused to make a sound about it. I couldn't look at Finn, and knew I wasn't supposed to, so to compensate for my total confusion and Finn's stinging smack of betrayal, I laid in the dirt in fetal position and covered my head with my hands. I hoped he didn't feel the need to kick me or something to prove he was a big man and that I was very, very small.

I felt small, and I didn't like it.

I told myself when we left Bev's trailer that I'd never let anyone hit me again. Suddenly without my permission, I was back in the trailer, unwilling to hit back and unable to escape.

"Fine, I'll take you on mine if you can't manage something as simple as riding a horse. I hope you prove more useful to King Kabayo than this." Finn lifted me up out of the dirt and placed me on the horse's saddle-less back, his hands firm and feeling all wrong on my hips. The backpack was worn around my front, giving me something to hold. I don't know how he mounted without a saddle or stirrups, but he managed just fine, scooting up behind me and wrapping his arms around my sides as the woman handed him the reins. The leather straps were attached to the bit, and I could tell by the irritable twitch of his ears that the horse wasn't used to the gear and didn't like it at all.

The woman watched me with pity.

Watched, and did nothing.

Finn gave her some BS grand parting words of thanks and kicked the horse's sides, taking us from a dead stop to a gallop I was unprepared for. I had nothing to cling to, so my hands found their way into the horse's mane. My gritted teeth let out a tiny squeak of fear, but I didn't utter a word beyond that. Though Terence the Taurus was far faster, I had doors, a seatbelt and a windshield to keep me from feeling the speed. This horse had no safety net for me, other than Finn's arms, which were not a safe place anymore.

I had no choice but to lean back against Finn when the horse's pace picked up yet again. "That's the way," he cooed in my ear. "Just relax. We'll be there before you know it."

I didn't pull away for fear of flying off the horse, but I didn't answer him. He wanted a silent slave, so that's what he'd get. I wouldn't slip up again. I'd been knocked around too many times as a kid. I knew how to play the game and lay low. I knew how to be invisible while standing right in front of a person. I was the amazing insignificant woman whose friends called her Bait. I'd thought Finn and I were starting to become friends. I saw the danger more clearly now, felt the bite of the back of his hand and knew that no matter how hard I tried to be a person to the people around me, I would always be Bait.

I don't know why this made me miss Von. Aside from our last encounter where I'd been short with him and he'd unloaded a crap-ton of venom onto me, we'd been good to each other. We'd been friends, and despite our opposite genders, we'd managed to hold onto each other even when we weren't pretty. It felt like this was the story of my life. As soon as I let myself get comfortable and allowed my guard to drop, I got popped in the gut. That Finn turned on me wasn't a giant shocker; we didn't know each other all that well. But it was the cherry on top of the avalanche that threatened to bury me alive, if I was still, in fact, alive.

I didn't feel alive.

I zoned out as Finn drove us forward, feeling nothing and hearing none of the words I could tell he was trying to soothe me with.

8

STONE IN THE WELL, EYES ON THE GROUND

My body felt like a limp noodle when the horse came to a stop so many hours later at a grim and foreboding stone palace. I didn't recall much of the ride, only that the barrier in my mind that kept me from feeling the sting of my fight with Von, Bev's deranged apology, Finn's backhand, or any of the other heart-wrenching things was starting to crumble. I was grateful I had a good excuse to be silent. I didn't want to spill all my dysfunction in a trail across Kabayo's land.

When suddenly we were at the castle that looked more evil kingdom than fairytale fun, I was still no more a person than I'd been when we started the ride. Finn leaned me forward so I didn't fall when he dismounted. When he reached up for me, I didn't understand what I was supposed to do. I kept my head down and refused to respond, melting off the horse when Finn gently pulled me down. I stood next to the horse, hugging the bowling ball inside the backpack. I wanted to chuck it into the ocean just to have done with it all.

Finn clicked his fingers, so I went where he led, hating myself on a level I couldn't reconcile. Finn led us past stone gargoyles who stood sentry with scowls. They wore expressions that were mid-yowl, telling me I super didn't belong here. Next to the gargoyles were rows of dozens of stone Goblins, frozen in various states of confusion and horror. If I thought I couldn't feel any lower, I'd been wrong on that point.

Finn led the way through the gate and into the castle, conversing with different guards and officials that let us through gateway after gateway. We finally reached an inner room that was guarded by a horseman who wouldn't let us pass until after a thorough pat-down and a demand that I open my backpack to show him the contents. I didn't know if I was allowed to obey this command, or if I'd get backhanded for trying to preserve the secret we'd been guarding. I started unzipping the backpack, hoping the plastic wrap hadn't ripped through.

Finn's command was sharp. "That gift is for no one but King Kabayo. Tell him I'm here with the girl and a grand gift. He'll come out, and I promise on my life he'll come to no harm."

The guard scoffed, but disappeared into the room to deliver the message. He came out with wide eyes and a grudging offer for us to pass through. "King Kabayo will see you now."

Finn muttered some disparaging comment about the guard's intelligence at keeping him waiting and brushed past with me following behind, my eyes on his boots. As soon as the door locked behind us, I heard Finn running forward. "We've got it! We did it, Kabayo! We brought the stone, and she's ready to put a portion into your well."

"I thought your journey hadn't begun yet! Really? It's here?" Kabayo's elation threatened to draw my eyes upward, but I remembered the sting of Finn's hand on my face and kept my head down, lingering toward the back of the room. "This one's supposed to be missing, so the mission was delayed until Ezra found her. Did you come in secret because one of us is a mole?" Kabayo snorted through his long snout. "Who is it?"

"No, no. We knew it would be a risk, so we thought we'd endanger fewer people this way. Sama's army is coming behind us. We've got to do it now and run. If Sama finds her here, it'll be over for us, and the stone will be lost."

"I heard word Sama was marching on our city. It's why I have so many security checkpoints to get to me now. I'm afraid my men aren't strong enough to fight against Sama's army, but I'll rest well knowing the sagrado stone fights for my people even after I close my eyes when Sama finishes with me."

Finn made a fist and pushed it to his own chest. "Don't

give up hope. We're here. We're here and we've got the best help there is."

Kabayo's voice turned toward me. "Lady October? Come here, kid. What do you need to split the rock?"

I kept my head down and turned it from side to side. I wouldn't be a person when it was convenient. I didn't want to play that game of being friends only in secret when it served everyone's best interest. My face was a little tender still, and I hoped it didn't bruise up on me, announcing to the world that I was small, and my fake master was big. Bruce Campbell would never have been so cruel. He fought zombies, not women who asked simple questions. Finn was no Bruce Campbell, and that thought sunk in me like a brick.

Finn sighed. "She's mad at me. We don't have time to get into it. She needs tools, so grab them quick."

Kabayo ran to the door, unlocked it and gave instructions on what we needed to the guard. He closed the doors and clapped me on the shoulder. "You brought me the grandest gift of all, and you won't even greet me? Must've been some fight you two got into."

I moved away from him and went to the corner, sinking down to sit on the floor where I didn't have to stand awkwardly and be the topic of conversation. To get them to both back up and leave me alone, I took the stone out of the bag and started unwrapping it, relaxing a little when they fell back at the big, bad weapon that they couldn't control.

When the guard returned with the tools, I set to work chipping off a piece of the stone, not caring if it was an even fifth or not. It was good enough. Maybe I'd grown, or maybe I was too devastated to care anymore. I had my medication in me, so that was helping me fake being normal easy enough.

I wrapped the remaining rock up again and zipped it inside the two backpacks, pulling it over my arms to hang off my front. I moved the other pack with my supplies to hang off my back. I stood without a word, holding the baseball-sized portion of the stone in my hands, waiting for them to direct me where to go.

Kabayo opened the door, calling out to his guards, "We need an escort to take us to the well in the main village. Be sure no one touches the girl, or even breathes near her."

I kept my head down, hoping I didn't trip and let the stone go flying. Knowing my luck I'd turn the one decent guard to stone or something. Whispers of, "Is that... It's the stone! She's got the sagrado stone! It's the Omen!"

Finn held up his hands. "Don't look on her face! She carries freedom from your famine in her hands. If Sama learns who she is, she'll never escape him. She has work to do, so forget who she is. Forget you saw her. Don't look on her face."

More horsemen joined the caravan, giving me a wide and reverent berth as we marched out of the palace and into the village. The soldiers flanked me on either side and shielded the way before and behind me, ensuring that passersby wouldn't see me and be subject to giving up my identity if tortured. I didn't like all this torture business. I wanted to go home and take a shower. Wash my hands. Lay in bed for a whole day, with no hint of riding a horse or sleeping on the dirt. You know, the good life when a day off actually meant a whole twenty-four hours where you didn't see your coworkers.

We marched through the village lit only by the moon, the blaze of stars, and the few torches the guards carried. They led us to the well outside of the castle. It was located in the middle of the gated inner city. The soldiers gathered around, their eyes glued to my hands as they waited for the stone to save them from famine and certain death. I wasn't sure if I was allowed to toss the stone inside, and waited for some sort of signal.

"Throw it in, Lady October. End the drought for us all," Kabayo instructed, tense with trepidation. The wind caught his mane, lifting it and showing off the three long braids he wore interspersed through his thick, black locks. Everyone was watching now, waiting with bated breath and balled fists.

I don't know what I expected when I dropped the one-fifth of the stone into the well. With all the buildup and running and secrecy, I guess I expected light beams to shoot up from the ground or something. Maybe I'd seen too many X-Files episodes (if such a thing were possible).

The men around me exhaled audibly and cheered with so much enthusiasm that before I knew it, I was swept up in Kabayo's arms, hoisted into the air on his shoulders for the soldiers to rally around. So much for the whole not seeing my face thing. Swords were thrust into the air too close to my body for my liking.

Finn's voice broke through the din. "I'm going to take her Topside now. She really shouldn't be here when Sama's army comes."

As if on cue, we heard marching in the distance, and the celebration mutated to alarm and duty. Kabayo ignored Finn and shouted to his men, "Sound the alarm and man your posts! If Sama wants a fight, then we'll give his dead a battle to remember! He won't take our land the moment it's been given back to us. Go! We have something grand to fight for now!"

The guards scattered, running with their king to the city gates to reinforce them and form a line that kept growing as more soldiers were summoned.

"I've got the Omen," Finn called to Kabayo. "She can't be near the battle."

"Take her to my safe room. Just don't port her out of here yet. If we end up needing you, you'll never make it back to us if you port her out," Kabayo ruled. Then he turned back to his men to give them further instructions on how best to fend off the undead army.

Finn placed his hand on my shoulder. "Come on, kid. Into the palace with you. I didn't work this hard to get here only to see you hit by a stray arrow."

I turned and followed him only because I knew I had

no other choice. I kept my head down and my mouth shut like a good little slave. We walked up many flights of stairs, taking the wind out of my sails as I carried too many burdens on my shoulders. They'd already been weighted enough for a lifetime of therapy and regret. We went into a smaller, windowless room that locked, and Finn seemed satisfied with the mini fortress' protection. He drew his sword, and I sank to the floor, waiting out my doom in silence.

9

HIT ME OR KISS ME

"Look, I know you're mad at me, but I told you not to talk." Finn's borrowed sword hung at his side as he paced the room. We couldn't hear any sounds of a battle being fought below outside the castle walls, but we knew they were coming. When I didn't answer, Finn kept going as if I'd argued back. "I laid it out for you, and you couldn't follow the simplest instructions. When I shadowed you Topside, I had to fall in line. I had to wear clothes like Ezra. I couldn't bring a sword. I had to follow along where you three led."

I pulled my knees to my chest, both packs beside me as I gave my body a much needed break. I was sitting in the corner, my head resting on the cool stone wall. It did wonders to relax me from the overwhelming heat I hadn't been able to escape for days.

"Okay, fine. I shouldn't have hit you. Are you happy now?"

I never understood how people could literally or figuratively hit you and then be frustrated when you stayed hurt longer than was convenient for their conscience to brush off. I didn't want to fight with Finn, who clearly saw himself as the dominant one. I didn't need him to repent or be wrong. I wanted to go home. I fished through my backpack for a portion of the *baga* root and swallowed it down, grimacing at the rancid licorice and lemon rind flavor that sat in my hollow stomach and threatened to vomit itself back up. It had been since breakfast that we'd eaten, though I didn't complain. I learned that lesson when I was little, and had to watch Allie cry when she told me there just plain wasn't any food. I'd watch Ollie disappear for hours and come back with enough scraps to scrape a meal together; I knew better than to ask where they came from. My tears hurt them, so I learned not to cry out loud. I sucked it all in and gouged my hands up when I was hungry or in need, burying deep the scars everyone could see, but no one could touch.

Finn was kneeling before me, and I didn't know how long he'd been there talking. Finally he put down his sword, reached forward and cupped my cheeks, tilting my head up to face him. I watched him wince at what he saw, and then I closed my eyes, not wanting to look at him. He leaned in and kissed my cheeks softly, a gentle brush of thick lips on dirty skin. "I'm sorry, October. I shouldn't have hit you, no matter what the circumstance. Your cheek's starting to swell. I didn't realize I hit you that hard." He kissed my face again, so I pulled away, shrinking into the corner and covering my head with my forearms. I had no need or desire to talk to him, or to talk at all.

Sama's army was coming, his zombies marching on Kabayo's land. Bruce Campbell would've known what to do, but I was at a loss. Had we waited that extra half a day, we never would've made it. Now Silo had a chance to repair itself. No matter what, I couldn't regret the decisions that led me to duck out of the group and go rogue with the jackhole from Dagat.

The army's steps grew closer, pounding the earth with purpose they didn't need to understand. Sama knew what he wanted, and his mindless army would obey, like good little girls who came when their master snapped his fingers.

Finn sat on the floor next to me and wrapped his arm around my back, leaning me in to rest my head on his shoulder. I don't know why Finn was trying to be nice now, and though I wished he was anyone else, I didn't have the wherewithal to pull away. Sama wanted the sagrado stone. He wanted Kabayo's head on a platter. He wanted to win and didn't tolerate disappointment. I'd never been this close to a war before, and my nerves were nearing their peak.

"I'll protect you with my life, little Omen. You've got a lot more work to do before you can really, truly rest. Until that day comes, I'll be here to make sure you have a path. Even if you do hate me."

I nodded, which I figured was just as good as speaking. I didn't know how we were going to get out of this, and I wished a thousand times over for Allie and Ollie. Allie would know the perfect thing to say, and Ollie would know the perfect thing to do. Somehow they would broker peace with Sama, or they'd get me the flip outta Terraway before I got too hurt.

Finn held me, his sword on the ground at his side as he pressed my head to his chest beneath his chin. He seemed relieved that I was near him, which made little sense to me. "I don't like hiding," he confessed. "I'm more anxious in here than I would be on the front lines. I wasn't meant for ducking while others fight. I want to stay with you, but I have to go stand with Kabayo's men."

I didn't know what to say to this, so I kept quiet.

"Sama wants Terraway under his thumb. That you have the sagrado stone means you're his number one target, though no one knows we're here. I don't get it. Maybe Sama's marching on Silo because he knows Kabayo's a member of the council, so he must know you. If he's targeting kings, we're all in trouble."

"I don't care why," I murmured. "I just want to go home."

Finn exhaled his relief that I was speaking again. "We'll go home just as soon as the battle's settled. It'll be alright."

"You shouldn't have hit me like that," I said quietly.

"You kissed my eyelashes last night, and then you hit me today. Lowest of the low, Finn. I told you I didn't know how to ride horses. You put me in a situation where I had to talk, and then you knocked me around when I did. It's mean."

Finn kissed my hair, brushing my cheek with his knuckles. "Oh, *kendi*. Don't you know by now? I *am* mean. But you're on the council, so no matter the setting, I shouldn't have hit you. I'm sorry."

"How many women's faces have you banged up?"

Finn stiffened and released me from the hug, leaning against the stone wall and staring ahead. "My world isn't like yours. Part of my job is keeping the slaves in line, bringing them to the king when he asks. They don't always go willingly." Finn ran his hand over his face, the weight of too many worlds crushing him down. "Sometimes I think Banak likes it better when they put up a fight."

I hung my head. "Ah, jeez. I'm not your slave. Banak didn't order you to hit me. You did that on your own. Quit blaming your curse for everything."

"You shouldn't talk back to me."

"You're deeper than this. Why do you try so hard not to have a conscience? Just because Banak owns your will doesn't mean he should get all of you."

"A conscience does no good on the battlefield. I've buried many men with that little voice inside that tells them not to do what they know they have to if they want to survive." He motioned behind us out where the horsemen were readying themselves to stand against the marching zombies. "It's win or die out here. Who knows? Maybe after you set things right, I'll be able to afford a conscience again."

"I don't think it works like that." I let out a heavy sigh as too many conflicting brands of ethics tumbled around inside of me.

"You don't understand. I've seen your house. You're not starving like these people are."

"I learned enough about being hungry when I was a child." I forgot how little Finn actually knew about me. "Look, I get being desperate and how that messes with your conscience. But Finn? Out there you weren't desperate, and you hauled off and hit me. There's a difference between doing what you have to and letting the darkness take over. Who knows how long you've been on autopilot. I bet Banak doesn't even have to give you orders anymore, or force you to obey him. You just do it on your own. You're the tyrant now." I paused when he linked his fingers through mine, stopping the shredding I was doing to my skin. I hadn't even noticed until he intervened. "It's time you started thinking again. The land will be healed soon, and all you'll be is the darkness because you're letting it make the decisions for you."

Finn squeezed my hand when I tried to pull it out of his. There were too many germs. "Stop hurting yourself. You're bleeding."

I looked up at him, not holding back my disappointment or sadness that this was what lay behind the curtain of the mysterious man. "You first. Stop hurting yourself. Stop hurting me."

Finn traced his thumb from my temple to my chin, giving me the shivers when I was trying to actually have a real conversation. His gaze lowered to my lips, and I felt butterflies tumbling around where a strict order or vomit should've been. Finn's mouth curled into a tender smile. "It just figures. The one time I really want to kiss someone, that pesky conscience resurrects itself and starts yammering in my ear."

My eyes widened and I turned my head to stare forward, my cheeks turning that traitor shade of pink. "Well, listen to the cricket on your shoulder, dude. You don't want me; I can promise you that right now. You're just confused."

Finn stiffened. "So you're the authority on my conscience *and* what I want?"

I didn't hesitate with a response. "Yup. My black eye says you don't have a hold on your conscience enough to make good decisions yet. You can't hit me and kiss me all in the same day. How low do you think my self-esteem is? If you actually gave a crap about me, you would want more for me than a guy who knocks me around."

Finn swore loudly, making me jump. "That was a better point than I thought you'd make."

"Trust me. You don't want me."

"Can't argue with logic like that." His hand found its

way to my back and started lightly scratching in circles to relax me. We listened to the pounding footsteps come nearer until something else took over. A different sound, sort of like a waterfall, but it was hard to pinpoint exactly what. "What is that?" Finn asked, craning his ear in the windowless room.

I listened closer, my heart picking up and my spirits beginning to lift. "Finn? I think it might be raining."

10

BRUCE CAMPBELL, WHERE ARE YOU?

Our heads snapped to look at each other before we scrambled to our feet. Our camping gear was thrown on the floor and Finn's sword was drawn. He slowly opened the heavy wooden door that creaked too loud for my liking. I walked on tiptoe behind Finn as I clutched the backpack with the stone in it. The rain was louder now, and despite our trepidation that zombies might be around every corner, we both gasped and ran to the nearest window cutout that overlooked the main village. The view let us see out to where the zombie army was still marching – their footsteps drowned out by the blissful sound of the rain. There were thousands of them, each dressed in black tunics and matching cinched pants with black boots that looked the right amount of no-joke. There was a man in white in the lead, and I guessed he was the commander, but didn't look impressive or big enough to be Sama himself. I reminded myself that Sama was sequestered to his island of solitude, and all this mayhem was controlled by Sama's spirit that he sent out to mind-warp the undead to do his bidding.

I don't know what I expected to see, but I wanted more detail through the rain that every minute seemed to fall heavier than the minute before. The gray zombie faces were obscured, even when I squinted to see how close the B horror movie directors had gotten to the truth. Ollie would've been floored at seeing a real, live zombie. I tried to take as many mental pictures as I could, blurred by the elements as they were.

The hard, dry ground didn't know what to do with itself, but it started by soaking up as much of the water as it could. The brown earth guzzled with its cracks and crevices to greedily gulp for more and still more. Kabayo's soldiers all wore grins beneath their elongated helmets that were fitted to their horse heads. No matter how the battle ended, Silo had been restored to them. Though I could tell we were outnumbered two to one, Kabayo's men looked ready for the fight, hungry for nothing but more rain and some fresh zombie guts.

Finn pulled me from the window, moving me to the right so I couldn't see the zombie army, and they sure as Sunday couldn't see me. He pointed to the sky, his jaw dropped open in shock. My gaze followed to whatever it was that stupefied him, and I saw the gray clouds beginning to gather in a swirl that looked like the beginnings of a cyclone in the sky. It was wider and flatter than a tornado, and it seemed to spin like a slow-moving record with ominous purpose. "What the flip is that?" I asked, my nose scrunched as I squinted at the sky.

"It's the Ganado. The centaurs are coming! They're going to fight with Kabayo!" Finn clutched me with excitement that was laced with fear. "They'll kill anything that isn't clearly on the side of Silo, and I don't want them guessing at our loyalties. We have to get to Kabayo right now, or we could be targeted."

"Wait, what? You want me to go down into the battle with the stone?"

"We have to, or we're as good as dead. Hide the stone in here and let's go." He brought me over to a trunk in the corner of the room we'd just vacated, and shut it after I placed the national treasure and our packs inside. "I'm from Dagat, and you're a Topsider. We look nothing like the Tikbalangs. Hurry! They're coming!" Finn grabbed my empty arms and spun me around toward the staircase, racing down the circular winding stone steps like we were running from a fire. I followed, hoping I didn't trip, and that Finn knew what he was doing.

We were four stories up, and almost to the bottom when Kabayo met us at the front gate, breathless with anticipation. "I was just coming to get you! Stand by me, no matter what. We can't have the Ganado going after you two. Hurry! They're almost here!"

I bolted outside, stopping short when the fat raindrops

pelted me so hard, I checked my arms for welts. I could barely see, but Finn stayed with me. He slowed his steps to match mine as we ran after Kabayo out through the gate where nearly a thousand horsemen were gathered in two tight rows. They stood between their capitol and Sama's encroaching army, muscles tensed and maws bent into thrilled grins that rallied my spirits.

Finn was in his element, standing near the ranks, sword drawn as he waved down four men with gills. I guessed they were in Silo already as the gesture of good-will, doling out water to the thirsty on his orders. They came running toward him, saluting and offering up words of pledge to whatever end Finn ordered them. "We fight with King Kabayo tonight." Then Finn raised his voice. "Let it be known that Dagat didn't run when Sama attacked Silo! We stand with you tonight as brothers!" This was met by a few salutes and cheers from horsemen in well-fitted brass armor.

Finn met the eyes of his kin as he gripped my shoulder. "This is the new Omen, and I want you to protect her with your lives. The whole of Terraway's survival depends on her." The men gaped at me for a few seconds with awe and confusion, and then nodded at their commander. Finn kept me tight to his side, and then inched in front of me, readying to impale and gut as needed. Not that we could see more than a few feet in front of us.

Kabayo took the lead, stomping back and forth along the row. He shouted for the men to hold their ground, and not to fight until the Ganado came out first. The zombie army was marching steadily, and soon a battle would be inevitable, whether or not the centaurs made an appearance.

My heart sank as I felt the ground tremble beneath my feet. The zombies weren't waiting for the centaurs to come down and fight; the commander in white was smarter than that. Suddenly I found myself smack in the middle of a war, seconds away from any number of swords deciding my fate. I didn't know if I'd see Ollie again. I didn't know if I would live to see if there would be yet more episodes of *Star Wars* that would come out in my lifetime. I didn't know if Darius would ever get out of his brother's illegal empire. I didn't know if Allie would ever come back to us.

I didn't know what to do; I'd never been in a battle before, much less unarmed. As if reading my mind, Finn turned and gripped my hand. "Behind the gates with you. Don't come out for anything. That'll be near enough so the Ganado don't come after you, but hopefully not so near that you'll see any action from the battle." He ran with me through the gate and positioned my back against the stone wall that separated the inner city from the battle. I gulped as the rain poked me all over, washing away the dirt and heat.

Finn reached down and pulled out an oversized switchblade knife from his belt. When he flicked it open, the wide janky and jagged blade was nearly a foot long, making me gasp at how evil the thing looked. The edges weren't one smooth crest, but rather a series of dips and sharp points along both sides, ensuring that once it stuck into someone, the journey out of the person would be the thing that ripped them to shreds. I'd always pictured switchblades to be much smaller, but this could do some serious damage.

Finn wrapped my fingers around the jade handle and pressed the steel to my breasts, shouting over the rain. "This is my balisong blade. If we're separated, show any of the soldiers my blade, and they'll know you're under my protection. Stay tight to the wall, *kendi*! Leave your conscience in the castle, and hope that you don't have to use this."

"Be careful!" I stood up on my toes and wrapped my arms around his neck, my heart racing against his. I'd never sent someone off to battle before, and the moment transcended how pissed I should've still been at him.

He smiled and kissed my unbruised cheek. "Don't you know by now? I'm never careful. It's how I'm still alive." With that, he ran out to join the army.

I was terrified, and that didn't often happen to me. A zombie army was bearing down on us, and I had what felt like a pretty butter knife to defend myself with. Okay, it was scarier and far larger than a butter knife, but it wasn't exactly an automatic rifle or something that could inflict damage without me having to get close to the danger. I inched along the edge of the stone gate and peered around the opening, blinking out at the army that was too close, too gruesome with their gray, torn leprous skin and slack-jawed roars.

My eyes searched for Finn among the ranks. He was easy to spot, as he and his four men were the only ones with human heads. Finn's knees were bent, his shoulders squared to the oncoming enemy as we waited for Kabayo's command to unleash his soldiers. I clutched the knife as if I totally knew what I was doing with it.

Bruce Campbell, where are you?

One Mississippi.

Two Mississippi.

Three Mississippi.

"Steady, men!" Kabayo yelled, his arm raised.

I whispered my brother's name and prayed that wherever Ollie was, that he knew I loved him.

Then I saw it. The commander in white for the zombie army drew his bow and let it fly, sinking it deep in the leg of one of Finn's men. Not just one of his men, but the man right next to Finn. He had dark skin, a flat nose and wide shoulders. A few inches off, and it would've been Finn hitting the ground, gritting his teeth through the agony of the arrow.

My heart dropped into my stomach when Kabayo shouted, "Attack!"

The Tikbalangs and Finn's men charged forward, vicious in all of their terrible glory. Finn's man who'd been hit sat on the ground, unable to do anything but wait to be finished off.

Not on my watch. I bolted onto the battlefield, clutched the hilt of my closed knife between my teeth, and gripped the man under his armpits. He was a sturdy fellow, so I relied on a fair amount of adrenaline to drag him back behind the wall. "What's your name?" I asked, propping him against the slick stone.

"Klavin, milady." He had the grace to answer with manners, even though I could see him cringing in pain.

I didn't wait for him to be ready; I ripped the arrow from his leg without warning or hesitation. He howled as I unlocked the balisong blade and cut off the fabric of his sleeve. Rolling his pant leg up, I made a quick bandage that would hopefully stem the bleeding until I had more time to treat it. "You'll be alright, but you're done fighting for now. Stay here. Can I borrow your sword?"

"Of course. You can take whatever you like." He was sweating now, and I prayed he wouldn't pass out.

Though I didn't know him, I gripped his hand as if gearing up for an arm wrestling match. His beautiful skin was the same color as Judge's, and my heart pinged when I pictured my Judge in this much pain. I leaned forward and kissed Klavin's cheek. "Stay strong, soldier."

"Wait, you can't go out there!" he cried after me as I stood, his sword in my right hand and the long, thick, jagged dagger from Finn clutched in my left. My muscles tensed for the fight Sama had coming.

I didn't listen to Klavin, but ran out onto the battlefield. I was done cowering and feeling scared. I wouldn't be made small. I wouldn't be stepped on by Sama or his zombies. Though I didn't know how to fight with a sword, I hoped my determination would make up for some of that. My name wasn't Bruce Campbell, but I wasn't about to let that stop me. I let my favorite superhero act as my guardian angel, driving me forward with confidence. I imagined him whispering, "You've got this, sweetheart," in my ear as I ran without pause or self-preservation.

I was determined to be a good soldier. Years of video games with Ollie and my casual guy Beto trained me for a zombie apocalypse. I wasn't about to chicken out now. Snarl in place, I charged into the fray, keeping low and hoping my knife and sword would be a decent challenge to the menace of their spears.

11

OCTOBER GRACE, ZOMBIE SLAYER

When the two sides met, it was with a crash of screaming metal and fury beneath the pelting rain. I could hardly see more than two feet in front of me, but when a zombie jabbed his spear in my direction, I ducked and lunged for his knees. My unexpected force toppled him backward and plunged my knife into his gut. He smelled like rotting garbage and looked like a science experiment gone horribly wrong. His gray face had holes in it like Swiss cheese, and drooped on one side. This one was about six feet tall, but they were all varying sizes. I could see one with gills, like Finn had, a few rows down. There was even a zombie Tikbalang fighting against his kin with dead eyes and a hunger for something meatier than *buhay* shoots.

I sat up atop my conquest's chest after he'd hit the

ground and set to making a path of destruction to be reckoned with. The zombie to my left got a quick stab to his thigh. I made the wound worse by dragging my knife upwards in a clean slit before retracting. It wasn't red blood that flowed out, but a thick, black tar-like substance that coated my knife and stank like sulfur, stinging my eyes. I indulged in a split second of conflict: part of me wanting to run from the disease-infested blood, and the other part was fascinated, wishing I could take a sample and study it under a microscope.

I wanted to vomit when the black blood came close to touching my fingers, but knew there'd be time for that later. Adrenaline trumped my neurosis, so I fed the machine inside of me that was hungry to be set loose.

Finn had three zombies on him, his sword swinging out and slicing with purpose and pleasure. Still on my knees, and probably harder to spot with all the rain, I thrust my knife into the calf muscle of the nearest zombie to give Finn a little breathing room. "Get behind the wall!" he bellowed at me.

The throng of gray-faced, open-mouthed soldiers filled my vision, and I knew I would be dealt with in the harshest way possible if I didn't get up quick. I hopped to my feet and dodged one of the spears that jabbed at me, grabbing it at the midpoint and yanking its owner forward so I could stab him through his throat.

Finn's eyes were wide with shock that was mingled

with appreciation. "Stay close to me," he said, amending his edict that I should run and hide.

The rampant germs scared me more than the murdering at my hands. I recognized that as much progress as I like to think I'd made, some part of me might always have this dysfunction without Von and Mason to suck it out of me.

One of the gilled men threw himself in front of me, letting out a roar of bloodlust as he gutted two zombies in one go. Finn's men were attempting to form a box around where I stood. Though part of me was scared, seeing their precision and tenacity made me act as if I was fearless. I shot out between two of them and tackled one that was gunning for Finn before he hit his mark.

I didn't know how to deal with my participation in the gore, so I put it on a shelf in my mind and kept going, following Kabayo's orders for his soldiers to attack until we were told otherwise. This led to more stabbing, swallowed screaming and a spear that missed its deadly mark and sliced my shoulder instead. My howl of pain scared even me, but Finn pulled my body tight to his side, reminding us that pain would have to wait until later to be acknowledged. "Keep fighting!" he urged everyone around him. The gilled man on my right swung wildly with his sword, so I made sure to give him a wide berth.

My jagged knife plunged into the stomach of a woman I didn't know. She'd tried to claw at my face, so I stabbed her. This was who I was now. The inmates had trained me well for the cruelty of this soulless fight.

As the battle grew to chaos around us, I was horrified that I wasn't horrified, and what that said about me.

12

FALLING BACK AND RUNNING
FORWARD

Blood was dripping down my back and over my chest, each movement reminding me of the slice that felt like the spear was still in me. I nearly cried when I heard a trumpet sound above the din. "Fall back!" Finn told me, grabbing my bad shoulder. "Run!"

I didn't need to be told twice. I spun on my heel and ran with Finn, the gilled soldiers and the horsemen I didn't know toward the village wall. I hoped there was some sort of plan other than for all of us to get skewered in the back.

Overhead I saw something that looked sort of like a brown cow dropping from the sky's gray cloud vortex as if it had been fired from a cannon. I turned and saw a real, live centaur land with what should've been a splat, but its purposeful crash to the rain-soaked earth gave way to a gallop. The beast charged straight into the undead heart of the enemy. I looked up as I ran and saw a peppering of centaurs flying down from the flat, dark cyclone that circled in the sky above us. I thought I was running fast before, but at this, my legs really started to fly. Kabayo's soldiers bolted into the main city like ants scurrying into their hill.

A few horsemen lingered, carrying their injured compatriots back. That's when I saw an olive-skinned gilled man limping toward the gate with too many zombies on his tail. I broke away from Finn and charged at the enemy as three of them jumped on my guy, biting his shoulder, arm and hand. He howled and fell seconds before I reached them, but I didn't stop. I flew at them with abandon, the rain and wind whipping through my hair and telling me it was all or nothing. I jumped and tackled one of the zombies on my guy, knocking him back with a groan. I had to do something to give Finn's man a second to fight the monsters that threatened his life. I stabbed my supine zombie through the neck, jumped up and sliced another through the back, hitting what I hoped was his kidney. I didn't stop until my jagged knife plunged the third through his eye socket.

I grimaced at that last one. I mean, totally gross.

"Run, October! Go back to the gate. I've got this!" Finn charged past us, knocking several more zombies over with sheer force, his sword swinging like a madman on a mission. The two remaining gilled men charged out to fight with their captain, their war cries resounding through the field.

The centaurs landed at random and began slaughtering the zombies with fierce expressions, hoofs of iron and swords swinging.

I lifted the gilled bloody guy by his armpits, not caring if I did more damage to his shoulder. The goal was to get him back behind the wall. He blinked and lifted his head, pulling out of my grip and staggering to his feet. "Run, Lady Omen!"

"We'll go together. Hurry!" I let him lean on my good shoulder and guided him toward the gate. I breathed far easier once I handed him over to the awaiting Tikbalangs. They dragged him to the nearest tavern with the other wounded, which was about half a block back from the stone wall.

I turned toward the gate and peeked out through the soldiers to find two horsemen, two gilled men and Finn still fighting as they tried to fall back without getting stabbed to death.

I couldn't take the standing and waiting for someone to get gutted. I ran back out, stabbing at random as I fought my way to Finn, who was quickly outnumbered. The centaurs were still landing, though not as close to us as to be super helpful just yet.

I didn't feel the slice on my shoulder. I didn't feel winded, and didn't notice the pelting rain anymore. I saw a zombie jump atop Finn, biting down hard on his neck, and lost my shiz. "No!" I screamed through the pouring rain, my feet sliding on the slick ground as I charged toward the fray with all the gusto in my much smaller body. I'd brought Finn in on this. He was here because of me. Because I wanted to run away from my problems. I couldn't stand the fighting, and now I was smack in the middle of a war.

In hindsight, I probably shouldn't have jumped at the zombie, knocking him sideways and putting me closer to the fight. I couldn't think about getting myself out; I only knew that if Finn died because of me, I wouldn't be able to live with myself. I stabbed and sliced until one of the gilled men ripped me off my prey. "Fall back!" he reminded me, carving through a zombie's tendon.

I glanced around, but could barely see any further than a few feet in front of me; the rain was so thick. "Is everyone safe? Where's Finn?"

"I'm here!" Finn shouted, stumbling beside me and dragging me by my arm toward the gate. "And you're crazy!"

13

FAKE ROYAL, REAL NURSE

Somehow we made it to the other side of the stone wall, leaving a trail of blood in our wake. From there I was immediately corralled into the tavern nearby with the wounded soldiers. There were around three dozen of them that were visibly injured. I set to work, going straight to the woman who I was told owned the tavern with her hubby. "Hi, I'm a nurse. Do you have a sewing kit and some clean rags? I can get started patching some of these guys up."

The woman was dumbfounded at all the wounded soldiers. Just as they were, she was torn between the devastation of war and the elation of the first rain they'd had in who knows how long. The centaurs coming to fight for the people made the tavern buzz with versions of "Did you see the big one with the dappled hide?" and "I saw one slaughter three of Sama's soldiers with a single blow!"

It was hard to get her to focus. "What's your name?" I asked, redirecting her attention.

She blinked at me, her glassy horse eyes wide as she wiped her dainty human hands on her apron. "I'm Bonito. Who are you?"

"My name's October, and I can help clean some of these guys up. Needle and thread?" I knew better than to ask for gloves, though I desperately craved them.

"Oh! Right, yes. Of course." She darted away, snapping to action and running up the stairs to retrieve what I needed.

I jogged into the kitchen and snatched up a pot, but knew there was no water around to fill it. I grabbed Finn, who was standing at the door. His hand was pressed to his bloody neck as he watched the centaurs work to full-on exterminate the zombie army out on the battlefield in the distance. "Finn? I need this pot filled with water. Help a girl out?"

"Uh, yeah. Sure." He didn't even look, but felt around for the pot and sprayed water inside from his hands as if he was using a hose.

"Thanks." I went back to the kitchen and hefted the pot atop the wood-burning stove, glad it was already hot. I went back out to the bar area just as Bonito was racing down the stairs, her pale blue shin-length dress flying out behind her. Her horse head was dappled, and her creamy arms were similarly freckled. When she thrust the sewing kit at me, I gave her another job before she grew overwhelmed with the crazy day and the men bleeding all over her bar's floor. "I need all the clean rags you've got, now. And some clean sheets we can rip into strips to make bandages, unless you happen to have a ton of bandages laying around somewhere."

"Yes, ma'am!" Bonito was happy to be given a concrete mission, and ran off to put herself to use.

I went to the kitchen and heated the needle, hoping that was enough to disinfect it in such a rural setting. Mason had told me that Terraway creatures didn't get diseases from germs, like humans did. I'm not sure if he was trying to pacify me or not, but I clung to that as the truth I needed to be able to do my job.

The rustic tavern was all roughly hewn wood and exposed nails. There wasn't a clean place to lay any of the patients, but I knew I couldn't worry about that now. I knelt beside the first horseman still in his leather armor, putting on my calm nurse smile as I rolled up his pant leg to reveal the source of all the blood staining his brown pants. "I'm sorry. I don't have anything to numb you with, but you really need stitches. Can you grit your teeth through it?"

I think he knew there was no other option. The slice was clean, but too long for a simple bandage. "Of course." He let out a brash whinny to show to his injured buddies that he wasn't a wuss. "Do what you need to."

I asked him his name, where he lived, what he wanted to be when he was a boy, and about a dozen other things to occupy his mind while I tugged on his skin. When I finished with a light smile I knew he needed, Bonito was ready with the sheets she'd shredded into long strips. She gently wrapped his leg while I set to work stitching up the next guy after threading a new needle. We went down the row of soldiers who were propped up against the bar, sitting on the floor and talking animatedly about the wonder of the rain and the return of the Ganado. They barely noticed me as I stitched, cleaned and treated their wounds as best I could. I wasn't exactly a veterinarian, and I wasn't totally sure if the facial abrasions should be treated like I would a patient, or like a vet might treat a horse. I did the best I could, frustrated only when I couldn't lift my arm without my sliced shoulder causing me a world of pain. Then my fingers started to tremble beyond what I could tolerate and still make a proper suture. I was determined not to scratch my hands in front of the soldiers.

The germs would not get me. The germs would not get me. I repeated my mantra over and over. I decided I could get through this because soon enough I'd be back in my bedroom, and my bedroom was perfect. I sighed through a gust of anxiety, promising myself that if I could get through this, my perfectly pristine bedroom would be waiting for me with no germs infesting it at all.

"Nurse October, are you alright?" Bonito asked as I clenched and unclenched my fist in an attempt to regain control over my slight tremor.

"Never better. Big day for you guys, right? So exciting." It was all I had to say for Bonito to get distracted with the monumental day we'd all been witness to. She started chatting animatedly with the horsemen around her about the miracle of the rain, leaving me to work in peace.

My next patient was the olive-skinned gilled man who'd fought next to me, and who I'd dragged back to the gate toward the end. He was unconscious, but breathing steadily. I checked his pulse, which was low, but even enough for me to concern myself only with the obvious wounds on his neck, shoulder and hand. The hand was easy enough to clean and bandage without rousing him, but the needle tugging on his shoulder brought him back to the land of excited commotion. "What? Where? Am I dead?"

"No. But you are a stranger. Can you tell me your name?" I took the candle Bonito had given me to sterilize my needles with and checked his pupils for responsiveness to light. *No concussion. That's good.*

"Ben. Benjamin of the Seventh Lake. And you're the Omen."

I cast him a baleful look, my voice quieting. "Alright, alright. Don't spread that around."

Bonito gasped. "You're what? I thought you were a slave of Captain Finn!"

"Potato-Potahto."

She hoisted me up seconds after I tied off Ben's last stitch. "You'll not crawl around on the floor like a dog. Oh, the king will have my head for this! Up on a stool with you. Here, let me fetch a fresh pail of rainwater to wash your feet. I've got several buckets hanging outside."

"Bonito, it's fine. I promise. Kabayo would probably rather I help these guys than sit here and watch everyone bleed out."

"My brother was one of the warriors who marched King Geon's land to rescue you, you know. He said you were the most beautiful maiden in their land." She motioned to the row of wounded I still had yet to tend to. "Many of these men were there that day."

I choked back the rising emotion that these were some of the soldiers who'd come to rescue me from the unending darkness of Geon's cell. I knelt back down and dabbed at the blood on Ben's neck. I tried to ignore Bonito's fretting and hand-wringing that Kabayo would be upset I was on my hands and knees in a bar.

"It's not too deep here," I said reassuringly to Ben. "Doesn't look like the zombie guy chomped down on anything too important. You fell pretty hard out there. Stretch out your arms for me. Now I'm going to push down, but you can't let me, okay?"

I tested the strength left in both his arms and judged the damage not to be too detrimental. Ben watched my face as I tested his leg reflexes. "You ran back out to save me."

I shrugged, unwilling to soak in the gratitude exuding from him. I kept my eyes on my work. "You fought next to me, too. Probably saved my life a dozen times. So I still owe you, like, eleven saves."

His black eyes studied me. "You're not from Dagat. You didn't even know my name. You're an Omen. You shouldn't have even been on that field, and you ran back out to rescue me."

"You're making it sound cooler than it was. We're war buddies now. Isn't that how it's supposed to work? Would you have left me to rot on the field?"

"No, but you're an Omen. We all depend on you to stay alive."

"Well, you helped keep me from biting it out there. It only seemed right to return the favor."

Ben's mouth fell open, as if I was telling him something that blew his mind, but to me felt like Fighting 101. As I finished cleaning him up, he took two fingers and placed them sideways across his heart, and then saluted me, like some sort of rite of passage. I returned the gesture, and he smiled, inclining his head to me humbly.

"What are you doing?" Finn asked, his tone curt as he came up and stood behind me.

"Calculus. What does it look like I'm friggin' doing?"

"Get up. Seriously. You're on the floor like a commoner. Don't you know anything about your position?"

"I know a fair bit about your position – laid out on the floor if you keep nagging me. These guys are injured, Finn. That's a little more important than waving around my fake royalty card."

"It's not a fake…" He rubbed his forehead in exasperation. "Fine. Have it your way, but don't leave my sight. And after this last one, you're done. You've got who knows how many people's blood on you. You're covered!"

I didn't tell him that a generous portion of the blood that stained my clothes was probably mine. My hands were shaking again, and if I stopped for too long, I felt short of breath and queasy. "Bonito, do you think you could get Finn something to eat? He gets crabby when he's hungry."

"Oh, shut it. I'm not hungry. Don't talk to me like I'm five."

"Then stop acting like you're five. And actually, a five-year-old knows how to get food for himself. So I was more treating you like you were three." I looked over my shoulder to Bonito. "See? He's already getting crabby."

"Of course!" Bonito ran into the kitchen while Finn grumbled under his breath.

He watched as I finished cleaning up the last Tikbalang in the row whose bash to the head needed more than I could give him at the moment. I cleared my throat and walked over to the olive-skinned Mer-soldier. "Ben? Could you keep an eye on this guy over here for me? No matter what, you have to keep him awake for a few hours. Can you do that for me? I'm pretty sure he's got a concussion."

"Anything. I owe you my life." He extended his arm and I helped him to stand, letting him use me as a crutch to walk over to the injured horseman who needed looking after.

I set him down gently and waved off his admiration with a weak hand as I knelt to check my patient's pupils again. "None of that kinda talk. Thanks for looking out. And if you start to feel woozy, let me know. You lost a decent amount of blood."

"Alright, you're done," Finn ruled. "Up off the floor with you."

I took the hand Finn offered me, but stood a little too quickly. *Stupid blood loss.* My knees were unsteady and the room started to spin, pulling me downward with too much gravity. My ebbing adrenaline plummeted, and my knees buckled.

"Whoa! Easy, now." Finn scooped me up in his arms that had various cuts marking them, and called over the bar into the kitchen. "Bonito, show us to your biggest room. The Omen needs to rest. I would take her to the palace, but until the Ganado finishes off Sama's army, I don't want my men or her stepping foot outside this tavern. They may not recognize us as allies, since we're not kin."

"Of course! Right this way."

I prayed Finn's muscular arms were a safe place, since there was precious little I could do to fend off an attack now. My heart rate stuttered as he clutched me to his chest, and carried me up the stairs to our room.

WHAT SCARED ME MOST

*B*onito grabbed a key off the wall and a tall brass candlestick, leading the way past the others who watched me with sympathetic "oh, how precious" expressions as I lay mostly limp in Finn's arms. I'd just fought a battle with them and killed my fair share of zombies, but now I looked weak and small, even to myself. I didn't much like the contrast.

She led us up the stairs to a long room that had its own fireplace, a four-poster bed with a handmade pink quilt, an empty washtub and a long black animal skin rug stretched out in the center of the room. Bonito lit the lamp that was attached to the wall, casting shadows on the wood floor and the bare stucco walls. "Would Lady October prefer a bath? I can draw one for her."

Finn answered "yes" at the same time I mumbled a feeble "no, thanks." Of course I wanted a bath, but not in a tub I'd not cleaned. I was so filthy, I would just be bathing in dirty water. "She'd like a bath and some human food, but I can take care of the water. Soap and towels, though. The battle's over for us, so no one's to call her for help. When King Kabayo comes to see his wounded, send him up here."

"Right away, Captain." Bonito curtsied and dipped her elongated head to the both of us.

The second Bonito exited, Finn leaned against the wall and sank to the floor with me still in his arms. He exhaled as if finally able to let down his mask of superiority, now that it was just us. "You shouldn't have run back out for Ben. I would've seen and gone for him. You nearly got yourself killed."

"But I didn't, so it's not a big deal."

"When will you learn that if you die, we all die? You can't be reckless with your life, October."

"Hello, that's all you people are asking me to do! Geon locked me in a dungeon and starved me, you took me with you right near the zombie apocalypse. You can't take it all back now just because you were scared."

"I was scared," Finn admitted, cradling me and leaning my head to his shoulder. I don't know if my temple felt so very right pressed to his body, or if I was simply too exhausted to protest. "I'm already going to be in deep with Ezra, but I can't imagine what would've happened if I tried to go Topside again without you."

Finn held me until Bonito returned. I decided to stay in his arms without examining why it was so easy to slip into a rhythm with him. Finn had thick biceps like Mason, his chest was hard and his body was used to driving itself to get whatever job needed doing, done. He didn't bother correcting Bonito's assumptions that we were more than sort of friends when she did the "Oh! Excuse me. I didn't realize."

"It's alright," Finn said, holding me tight as Bonito set a tray of bread, cheese and what smelled like super hoppy beer on the nightstand next to the bed.

"Bonito, could I borrow your sewing kit again?" I asked, clinging to Finn as if he was my lifeline.

"Of course." She pulled the small pouch filled with the needle and thread from her apron pocket and set it atop the towels next to the wash basin, curtsying again before she left.

I did my best to take charge of the situation. "Okay, I'm a little steadier now. Let me take a look at your neck."

"I'm not hurt."

"Hello, you've got blood on your collar." I didn't expect Finn to take off his shirt, but he pulled it over his head while still balancing me on his lap.

It was like looking into the sun, seeing Finn without his shirt on. I turned my head to the side so I didn't do a teenager, and ogle him with my mouth hanging open. He was too good looking, too trained for a zombie apocalypse, too... Just too much to look at directly.

I stood carefully, so as not to collapse this time. "Steady," Finn warned.

"I'm fine. Just disinfecting the needle first." I cursed my trembling fingers, but kept my chin up as I heated the needle in the lamp's flame. I repeated Ollie's mantra in my head. *Keep your chin up, take it slow.*

I grabbed a rag and tossed it to him, kneeling at his side while he moistened the cloth with a few squeezes. He winced when I dabbed at his neck. When I got the blood out of the way, I saw one of his gills was torn. "Oh, man. Finn, this is above my paygrade. I don't know how to stitch a gill. Ben's bite was below his."

"It's just like regular skin, only a little thinner and more flexible. You can sew it like anything else. Just don't stitch it shut," he joked with a slight upward twitch to the corner of his mouth. "You don't have to. I can get someone else to look at it if it scares you."

I bit down on my lower lip and inched closer, praying I didn't get a tremor in my hand and rip one of the rows of thin flesh clean off. With great care, I sewed his torn gill flap back into place, chewing my lip against the vomit that welled up in me to contrast with the idle curiosity. Ollie would never believe this.

Finn glance sideways at me. "What, no bedside manner? No fifty questions to distract me from the needle? All the other soldiers got the special treatment, I guess. None left over for me."

"Dude, I'm about five seconds away from ralphing all

over you, here. Let me do my thing, and then you can go back down there with your guys." I tied off the last stitch with a gust of relief that I hadn't made the whole mess worse. I glanced down at his arms that had various nicks and gouges. "These need a cleaning, but none of them are deep enough for stitches. Go on down. Kabayo might need help at some point. And make sure he grabs the sagrado stone from its hiding place."

"Alright. Thanks." He kissed my forehead and stood, filling the steel bathtub in the corner of the room for me, and then leaving me alone in the lamplight.

The moment the door shut, all my feigned calm gusted out of me in a sob I couldn't hold inside anymore. The flesh wounds were one thing; I was used to them from patching up inmates, but zombies trying to claw at people and eat me? Whether they were undead or not, they looked human enough to tear up my conscience and leave me a blubbering mess on the wood floor.

What scared me most of all on the battlefield was me. That I could kill so easily, and what that must say about the person I'd devolved into since starting this job. I could still see the zombie faces coming at me, and try as I wanted to, I knew I couldn't save them. I couldn't resurrect them or bring their drooling mouths any sort of joy.

The rain was punishing the earth, angry that it had been kept at bay for so long. I could hear it all around me, and it brought about that eerily calm feeling you get when it rains too hard and you can actually sit inside and enjoy it from a distance. I let the pounding soothe me as it hit the roof in waterfall-like sheets. I wanted to lay down on the bed, but I was filthy, and too tired to bathe in a tub that was probably crawling with germs. I curled up in a ball on the floor and closed my eyes, not intending on opening them for as long as I possibly could.

15

FINN'S PECULIAR FETISH

When I awoke a handful of hours later, it was to a knock on the door. "October? Open up. It's me."

"It's not locked," I said by way of a greeting. My neck was stiff and my whole body grumpily reminded me of why it wasn't a good idea to fall asleep on a wooden floor.

Finn entered, looking around in confusion until his eyes widened. "What are you doing? Why are you on the floor?" He shut the door behind him and offered his hand to get me up. He was freshly bathed and in clean clothes that looked more like palace wear than the outdoor stuff we'd been in. He had on a high-collared white dress shirt with gold cufflinks. His fitted beige pants looked like something Ezra might wear. He shook his head at me in dismay. "What happened?"

"I fell asleep."

"I got you a room with the nicest bed in the place. Not good enough, your highness?" he tempted with a smile that bespoke of lighter things happening on the floor below.

"Hello, I'm filthy. I didn't want to get in the bed like this."

He motioned to the basin. "I filled the tub for you!"

"I can't be sure how clean that tub is. I have a thing about germs."

"Well, the tub's cleaner than you. In you get. Kabayo wants to see you in the palace later, and you can't go like that." He watched me look around the room, lost in the simple task that felt like one step too far. He motioned to the tub. "In you go."

"In where?"

His shoulders deflated from his perfect posture that the nice clothes naturally drew him into. "Oh, sweetheart. You make it easy to forget this isn't your world. Today tipped it, huh."

"Can you take me home?"

"Yes. But not before you talk with Kabayo, and he's still seeing to his men. I think he'll have time to slip away later today, which means we can get some sleep now, but not on the floor."

"Okay." I moved in the direction Finn aimed me, and landed in front of the tub, blinking down into the water. There was a screen behind the tub that Finn moved to separate me from him to give me the illusion of privacy. I peeled off my bottoms, knowing no matter how many times I washed them, I wouldn't be able to wear this outfit again. My shirt proved problematic, since my shoulder felt like the knife was still slicing me whenever I moved it more than an inch.

Finn was regaling me with details about the total obliteration of Sama's army. Though Sama could always raise more soldiers with the death that was in fresh supply in Terraway, for now they were vanquished. The rain was making up for lost time, and the centaurs were making themselves useful hauling the dead zombies into mass graves they were digging. The bodies were being given a proper burial so they didn't reanimate again.

I gave up on trying to get my shirt off and stepped into the tub, letting the water come up to my ribs. I chewed on my lower lip as the germs surrounded me, pressing into my pores and cuts. I tried to breathe through the flare-up, reminding myself that my bedroom was perfect, and I'd be there soon enough.

I tried again to get my shirt all the way off without harming my shoulder. The Band-Aid method of yanking it over my head didn't work, and hurt far worse than I anticipated, pushing a noise of duress from my lips that alarmed Finn. "What's wrong?"

"Nothing!" I lied. "I'm just having some trouble with my shoulder. It's no big deal."

"How about I take a look at it?"

"I... um... Yeah, alright. I'm in the tub though, so be cool."

Finn came around the partition with his eyes closed, feeling around like a blind man before he opened one eye to peek at me with a grin that quickly fell. "I thought you said you were in the tub. You've still got your clothes on. What sort of fun is that?"

"The kind of fun you won't get beaten up for. I can't get my shirt off. My shoulder's not doing so hot. Could you help without being pervy? Is that within the realm of your abilities, or should you send up Bonito?"

Finn unbuttoned his perfect white shirt, glancing down at me with a look that had barely contained laughter laced all through it. "I honestly don't know. You're not giving me a whole lot to help with my self-control. Victory on the battlefield followed by a sexy woman in the tub who 'just has to' have me help her take her clothes off? I can't promise anything. I'm in too good a mood."

"Alright, out you go. I'll figure this out myself."

Finn held up his hands. "I'm only kidding. How can I help?"

"Can I borrow your knife again? I can't lift my arm, so I'm thinking I should just cut myself out of this shirt. It's ruined anyway."

"I'll do you one better. Tip your head back and get as far down under the water to cover the parts you don't want me to see." Finn reached down and ripped open my shirt the second I obeyed, startling me. I made a grab for my breasts, which were safely hidden under the filthy water. He gently worked the shirt off one arm, but paused at my bitten off scream when he tried to slide it off the other. "Oh, *hani*. It's stuck to your skin. Did you get a little cut out there?"

"Something like that." I cringed at the anticipation of the rip I knew was coming. "Just yank it off."

He didn't do the obligatory countdown, which I appreciated. My scream could not be helped. My shoulder started bleeding afresh when the clotted mess was ripped open. Finn swore as he tossed my shredded shirt to the floor. "I didn't know all that was *your* blood! I thought it was from the soldiers you were treating. Why didn't you say something? Oh, it's really gushing."

"Can you get me a mirror or something so I can stitch myself up?"

"I can do it. But let's get you cleaned up first. Give your shoulder a chance to stop bleeding."

I expected Finn to go back behind the partition, but he sat on the ground next to the tub, his arms looped around his knees just as mine were as he faced me. He handed me a bar of hard soap, smirking at my discreet shifts in the water.

"How many soldiers did we lose?" I asked as I started at my arms, scrubbing the layers of grime off myself as best I could. I had dubious hopes that the soap had any sort of antibacterial properties.

"Fifteen Tikbalangs down. It's a hard thing to lose

anyone so close to the finish line, but it could've been a massacre, so Kabayo's taking it all in stride. You saw to patching up the injured ones so the number didn't grow any higher. I'm sure Kabayo will be thanking you for that."

I washed my face, handing Finn the soap as I untied my hair. I dunked myself completely under the water, letting my muddy auburn curls float on the surface. It was the one place I couldn't hear the rain, couldn't hear anything, and though I was encased in dirty water and germs, I commanded myself to remain calm as my shoulder burned.

When I resurfaced, Finn said, "There you are. I was beginning to miss your face. You've been dirty for so long. Utter waste of a beautiful woman, if you ask me."

I pushed the creeping OCD off me from the germy water and smiled. "Thanks. You should really settle down with someone. Spend those compliments on a girl you can invest in."

Finn nodded noncommittally, holding the soap just out of reach. His voice quieted, a note of insecurity creeping through. "Can I ask you something private without you losing it on me?"

"If I haven't freaked out yet, I highly doubt your questions will be the tipping point. Hit me."

"There aren't any women who can walk in Dagat, you know. They're all Mermaids. I only get to see women's legs Topside, or when I'm sent to visit the other countries.

Everyone in Terraway fears the Kataw, so I don't get too near all that often."

"You want to know how you'd look in heels? Can't say I'm surprised," I teased him.

When his request finally bubbled out, I had to strain to hear him. His voice was laced with an unfamiliar note of timidity that sounded foreign on him. "Would you let me wash your feet? Just your feet. Promise."

I wasn't sure what I was expecting him to say, but it surely wasn't that. My brows furrowed as my mouth drew to the side. "Um, you want to wash my feet? I mean, they're pretty disgusting right now."

He waved off the request as if he meant to vanish the words from the air between us. "Never mind. Forget I said anything." He stood up, clearly embarrassed, which was a strange color to see on him. "Call me back when you're finished, and I'll stitch up your shoulder."

I sat a little straighter. "Wait. I guess that'd be okay. No one's ever washed my feet before."

"Really? I find that hard to believe." He knelt next to the tub, nervously running his hands through his brownish-blond hair. The candlelight barely lit his face, but it was just enough for me to see his anticipatory expression over... my feet. "Hold on. Let me change the water first. This is getting pretty dirty."

"I, but I... You can't look."

"I won't." He closed his eyes and turned his head to the side, pressing his hands to the surface of the water. Like turning on a vacuum, the water sucked into his hands in half a minute flat, leaving me clutching myself in a ball as I shivered. Then as if turning on two faucets, water poured out from his palms and filled the tub with warmth that relaxed my muscles enough to loosen the hold I had on my body. The candlelight didn't fall anywhere on me other than my head, so I wasn't worried about Finn seeing anything too sexy for his own good. "Better?"

"Yeah. Thanks. I like the water heated like this."

He extended his hand to me, picking up the soap with his other one as he waited uneasily, as if he was the naked one. The candlelight danced across his bare chest, lighting the abrasions from the battle that smattered across his pectorals, and several scars from wars long ago.

When my toes broke the surface of the water, his eyes saw only my feet. He ran the soap over the top and then down the arch, working up a decent lather. I wasn't expecting a foot massage, and I'm sure he didn't expect my unladylike groan at the pampering that felt too good for coherent words. "You were amazing out there," he said quietly. "I thought you'd stay behind the wall. Then you came tearing out with this crazy, focused look on your face. I'd hoped you'd stay behind me, and I'd have the job of shielding you, but a couple times, you saved me. Ben, too. And you risked your neck to pull Klavin off the field when he was injured." He shook his head, torn between impressed and frustrated. "Where'd you learn to fight like that?"

My eyes were closed as I leaned back in the oval basin. "Seriously? I didn't have any clue what I was doing. I'm just glad it's over."

"You've fought before."

I did a one-shoulder shrug. "I've taken loads of self-defense classes for my old job. Been in a fair few fights, but never a war."

Finn soaped up my foot all over again instead of moving to the next one, rubbing in between each toe as if he expected to eat off of them later. He studied my foot from every angle, bending my leg up as needed to get a better look. "I don't forget the people who save my life in battle."

"Well, you saved me too, so we're square."

He rested my heel on his shoulder as he leaned over the edge of the steel tub, soaping up my ankle and calf. Droplets of water slid down his chest, which really wasn't fair. I mean, he was already completely sexy without all the trappings. He dug his knuckles into my muscles, giving the best kind of deep-tissue massage that set loose too many things I'd been holding onto. Every pass of his hands on my calf felt like I was floating one inch higher. I gripped the edge of the steel tub and bit my lip to keep from groaning like a porn star. "That feels amazing."

"Good. It looks amazing." He stopped at my kneecap, trilling his fingers over my knee that was just above the water's surface. It reminded me that I was naked, and this was more than a simple bath. He carefully rested my foot in the water and moved to the other, starting at my toes as he examined the tops from every angle.

"I've never seen anyone so fascinated with my feet before."

"Wait till you come to Dagat. They'll be fighting to get at you. Lady Mariang won't travel there anymore."

"Seriously? I guess I never thought much about my feet before, other than the usual grossness factor."

"See this?" He traced a small line atop my foot. "What is that?"

"It's the tarsal. You have one, too."

"What about this one?"

I took my time naming every bone in my foot for him, leaning forward to point out each part. It turned the sexy bath time into a medical lesson. What can I say? I have a gift.

Finn massaged and lathered until I was a puddle of limbs. He even stuck his finger in the water every now and then to reheat it for me. It was luxury smack in the middle of the rural setting, and I lapped it up like a glutton. My eyes were closed as he rubbed my calf. My heel was looped on his shoulder as he kneaded my sore muscles that now felt weightless and unbearably sexy. I didn't often feel sexy. I'd prided myself on my shapeless scrubs and my who-cares-what-I-look-like daywear. Now I was naked in a tub while a military captain worked my legs. I don't totally know how I ended up here, but man, the massage felt amazing.

A tiny gasp escaped me when Finn brought the sole of my foot to his mouth and kissed it. "Is that okay?" he asked, his eyes lidded.

My heart started beating faster as I swallowed the lump in my throat. "Um, I think so."

His full lips brushed over each of my toes several times before he licked my big toe, causing me to jerk my foot out of his grip. "Sorry," he murmured, clearly embarrassed.

"It's fine, but that's where I get off the train. Thanks for the massage. Sincerely. Hands down, best massage of my life. If that whole second in command thing doesn't work out for you, you should totally become a masseur."

"I'll keep that in mind, if you can keep this to yourself."

"You overestimate how many friends I have."

"Your Reapers wouldn't approve of... Well, any of this."

I shot him a baleful look. "Hello, Mason and Von aren't my parents. I went here without them, didn't I? But your secret fetish is safe with me. Everyone's got a weird sex thing. It's nothing to be embarrassed about. I've got a thing for Mr. Brady from the Brady Bunch, so no judgment here. Towel?"

I expected him to put it in my outstretched hand, but he opened it and turned his head. I dunked myself under one more time before getting out. The heat from our close proximity warmed my skin when Finn wrap me in the towel. He rubbed the material into my flesh as he pulled me forward to lean into him. He held me against his bare chest, my hair dripping down on his arms that were banded around me. Just as I'd suspected, I'd become a contact junky, which was completely the fault of Von and Mason.

"October?" he said softly as he rubbed my lower back.

"Yeah, Finn?" I pried my face from his chest and looked up into his earnest expression. His face was lit only by the errant flicker of the candle on the other side of the room. He was handsome in that I-just-killed-a-zombie way.

His right hand came up between us as he held me with his left. His thumb and forefinger spread out to make a V on my chin. His slight squeeze had the note of a command to it as he held my face just how he liked to. "Kiss me."

16

INCHES FROM REGRET

It wasn't a request, and I wasn't sure. I didn't know what I was doing anymore. I was seduced and curious and very, very tired. I leaned into his hand, letting him guide my face closer to his until our lips met in a gentle thrum of confusion and desire. The rain pelted the roof to warn us that the danger was inside the candlelit room, and I'd walked smack into it.

Something that smelled like green flooded my nose as Finn parted my lips. His eyes fluttered shut as we took each other down into the abyss of the psychedelic kiss. "Something's happening!" he whispered, half in the throes of desire, and half in distress.

He tasted like the rain and green mixed with silver. His voice sounded like a lusty heartbeat as he deepened the kiss. The V on my face migrated to the back of my head as our passion for fighting with each other mutated into something far more treacherous that would surely take us both under. Glittering green swirls started dancing around us, enticing me to follow the silver and green swells off into the bliss that beckoned me deeper, always deeper.

I heard nothing but Finn's panting and the rain as he began moving us toward the bed, breaking the earthshattering kiss only when I toppled backward onto the straw mattress. His eyes were wide, his pupils dilated as he tried to make sense of the colors and the music. "It's never felt like this before. Are you doing something to me?"

"I'm about to," I admitted. I grabbed him and pulled him down atop me, biting his lip just so I could suck on it and keep it as my treasure. We'd just been through a battle, and I was drunk on the victory. The room seemed to darken with the flickering shadows. The green kept glittering as trumpets announced a song that was only ours. He tasted like the ocean and somehow delicious. My heart raced with adrenaline and conquest as his fingers laced through mine. He played with the top of my towel when we both knew he shouldn't.

"I want you," Finn growled into my mouth, turning from soldier to a veteran of taking foreign women to bed. He ripped my arms over my head, his eyes widening and the spell lifting when he took in my unexpected scream.

"My shoulder!" I explained, the memory of the hot steel slicing me afresh.

His hands quaked as he rubbed my bicep, rolling off me and laying at my side on the bed while we caught our breath, staring guiltily at the wooden ceiling. "Are you alright? I didn't mean to hurt you. I forgot about your shoulder. I think I forgot my own name for a second there."

My hand went to my chest to steady my rapidly beating heart. "No, no. It was the wakeup call we both needed. Nothing good could've come from that. Holy Ian Somerhalder, Batman. That was amazing."

"You're telling me. That's what it's like to kiss an Omen? That's what Danny's been keeping to himself all these years?"

"It would've been even crazier if we were in love. Apparently you see visions and hallucinate even more when that happens. That's why Mason and I stopped things."

Finn was still catching his breath. "Because you started seeing visions?"

"Not me. Him." My elation darkened as reality started pulling me back down to earth. Or, well, to Terraway. "He had visions of his late wife whenever he kissed me, but I didn't know. It got to be to where he started kissing me so he could see her again. Then he started falling in love with her all over again, which made him fall out of love with me. He got frustrated when the visions stopped and he couldn't see her anymore. It was pretty messed up." I pressed my fist to my forehead. "I told myself I wouldn't kiss anyone else. I can't believe I already slipped up. Only kissed one other guy my whole life, and now it's like I can't keep it under control."

Finn let out a low whistle. "I knew things were weird between the three of you, but I never would've guessed all that. No wonder you wanted to run away."

"It's fine, but I have to be careful about who I kiss. Sorry for letting it get so crazy. That foot massage really scrambled my brains."

Finn laced his fingers through mine, still breathless. "Then let me suck on your toes for a while. We're doing that again. That was the best kiss of my life. Deserves a replay."

"No, no. We can't. It gets out of hand really quick, and I don't want that. My life's complicated enough."

"What about Von?"

I did a one-shoulder shrug, trying unsuccessfully to suppress a shudder as the after-effects of the kiss rippled over my skin. "What about him?"

"Did he hallucinate? Did you?"

I turned my head to look at him. "Now it's your brains that're scrambled. Von and I are friends. We've never kissed."

"Fine, keep your secrets. I'm too overstimulated to care right now. It's like your lips are everywhere still." He hmmed with his eyes closed, still enjoying the heady sensation.

"Yours, too."

Finn turned on his side and carefully rolled atop me,

his knees on either side of my thighs. "If I promise not to fall in love with you, can we do that again?"

I leaned up and pecked his cheek. "Not a chance. But thanks for the promise not to fall in love with me. Maybe the worst come-on I've ever gotten, and I've had a fair few sour ones."

Finn deflated and rolled off of me, giving us both a few more seconds to calm down from the huge mistake that luckily hadn't gone past the point of no return. "Well, then let me take a look at your shoulder. I'll get the sewing kit."

"Say that again while you lick your lips," I teased as I sat up on the bed.

He indulged me, making us both laugh. Finn looked younger when he laughed without cruelty, which didn't happen very often apart from his time with me. He twisted my hair and draped it over my good shoulder as he sat back down on the bed, situating himself to sit behind me. I wasn't expecting the kiss to the base of my neck, nor the smile that played on my lips. I warred with the pleasure that rose up inside of me when his affections made my toes curl. I waved off his advance. "Alright, alright. Knock it off. We hate each other, remember? Don't go getting confused."

"You've never had hate sex?" Finn inquired. "It's exquisite."

"I'm a virgin, so no. And my first time's going to be when I get married. So you know, never."

Finn chuckled as his lips found the back of my good

shoulder just to taunt me with the seduction he knew we both wanted. "You're young. You'll make love like a heartbreaker someday. I'm sure of it."

"Thanks." Though Finn was sure, I was not. I wanted to hope that someday I'd be happy with a husband and a home far away from the crazy that always managed to track me down, but my experiences thus far didn't give much credence to that hope.

Finn heard the dubious note in my reply. "You don't think so? I know so. One day when Von grows up and you stop being so... the way you are, you'll see."

I stiffened, and though it was obvious to both of us Finn had said the wrong thing, he was unapologetic. "There's about eleven things wrong with that statement, chief. Try again."

His arm wrapped around me, clutching the cinched part of the towel at my breasts. My heart pounded anew and my back arched when his lips dragged to my ear. "I want to get this towel off of you. Just one tug, and I'd get a clear view of everything I pretended I couldn't see when you were hiding in the water over there."

I gasped. "Are you serious?"

"I'm Kataw. Of course I can see through water," he said with a shrug, as if I was an idiot to think otherwise.

I shivered, fishing for a change of subject so my towel remained in place. "Um, I've got your dagger over there on the nightstand. Thanks for letting me borrow it. Dead useful. I felt clumsy with the sword, but your knife was way easier to maneuver."

Finn moved to the nightstand and picked up his knife. He examined the jagged edges and the jade handle as if it was something precious to him. "I want you to keep this. It's saved my life too many times to count. I'll sleep better knowing it's being put to use defending your life."

I blinked at him, flummoxed. "I... I don't know what to say to that. Don't you need it? Isn't that something that would be better for your country if you had it?"

Finn frowned, confused at his own actions as he rubbed a hand across his chest. "Maybe. Banak gave it to me. Wanted me to use it to defend his throne, but I've got plenty of weapons." He tore his gaze from the blade and met my eyes. "I don't want to defend his throne anymore. I want this blade to protect all of Terraway, not just one nation."

I softened at the sweetness. "Finn, you don't have to do that. I can tell that knife's important to you."

"It's mine, and I'll do with it as I please. It's my way of keeping you safe when I'm not around."

"I mean, that's real generous of you. Thank you. Are you sure? I don't exactly know what I'm doing with it."

"I'm sure." He rested it back on the nightstand and situated himself behind me on the bed again. "Hold still while I work. I don't actually do many healer tasks, so now's a good time not to be annoying."

"Did anyone ever tell you that you're a full-on Prince Charming?"

Finn sniggered as he threaded the needle. "You're the only one who gets to see my charming side. The others get a heavy dose of Captain Finn."

"Not Captain Finn: Pretty Princess?"

"Nah. He only exists around you."

I chewed on this a moment, weighing which personality was his real one, and if it even mattered, since he was bent on being a cruel slave trader. "Well, it was a pleasure to meet you, Prince. Even if you'll have to go away in the morning when other people are around, this was nice. I admit, I don't much like it when life does its magical disappearing act on the sweeter parts of your personality."

Finn paused his needle midair. "You've got quite the mouth on you."

"I happen to think you like me that way."

He leaned in, banding one arm around my middle and pressing his lips to a sensitive spot behind my ear. "I very much do."

I shivered at the kiss and the seduction from the man I knew I could never trust. No matter what happened with the stone, I couldn't allow myself to be alone with Finn much longer if I wanted to respect myself in the morning.

17

MASON'S RUDE AWAKENING

Morning came too early for my liking, and once again I awoke to Finn's hand cupping my breast. I didn't punch him this time, but I did slide his arm down so his hand was around my stomach. The pink quilted comforter was warm and soft, cocooning us in a hazy bliss that felt like a luxury we both craved. I wasn't sure how long we'd slept, but it felt like a solid day and night of no one bugging us.

When a knock sounded impatiently on the door, I realized it might not have been Finn's hand that had woken me. I had gone to sleep in Finn's white palace shirt that fit me like a party dress I'd never had the guts to wear.

When I sat up, Finn moaned. "I'll get it. You don't answer doors here. One wrong move, and the kingdom goes up in flames." He rubbed the sleep from his eyes and sat up, his full lips even puffier in the morning before he'd properly awoken. He brushed his hand down my thigh and kissed my knee, giving us both the guilty shivers before he got out of bed, opening the door in only his trousers. I watched his shoulders tense and the veil of d-bag Finn slide into place. "I was wondering when you'd find us. October? You've got a visitor."

"Huh?" was all I worked out before Mason barreled into the room and took a swing at Finn. Finn dodged and grabbed at Mason's arm, but Mason was used to fighting janky zombies, so he was pretty much prepared for any kind of attack. The two were evenly matched, so the only thing that ended the escalating brawl was me running in between them, placing a hand on either man's chest. Mason seethed while Finn snarled. "Knock it off, both of you! Mason, how'd you find us?"

"How'd I find you?" Mason reared back, affronted. He was soaking wet in his t-shirt, jeans and sturdy black boots. "That's quite a thing to say to me after you ran out on us! We've been looking everywhere. Everywhere! How could you run away like that?" He was shouting, which didn't ever go over well with me. He looked down at my bare legs and cast aside any pretense at playing nice. "Put on some clothes!" He pointed to Finn with too much purpose. "You and I are settling this outside."

"Fine by me. It's been a while since I kicked your hairy butt."

I clapped my hands to stop the posturing and yelling. "Enough! Now sit down, both of you." I waited until they complied, both leaning forward on opposite ends of the side of the bed while I dug in my pack for a pair of shorts. I slid them on and glared at the two. "We're not going to get anywhere fighting like this. Mason, I can't believe you're surprised I ran away. The only shocking thing about it is that I didn't do it the second after you and I imploded."

"That's got nothing to do with this! That was weeks ago."

"Well, it's done. I would've gone off by myself, but I didn't know the way, so I made Finn take me here. We fixed Kabayo's land with the stone, and that's that."

"Are you kidding me with this? 'That's that'? You ran away! You have responsibilities, October. You can't just leave the group, act without council approval and go off without your Pullers! Do you understand that if Sama's army had found you, you could've died? Then where would Terraway be? We've been driving ourselves crazy looking for you. Then I find you in bed with Finn? Finn?!"

"Hey!" Finn groused. "She could do a lot worse."

"Watch yourself," Mason warned, jabbing his finger toward Finn to punctuate this threat. "I raced across Silo on a horse, and I haven't slept in a long time. I can't make any guarantees I won't slit your gills just to shut you up."

Finn's evil tease was back with the squint of his eye at Mason. "You're tired? Lay down in our bed. October warmed me up nice and good last night. Though I'm not sure she'd be open to doing the same for you."

I gasped, letting Finn know he'd hit *me* with his words instead of cutting Mason. His conscience tore him from his fight with Mason to cast me an apologetic look.

Mason was not amused. He stood, towering over me. "October's free to warm any bed she likes. What she's not free to do is run off and jeopardize the kingdom on a whim." He looked down on me with the hardness of barely controlled anger. "Pack up your things. Kabayo needs to see you, and then we're leaving. We're falling behind on the quota of souls."

"You know she's more than ahead on the quota after the mass reaping at the carnival," Finn argued.

Mason was furious at being corrected, his fists clenching. "Omen work takes precedence over everything else. You know that, Finn. The only reason you've been keeping her here after the work was done was so that you could cozy up to her and manipulate her into bed. Well done, old friend, but the fun's over now."

I couldn't believe what a jerk Mason was being. "Get out!" I ordered, pointing to the door.

Mason was temporarily startled that I raised my voice, but recovered quickly. "You don't leave my sight. Pack up, and I'll take you to Kabayo." When I opened my mouth to argue, Mason shook his head. "Four days, October! You've been gone four days! We've been out of our minds for four days trying to find you! If you die or go missing, it falls on

Von and me. All the blame, all the lost lives if our Omen goes down. You can't do that! We're giving up just as much as you, so stop being a baby about it!" His fingers straightened. "I can't even pull from you right now because I'm so mad!"

With my scowl fixed on my face, I shoved the few things back into my pack, angry at the life sentence I'd been given. I shoved on a pair of socks and my shoes with jerking movements. I took the apple Finn handed me from a platter of food on the table, then I stomped behind the partition and changed into one of my shirts, so Finn could have his back.

I couldn't look at either one of them as we made our way down the stairs. Finn paid for the room we rented, and I could feel Mason's eyes on me with every movement I made. He walked behind us, ensuring I didn't breathe without him witnessing the event. I had never felt the desire to run more than I did when Mason watched me like the attack dog he was.

Finn tried to hold my hand, though for what purpose, I couldn't tell you. I batted his advance away, angry that he'd let Mason think we were hooking up, when just kissing was at the furthest edge of my capabilities. "I guess I deserved that."

"Don't talk to me," I seethed. "I'm not some slave girl you can pimp out when it's good for a laugh. You don't get to make me feel like your whore for sleeping in the same bed as you instead of sleeping on the floor."

That was the extent of the conversation I shared with either one of them as we made our way to the castle. The unspoken tension between the three of us only built with every step we took as we walked together through the pouring rain.

18

BOYS, BULLIES AND BRAIDS

For all the "King Kabayo" talk that was tossed around, I'd never pictured Kabayo on an actual throne. The stone palace was simple but ominous on the inside, with many horse-shaped helmets lining the walls that led up to the oversized metal-hewn throne. Kabayo's grand chair had a bearskin thrown over it, sealing the look of luxury without bedecking everything in blinged-out gold and diamonds. It was gritty and precise, which suited the surly horseman perfectly.

There were four guards at attention flanking the throne when the three of us were let in. Mason pushed ahead, his shoulders forward as he geared up to start yet another fight. "How long did you know she was here? How many days without reporting it to the council?"

Kabayo didn't bother standing at Mason's verbal assault. His smug smile couldn't be contained, and he refused to be ruffled by Mason's accusations. "For all I knew, she'd only made better time than we all thought she would. Why would I assume you and Von couldn't keep track of one small girl?"

"You assumed we sent her down into Terraway without us? That's how you're playing this?"

"Children play, men plan. I think I'll take my piece of the stone and concentrate on rebuilding my kingdom. We'll be off of Sama's rations in no time with the rain falling on our land again." When Mason cast a venomous look at Kabayo, the king responded with a brazen, "If you can't keep track of your charge, it's nothing to do with me."

"You let her stay here knowing she didn't have her Reapers. There was a battle not half a mile from here! What if she'd been near the battlefield? What if you'd lost and they came after her here? What then? What comes of Terraway if the Omen goes down? Or don't you care, now that you've got your bit of the stone?"

I cringed, hoping Mason wouldn't find out I'd been fighting. He was already so angry.

Instead of arguing back, Kabayo turned to look at me with a teasing smile drawing up the sides of his elongated mouth. "Have you been keeping secrets from your Puller?" He tsked me as if I was five.

Mason's head whipped to me, and I could practically see steam billowing out of his ears. "What kind of secrets?"

"This is who you are?" I cocked my head to the side, my arms akimbo, daring Kabayo to mention that I'd been in the battle. "Seriously? You want to start a fight with me after everything I just did for you?"

Kabayo was too pleased with himself to hold back. "Now, now. I'm sure Captain Finn made certain to keep her far from the battlefield, tucked safely in his bed."

"Shut up," Finn murmured to Kabayo, the tips of his ears turning pink.

Mason looked on the verge of either vomiting or Hulked-out raging. His voice was low and gravelly when he addressed Kabayo. "Have all the laughs you want. You've got two minutes before I port her back to the mansion so Ezra can deal with her. I fear if I deal with her, we'll be short an Omen, a Kataw captain and a Tikbalang king."

"Well, since you asked so nicely." Kabayo was enjoying his upper hand, finally on top instead of begging from other countries for food and water. "I need a moment with October first, and then you and Finn can take her back to Ezra."

"I'll be staying here," Finn said, his hands behind his back as he stood at attention.

"If Ezra needs you, I won't risk his wrath. I had no idea the girl snuck away without Daddy's permission," Kabayo taunted me. "Now that the situation's been brought to my attention, I'll act as a member of the council and send you on back to the mansion to answer for your crime. It's my duty, you understand."

Finn's jaw clenched. "Oh, I understand. Now that

you've got rain, all the service my men have done you is forgotten. We risked everything for your kingdom to bring you the stone. I won't be returning to the council if you're on it."

"Now that I have rain, I don't have a need for the council," Kabayo ruled.

"You're a bastard!" I raged, breaking out from the background and stomping up to the throne. "How dare you treat what we did like you don't owe us the world! I could've died for this, and we're both gonna get it from Ezra. Get off your stupid throne and come stand down here like you're one of us." I looked to the soldiers I could tell Kabayo was posturing for like an insecure freshman. "Tell your men to give us a minute so you can stop talking like a fool."

When Kabayo hesitated, Mason roared, "You know the Omen is above you! You know she can command your army whether or not you're fit to rule!"

Well, that was sure news to me.

"Give us a minute," Kabayo said to his men, his bravado falling slowly, like a feather losing its flight midway to greatness. When the soldiers left us with wary expressions, Kabayo's voice lowered to a humbler tone. "I have a score to settle with you, Omen."

My upper lip curled as I readied for whatever ridiculous bone Kabayo wanted to pick with me. "Settle it, then. I friggin' dare you."

Mason's fists were clenched. "Then we leave after this.

Ezra can deal with Finn and the Omen."

My head snapped to glare at Mason and his no-name address of me. "So that's how it is?"

"That's how you made it. You treated Von and me like strangers, running out on us. You wanted to go rogue? Then I'm the guard, and you're the charge. My only duty to you is keeping you fit for your post."

"Fine!" I spouted with too much attitude.

"Fine!"

Finn rolled his eyes, relaxing his perfect posture. "Oh, will the both of you just shut up?"

Kabayo stepped off the raised platform his throne was on and stalked toward us, his glassy bulging eyes on me. He stopped directly in front of me and spoke as if there was no one else in the room. "You ignored the council, ignored the schedule we all agreed on, stole the stone and went on the mission without your Pullers and without proper supervision."

"Hey!" Finn argued, but Kabayo ignored him.

I kept my chin high in defiance. "I did. All except the stealing part. It's my stone. I don't need permission to move my own belongings from one place to another. So, you know, suck it."

Okay, maybe that was crass, but I knew Von would've laughed if he was still talking to me.

Kabayo was not amused. He squared his shoulders to mine. "You misunderstand me. I didn't list those as marks against you. Those are the reasons I respect you. You did all that for my people, for my land that you'd never even seen before this week. You saw our land at our worst, and me at mine, and you still sacrificed yourself for us. I can't repay you for that, but I can try."

"Oh, um, thanks. Sorry about the 'suck it' comment, then. And it's cool. It was good timing all the way around. I wanted to get out of my situation for a little bit anyway, so it's no big deal."

Finn took a step forward to stand next to me as Mason grumbled under his breath about my AWOL status. "It *is* a big deal, and no matter what she says, you'll treat her like the queen who just saved your land."

I sighed, letting the men broker whatever needed to be postured about so we could be done with this already. Kabayo waved Finn off and placed both his hands on my arms, gearing up for the business. "I owe you something equal to the redemption of my land, but I don't know what that would be. So instead, I'll give you the next best thing." He reached up behind his head, running his hand through his mane. He looked like an odd half-horse half-man caught mid-lather in the shower or something. Mason gasped and Finn took a step back when Kabayo yanked one of the three braids from his head out by the root. It was about as thick as a rope. He held it out between his hands, long and black, presenting it like a glorious sword.

I didn't know what to say. I mean, it was a braid of his hair. I tried to be respectful of what I'm sure was a nice gesture, judging by the identical "holy crap" looks Mason and Finn wore. "Um, thanks. I don't own any horse hair, so this will be my first."

Mason forgot about his anger toward me, consumed with wonder at the braid. "This isn't just a piece of hair. This is his token. Every Tikbalang king has three tokens in their hair, and whoever they give one to gets special protection."

Finn had equal rapture in his voice. "Some people used to try to steal the tokens, and they got a severe curse. This... this is a grand gift, October."

I'd been jerked around enough with not being told anything about anything and being forced into it. I knew better than to accept a horse hair I wasn't totally educated on just yet. "Wait. What kind of protection?"

Kabayo was patient with my questions, which was a rare show of kindness from him. "You'll be able to contact me without going through Ezra because I'll be able to feel your stronger emotions, the danger around you. That would unite my kingdom with yours. So if you're in trouble, I can feel that and act on it."

"Sort of like extra insurance?"

"Yes. It also might give you certain enhancements. Time will tell on that front."

I didn't know what to say. "This is a gift? It doesn't make things more complicated?"

Kabayo smiled down at me. "I can't imagine anything making your life *more* complicated. No, this would help."

"Well, thank you. That's right nice of you." I tightened

my fist. "But I won't take it if you turn on the council. Don't you dare turn on Ezra just because you're the coolest kid in school again. You were with us when you were in need, so you should be with us when you have. Anything in between's just plain cowardly, and I won't accept gifts from a coward."

Kabayo's eyes glinted with anger at me. "Cowardly?"

I ignored Finn's hiss that I was skating on very thin and oh-so-breakable ice. "You couldn't risk yourself to help the other kingdoms before, but now you can. Now you have something to give. If you don't help now, it's because you're afraid to get your hands dirty. Either that or you're a child. I can't decide which one's worse to have on a throne – a child or a coward."

We glared at each other for several long beats in which neither Finn nor Mason breathed. "You're treading on dangerous ground, Omen."

"And you're running headfirst into quicksand if you think you can disrespect the council my dad sits on and expect me to take presents from you. You turn your back on my family, and you can forget any sort of alliance with me." I couldn't pinpoint when exactly a fierce protectiveness toward Ezra seared my heart, but somewhere along the road, Ezra Manaul had become my father.

Kabayo glared at me, weighing his limited options. "Fine. I'll remain on the council and help how I can."

"Glad to hear you'll do the bare minimum. I didn't have to come here, you know. If I hadn't, you'd be dead by now.

You and everything you worked for. Be better than this. You got a second chance at serving Terraway. Be a good man, Kabayo."

"Are you quite finished lecturing me?"

"For now. Unless you piss me off more. Then I've got a whole riot act I can read you with plenty of this." I mimed shaking my fists in the air and throwing a fit.

"Give me your arm then." Kabayo took his braid that was easily two feet long and wrapped it around my forearm in a crisscross that made X's on both the inside and the outside of my forearm from wrist to elbow. Then he tied it off around my wrist like a bracelet. He picked up my hand, examining the back of it with dismay. "These scrapes, you're still doing it? I thought your Pullers would've put a stop to this."

Mason grumbled, "She's been without Pullers for four days, and she was resisting me before that."

"I wonder why that is," Finn mused with a touch of evil to his smile. "Sounds like it was one bad kiss you gave her."

Mason pointed his hand aggressively at Finn. "You'll shut your mouth about it! You don't know anything about her or me."

"Oh, I know enough about her. I think I know exactly what you know about her."

The cockiness Finn exuded made me lash out. "Both of you, get out! I mean it. I don't need you two barking in my ear about stupid stuff that should never have happened. Had I known you'd both devolve into such jackholes, it wouldn't have gone down like it did. Neither of you actually love me or want me; you're just using me as something to fight over. Fight over sports teams, like normal men! Get a hobby and get out!"

They both narrowed their eyes at me with varying degrees of scoffing and anger. Kabayo took in their lack of movement toward the door and raised his voice to enforce my rule. "The Omen told you to leave. If you don't obey, I'll send in my guards to make it happen as she wishes."

Mason and Finn grumbled, shoving each other like petulant children as they left.

19

SCARRED AND SCARED

The second the heavy doors closed behind them, I breathed out the heaviness that never seemed to completely go away. "Thanks for that."

Kabayo surprised me by wrapping his arm around my waist, holding me in a way that confused me and made me blush before I started squirming. When this seemed to be the extent of the touch, I relaxed, resting my head on Kabayo's firm chest as he spoke quietly to me. "It's a different level we're on. It's hard to know when to rule and when to let your guard down." After I put him in his place, Kabayo seemed to take a shine to me more than usual.

Men are weird.

I closed my eyes and tried to center myself. "Does it get easier? I don't want to rule. I just want my life back."

"I know, *hani*." Kabayo held me tenderly to his chest. It

was a sweet gesture I wasn't expecting, but surprisingly needed. "Hold still. The transfer stings a little."

"The what?" was all I worked out before my arm started tingling. He held me still even as I tried to jerk away to itch the bite of the braid as it traveled up my arm and began to trickle through my whole body. The irritation turned from a nuisance to a slow-building fire I couldn't extinguish. "It's supposed to feel like my arm's burning? Ow!" I began to understand why he'd initiated the hug – he needed to hold me in place and keep me from thrashing around.

"Squeeze my hand. It'll pass." The fire built up in me, feeling like white and blue flickering through my veins. I gritted my teeth and closed my mouth through the scream that welled up in me. I buried it in Kabayo's shoulder while he held me tight.

Then just as quick as it built, the invisible flames began to diminish. He held me as my body deflated, looping his long horse head over my good shoulder. I tried not to worry about barn germs, but I knew they were there, crawling all over me now. I went to take the lock of hair from my arm, but it had vanished. In place of the hair was a red burn mark in the exact loopy X pattern. "Is... Is that permanent?" I asked, trying to keep my panic at bay.

"It'll fade a little in time, but it'll turn black when I'm in danger, and mine will turn black when you're in danger." He displayed his forearm to me, revealing an exact match of my burn on his arm.

"Oh, your arm! Are you okay?"

Kabayo's amused expression didn't fade as he watched me fawn over him. "You're just as burned as I am, but you're concerned about me? I can see why Ezra's so taken with you."

"He won't be after what I pulled. Whatever. Father of the Year time had to end someday, right?"

"Let me show you how this works." He patted my back and stepped aside so I could have some breathing room. "I didn't want to tell you this until my land was secure, but I got word that Von, well, he was killed by a Matruculan vamp hunter while you were here moving the stone."

He said those words, exactly like that. Like he hadn't shattered everything. Like he hadn't ripped something precious away from me. Like my insides weren't bleeding all over his throne room floor.

The world stopped spinning, cotton filled my ears and all the revulsions in the world felt like a distant playground. Everything horrible and hefty hit me over the head at once, knocking me like a ton of bricks dipped in heavy metal. I clutched my chest and stumbled back, too beyond coherency for tears. "What? He... Von... No! No!"

"He was out looking for you, and got caught without Mason or you there for backup. It was quick, if that helps you. The hunter brought Ezra Von's severed head, if you wanted to say goodbye."

Guilt I couldn't process tumbled over me, pushing me

onto the ground as I screamed the only word that found its way to my lips. "No! No!"

Mason came busting in through the wood double doors, his shoulders forward as if readying for a fight, with Finn following on his heels. "What?! What's wrong? What did you do to her?"

"Von! How could you not tell me? He was my... No!" My heart felt like there was a vice around it, keeping normal beats on hold and less potent than they were supposed to be. Von added color and warmth to my cold and focused life. He was good for me, and up until our last conversation, he'd been good *to* me. I didn't have many people around who were both.

"What about Von?" Mason asked, scrunching his nose at me in confusion.

"I was just making sure it worked. You're the first person I've ever bound myself to." Kabayo displayed his arm to me. The pink burned loops had turned a horrible black with a blue glow around the scar, looking like an alien infection had taken over his arm in a decorative X-shaped fashion. "See? You're in agony, so I got a signal that you need help. I'll get that whenever you're like this, and I can be there." He waved his hand to dismiss my angst. "Von's perfectly fine. He's not dead. I was just testing the connection."

I looked up, my vision going from foggy to seeing red. "You... You what? You made that up just to jerk me around? You're a bastard!" I picked myself up off the floor, unsure if I wanted to lunge at Kabayo to choke him, or if I wanted to run home to find Von and make sure it wasn't real.

Kabayo shrugged unapologetically at my accusation. "That may be. But this connection is the best gift I can give you. If you need me, I'll be there." He picked up my backpack, which I hadn't seen on the floor, tucked behind his throne. He handed it to me by the straps, afraid to touch the bag itself.

"The only thing I need you for is if I wanted to make some glue the old fashioned way," I jabbed, speaking through gritted teeth, my fists clenched at my sides. "That was below the belt, Kabayo."

"I wish you all the luck in both our worlds when you have to go before Ezra. You'll certainly need it."

I gulped, never having known a father who I'd disappointed for legit reasons. I held my head high and nodded once at Mason. "Do it to it. Let's go home."

20

CRAPPY JEWELRY FROM EZRA

We landed ungracefully in a heap of limbs smack in the middle of the council room in Ezra's mansion. I groaned without apology. "Oh, man! I meant my home, not here. You did that on purpose," I accused Mason, who was the first to stand.

I was a little nervous about the whole Ezra thing, but knew I could handle myself in a fistfight. If Ezra threw the first punch, no matter how much bigger than me he was, I could figure something out. My biggest concern was finding Von. I tore open the doors and bolted out into the mansion. "Von? Von?" I called, hoping to see his face to confirm Kabayo had been lying. I entertained a brick of anxiety that sank in my stomach and wouldn't dissolve until I saw Von with my own two eyes.

When I rounded the corner that led to the foyer, I ran

smack into Ezra. I backed up in surprise, my hands raised in a defensive position in case Ezra decided to haul off and hit me instead of yelling first. His hands flew to my arms, and I knocked them away in an outward sweeping motion. This time my hands balled into loose fists, hovering a few inches in front of my chin, ready to fend him off if he struck me.

Ezra held up his hands in surrender. "Steady, darling! You're here? Who found you? Where have you been?" Then he wrapped me in a hug that crushed the breath from me and confused my fight.

"Huh? What's happening? What is this?" I was stiff, unsure if this was part of the attack, or if he really was genuinely glad to see me.

"It's a hug, you daft girl." Ezra pulled back but did not release me, his hands gripping my biceps. "You gave me such a fright! I didn't know if you'd been abducted or if you'd run off! I didn't even know which world or which country you were in. You can't do that to me!"

I let him shake me, since it seemed he needed the release, and I needed a few seconds to catch up. "You're not mad?"

"Of course I'm mad!" he shouted, though his eyes said worry, not anger. "I take Bev to the hospital, I turn around and you're gone! You and the stone, just gone! Where were you? Who found you?"

"Mason."

"What happened? Did someone abduct you? No one's been able to find Captain Finn, either." He shook his head, flustered, and pulled out his phone to call someone. "Danny? We found her. Yes. I have no idea. You can come home, though." He brought me to the living room and called Lynna to bring me some tea. Then he left a message on Von's phone before sitting me down on the white leather sofa, his earnest eyes imploring me to talk to him. "Are you hurt? Your face! It's swollen across your cheekbone. And your hands and arms are all torn up. Is that a bruise? You can't take off without a Puller!"

"I'm fine. And Finn didn't abduct me. If anything, it's the other way around."

"When you say it like that, it makes me sound like the damsel in distress," Finn said, making his presence known as he rounded the corner, his hands shoved behind his back, like he was restraining himself to endure a flogging. "Good afternoon, Ezra."

Mason followed in behind him, his angry expression telling me that even though he was on two legs, I was sitting in the company of a wolf, not the man I'd made out with.

"'Good afternoon'? You make off with my daughter, and then stroll into my home with a 'good afternoon'?"

"'Make off' sounds so cheap. Can't we say I ran away with your daughter? Far more the-other-side-of-the-tracks, if you ask me."

The fire in Ezra's eyes matched the fight I feared from

him. I didn't know what to expect, so I opted for explaining before he could get too worked up. "Finn, knock it off. Seriously, do you have any friends? Ezra, I left to get a jump on things, sneak in with only one guide rather than take the whole entourage." I explained to Ezra my side of the story, and our subsequent journey through Silo that only knit his eyebrows closer together in what I swore looked like concern. I left out my part in the whole zombie war thing, pretty sure that might push him over the edge. My story skipped from dropping the stone in the well to Mason showing up and bringing us to the mansion.

Mason was furious. He stomped behind the couch, placed one hand on my shoulder and jerked my head to the opposite one. "Then how do you explain this?" he roared, exposing my stitches to Ezra.

I would not be the small one. I didn't care how big Mason was, he stretched my stitches on purpose, tearing at the tender skin just enough to make me wince. What's worse is that he spoke like he had the right to scold me.

I twisted out of his grip and stood, jumping away from him with my fists raised, just in case. We fumed at each other, upper lips curled in loathing we couldn't get a cap on. "You want to jerk me around? Come and get it, jackhole! Don't sneak behind me. Look me in the eye when you try to rip my stitches!"

Mason fumbled, which I hadn't been expecting. "Clearly I didn't mean to rip your stitches."

"Clearly? Clearly?!" Anxiety swarmed up and choked

me around the neck. It was pretty good timing, actually. Kept the string of nonsense curse words trapped inside of me for the time being.

Ezra held up his hands, the sweeping movement in my periphery making me flinch as I prepared for a blow. His face fell to pity as he took in my defensive stance that was aimed in too many directions. His voice was gentle as he lowered his hands at a snail's pace. "Sweetheart, you don't have to be afraid of me. I've never raised my hand to a woman."

"I don't know the first thing about you to know if that's even the truth," I pointed out.

Ezra squared his shoulders and drew something black out of his pocket. "Then let's start with the basics. I'm the ruler of the residents of Terraway who live Topside, and that includes their descendants. Give me your hand." He extended his arm slowly, and I hoped as much as I guessed that he wouldn't hurt me. I placed my hand in his, retracting it twice like a gun-shy animal before I let it rest there. He lifted the black bit of leather that looked sort of like a bracelet with swirls burned into the sides, turning it left and right to show me it wasn't anything more than a strip of leather. Finn and Mason both gasped as Ezra tied the bracelet around my wrist, working on a complicated knot as he spoke. "This is a *karsel* bracelet. I would imagine it works much like an anklet a prisoner would wear, only you're of course not a prisoner here."

"What?"

Ezra finished off the knot and traced his finger along the burn marks on the leather. "These are parts of a charm meant to keep you here. I lost you and the stone once; I won't lose you both again."

"What are you talking about?" I started picking at the leather lace to untie it, but it was proving more problematic than I anticipated.

"That leather's bound to the mansion. You can go anywhere you wish in my home, but the bracelet won't let you leave." My dubious look drew out more explanation from him. "You can try to walk out the door, but the bracelet will remain here. It's attached to your arm until I remove it. Not Mason, not Von. Only me."

I stared up at him, doubtful. "I've got news for you, Ezra. I'm just going to cut it off the second you leave. It's a piece of leather, not titanium."

"I would advise against that. Whatever pain you inflict on the leather will mirror itself onto you. If you try to cut the leather, the knife will only slice into you, leaving the bracelet untouched."

My nostrils flared as I fumed. "I'm not your prisoner! I don't belong to you! I didn't even mean to come back here. Mason screwed me over on purpose."

Ezra stood straighter, looking down on me imperiously. "You did this to yourself the second you went to Terraway on your own. The stone belongs to Terraway, and the council speaks on their behalf. Going off without informing us? Unacceptable and irresponsible. Sitting on the council, as you have, means you're accountable to them, as well. You'll stay here until I say otherwise."

"We'll see about that." I was livid. I was girl on a mission. I had never been grounded before, and this felt like that kind of punishment. There was no thanks, no job well done. There wasn't even a "Hey, that sounds rough. You alright?" It was a swift and harsh judgment I didn't have the patience for. I clawed at the backs of my hands as I marched away from the guys. I tried the front door, just to see if the whole thing was a bluff. I flung open the door with a triumphant smile, but the second I tried to step a toe out onto the porch, my foot bounced back, like it had hit an invisible trampoline. Frustrated, I kicked over and over, drawing eyes and sniggers from the peanut gallery. I whirled on Ezra. "Let me out! I don't live here, and I'm not your prisoner!"

"Would you feel more comfortable resting in your bedroom? It's been fully stocked for your use for months now. New clothes, new shoes, whatever you need will be ordered for you. But until I can trust that you won't disappear the second my back is turned, you're staying right here. My house is more secure than yours anyway. It was only a matter of time before you moved in. Your mother will be living here, too, as soon as she's given a clean bill of health."

Ice banged around in my veins at mention of the

person I'd run from in the first place. My voice was level, lest I speak too loudly and tear a hole through the roof. "I will not live with Bev ever again. I made a promise to myself, and you won't make me break it."

"You have to stop!" Ezra exclaimed, motioning to my hands. "You're bleeding! Don't you feel that? Mason, do something!"

Mason ran for me, and I panicked. "No! Don't touch me!" I didn't want him to pull so much anxiety that I submitted to incarceration.

His arms were rough as he tried to get a grip on me for a decent pull. I twisted away, but he was persistent, and ended up accidentally knocking me backwards into the wall.

I didn't think it through. I didn't think at all. Before I knew it, my hand swung out and slapped him across the face. Mason dropped his grip on me, and I gasped at the horrible thing I'd done. Sure, I'd gutted zombies, but slapping Mason was a level of violence I was ashamed of.

I was Bev. I hit someone instead of using my words. I hit Mason, who despite everything, I cared a great deal for. My voice was quiet with disgrace. "Mason, I'm sorry. That was awful. I... let me get you some ice."

"Don't. Move." Mason snarled at me, holding his cheek as it throbbed in betrayal.

Ezra's voice was laced with disappointment. "You have every right to defend yourself when a full-grown man throws you up against the wall. The Omen-Puller bond is based on trust, not force."

"Trust? You want to talk about trust? I turn my back and she's gone!" Mason turned to aim his hurt in my direction. "No note, no message, nothing! You know this is my job now. You're jeopardizing my career and Von's! I get that you were mad at me, but Von? You did this to him, too. And what about Ollie? You brought him in on the secret, and then left him to deal with all of it by himself. You know what I was doing when you ditched? I was taking care of *your* mother, because that's what friends do." He shook his head and exhaled, his cheeks puffed out. "I don't know what I ever saw in you."

I hung my head as the guilt washed over me. My lower lip quivered at the public recitation of my sins, but I kept my tears tucked tight inside me. "I'm sorry, Mason. I shouldn't have run. You're right. It was selfish."

Finn gave a disgusted "pfft." "Nothing about your trek through Silo was selfish. You did right by the council, and right by Terraway. You ran away to keep the people you love away from danger. Ending a famine and a drought while keeping your family safe isn't selfish."

I was a person who could hit her friends. I couldn't think of anything worse. Sure, Mason had been rough, but I could've gotten out of the hold a dozen different ways. "I'm sorry, Mason. I'll fix it." I turned on my heel and darted for the kitchen, yanking open the freezer and pulling out a bag of frozen peas.

"What are you doing?" Mason shouted, making me jump when he stomped into the kitchen, not stopping until he was in my face.

I dropped the bag of peas, afraid of too many things in that moment. I was afraid Mason would lose his temper and shove me, sure. I was more afraid that I would become a person who struck the people she loved. "P-Peas," I explained, reaching down and retrieving the bag with trembling fingers. "For your cheek."

"Huh?"

I pointed to the place I'd struck him. "I h-hit you. Mason, I'm so sorry."

Mason studied my sorrow, and his shoulders dropped a noticeable amount. "What are the peas supposed to do? Is that some Topsider remedy?"

Carefully, I placed the cold bag on his cheek. "Takes the sting out."

Despite our feud, Mason chuckled. "Well, whataya know. I'm cured." He took the bag off his face and set it on the counter. "You shouldn't have run. You hurt me."

I nodded, keeping my chin down so I didn't appear to be arguing. "I'm sorry. I didn't mean to upset you, but that's exactly what I did."

He ran his hands over his face, exhaustion dawning on his senses when the fight finally reached a crest. "I was too rough out there. I'm surprised you only slapped me. You should punch me next time I lose my temper like that."

"I can't believe I hit you. I'm so ashamed. Please forgive me."

"Come here." Mason motioned me forward, but I was hesitant to sink into his open arms.

"I don't want you to pull. I'm serious. I deserve to feel terrible for hitting you. Don't take that away from me."

Mason nodded, but still beckoned me to him. The solid embrace didn't solve everything, but it was a start. He forgave me enough to be kind, and I trusted him enough to hug me without pulling.

"Are the two of you quite finished?" Ezra rubbed his forehead, exasperated. I wasn't sure how long he and Finn had been watching our exchange, but suddenly there they were. "October, you've been four days without a Puller. You look haggard, darling. Let Mason help you."

I kept my voice low, but laid down the law all the same. "I don't care how I look. Pretty matters zero in this line of work. I'm a person, not a show dog."

"You're still scratching your arms!" Ezra pointed out, flustered.

Crap. I really needed to start paying better attention to that.

Ezra moved slowly toward me, his hands up in surrender. "This isn't how I want things. We were starting to understand each other, and now we're here. I was taking care of your mother in the emergency room, and what happened? Did I do something to upset you?"

"Hello. You're holding me here against my will. That's pretty upsetting."

Ezra squinted his left eye at me, sizing me up. "Mason, Finn, why don't you two go get something to eat? October and I need to have a few words."

Finn strolled past, clapping me twice on my good shoulder, no doubt thrilled Ezra hadn't laid into him yet. Mason followed after, avoiding my penitent gaze.

21

THE MONSTER YOU THINK I AM

"**A**re you hungry, October Grace?" Ezra inquired politely, as though there had never been any tension between us. He'd given me the privacy to call Ollie for a few minutes, but it did little to diffuse the fuming that clenched my jaw. "I can ask Lynna to make you whatever you like."

"I can cook for myself in my own home," I answered, reminding him that diplomacy wouldn't be enough to diffuse our fight. I extended my arm, clenching my fist. "Now take this thing off me and let me go." My eye caught on the red dripping from the scabs on my arms, and I gasped without meaning to.

"Yes, it's bad, isn't it?" Ezra looked forlornly at my hands and arms, as if the scratches hurt him just as much as they stung me. "I daresay sometimes you may not even realize you're doing it. I've been through quite the ordeal with your mother. I might have some insight on why you're hurting yourself, and why she was the way she was."

"Huh? 'Was'? What are you talking about?"

"You've been carrying the sagrado stone through Silo, correct?"

"Yeah."

He turned and extended his elbow to me, silently asking if he could escort me like a gentleman. I was having a hard time getting a read on this guy. "Let's sit at the table. Let me dress your wounds while I tell you all that you've missed on your little adventure."

"Thanks, but I'm all bloody. I don't want to ruin your nice clothes." I walked next to him instead of holding onto his arm. Everything felt weird here. The second I decided he was a bad guy, he acted all civil, making my head spin.

When we reached the conference room used for council meetings, Ezra pulled a chair out for me, calling Lynna to bring him the first aid kit. He was polite and thought through his words before they birthed from his serene mouth. He was the picture of decorum, and I was a harried mess. "Your mother signed herself into a psychiatric facility after they released her from the hospital. Oliver's going through quite the shock himself."

I leaned my elbow on the long oval table. "Just so you know, nothing of what you're saying makes a lick of sense to me."

Ezra took the kit from Lynna, thanked her and shut the door to give us privacy. "I'm sorry. Let me start from the beginning. The sagrado stone has many magical properties, but it was never meant to be touched. Hence, why it turns people into stone."

Of course Ezra would say "hence" like it belonged in normal conversation. "Sure. That much I get."

"You, Oliver and Allison are immune to the dangers of touching the stone because of the rare magic in your blood. Bev, however, doesn't have magic in her. She's purely human. While the stone doesn't turn humans into rock, I'm learning that it does warp their minds the longer they're around it. You all lived with the stone in your trailer for years, and from what I understand, Bev had the most contact with it."

"That's true. When I was younger, Ollie boarded up the door to our room, so we got in and out through the window. It wasn't until we moved out that I started using the front door to visit her once a week. The stone was in her part of the trailer, not ours."

"And Oliver and Allison didn't visit her, did they?" He rolled up his sleeves and started cleaning the scrapes on my arms. I was embarrassed, and retracted my hands. "October Grace, you're cut. Please let me help you. I'm not the monster you think I am."

It took a few starts and stops, but eventually my arms landed on the table, though I couldn't look at him as he cleaned my cuts. It was too nice, too paternal. I swallowed a lump in my throat and went back to the conversation. "Ollie and Allie didn't go back after we moved out. They both swore they'd never set foot in the trailer ever again. When we found Bev last week, it was the first time Ollie had been inside the trailer since we moved out."

Light fell on Ezra as I confirmed something for him. "I suspected as much. Oliver's so put together. You'd never guess at the things that haunted him. I would venture to say that Allison's much the same, unaffected now in her adult life. She escaped the torment that held onto you and keeps Bev prisoner."

"Affected by what?" I asked, staring at my jeans.

"Affected by the stone's magic. It was never around humans, so we don't have the data to study. But over the last few days I've been watching Bev, listening to Oliver and putting pieces together to make sense of the mess you grew up in."

I swallowed the lump in my throat. "Thanks, but I've been in therapy before. I already know why I am the way I am."

"Ah, but there's more to it than you like things clean because you were born into a mess. And there's far more to these cuts on your arms than the pain inside being too much to handle."

I jerked my hands back. "Don't psychoanalyze me. I'm not your science experiment."

"Of course, dear. Apologies." Ezra waited for me to set my arms back on the table before he continued cleaning them. "This isn't your fault," he said quietly, drawing a roll of gauze out of the kit.

My voice was quiet, and I felt very far away from reality. It was almost like we were in a cave, and no one could hear my confessions. "Yes, it is. I cut myself. No one else did. It's my fault."

He held up my hands so I could see the marks I'd dug. "This isn't your fault."

"I make sure the pain's my fault. I can control that. I can live in something if I can control a little piece of it."

Ezra dropped my hands, leaned forward and crushed me to him in a hug that felt like being dunked underwater.

I wiggled out of his hug before it could make me tear up. "I'm fine. I don't need that like you think I do. I can handle myself."

Ezra straightened, composing himself. "It's not your fault, these cuts. It's the stone."

I sighed at his explanation, dubious. "Look. No disrespect to your awesome connection with Bev, but I know exactly why I am the way I am, and it's got nothing to do with any old doorstop."

Ezra ignored my sass. "Since you took the sagrado stone out of the trailer, Bev's been slowly coming out of her fog. It took a while since she's been nonstop poisoned by it for decades. She can see your brother clearly now. She can see herself clearly. It's why she checked herself into the facility. She's afraid of what she might do to herself now that she can feel the guilt of all she put you three through. The stone warped her mind. You taking the stone to Silo did her a great favor. She'd never been away from it for that long. The longer she's far, far away from it, the more she can heal – become the person she truly was before her mind was poisoned. She took a long time to come out of her fog, but it's lifting." He pointed to my arms. "You've had direct contact with the stone for several days straight, and look at what it's done to your mind. You're slowly being warped by it."

I churned this logic over in my brain. "Then why didn't it hit me this hard when I was walking through Sakuna? I was holding it then, too, and I only started going off the rails when my meds wore out."

"You had your Pullers, if you recall. They kept things in step. Almost like an extra dose of your medication."

My frown couldn't be helped; it was all so strange when filtered through Ezra's new logic. "And you think Bev's been warped by the stone? I took it to Terraway, so she started to heal?"

"That's exactly right."

I shook my head as Ezra finished wrapping my arms. "You're trying to explain away years of abuse by blaming it on a rock. I get that you want to be with her, and that she's going through some sort of mental breakdown, but it can't be as simple as shifting the blame to an inanimate object. Life doesn't work that way."

"I assure you, Bev is taking full responsibility for her actions, perhaps more than she should. It's why she's in a facility where she can be monitored, and where I plan on going back to after you're settled in here."

I raised my hands to fend off the lecture I could smell coming like a stinky piece of old chicken. "I'll go check in on her and see how she's doing. Promise. Trust me, no matter what her mental state's been, I never turned my back on her."

"Oh, you're not going to be able to visit your mother until that bracelet comes off. Not for at least a couple days."

"You're joking." I stood and backed away from the table, glaring down at him.

"I assure you, I'm not. I care about your feelings in this, of course, but I'm in charge of the Terraway events that occur Topside. You absconding with the stone is cause for concern. What if you did it again? What if you ran off with Captain Finn, of all people, and got yourself killed? Aside from my personal grief, Terraway would never recover if the stone was lost and the most powerful Omen gone. It would leave Mariang to reap for the whole of Terraway, which she cannot survive."

Anger flooded through me that this was the reason he was holding me hostage. I took a steadying breath so my words weren't tainted with aggression. "Good to have all the cards on the table finally. Yes, I know you and the whole friggin' world would gladly throw me to the wolves if it would save Mariang. You'll happily shove me in harm's way, putting more than double the workload on me if it saves her."

I stared up at the ceiling as Ezra spluttered. I tried to

collect my anger that seemed to swing out like a punch with no conscience. This wasn't me. I don't know what my deal was.

I took a few steadying breaths before continuing. "Don't get me wrong, I like her a lot. I get why she's worth saving, and I'm doing all I can." Emotion resounded in my words that I wished I could iron out, but it all welled up in me without any chance of coming out in a nicely put-together box. "Just once, I want a dad to care about me. I want any parent in the world to want good things for me that have nothing to do with beauty pageants, saving the world or furthering an agenda. I want someone to stop me when I volunteer to jump off a cliff to save someone else's life. Not because they need me for another job, but because they love me!" Stupid, disgusting tears fell down my cheeks, and I wished for about five more hours of sleep to be able to fend off such annoying meltdowns. "Boy, did you have me fooled. I thought you were that guy. I thought you were that dad."

Ezra was on his feet, and before I could defend myself, he wrapped me in a tight hug, squeezing me with passion to match my heightened hysteria. "I'm sorry, sweetheart. I'm so sorry. You're right. I was focused on the mission, on the job."

I pounded my fist into his chest, expecting him to let go. He didn't let go, but held me, which only confused me in my already turned around state. "You were supposed to be the dad who reads the paper and says things like 'those darn kids are cutting across my lawn.' You're not supposed to let me get locked in a dungeon! You're not supposed to let me get mind-warped by a rock! You're not supposed to let me anywhere near something this dangerous!"

Ezra didn't loosen his grip, even when I yelled for him to let me go. He didn't stop holding me even when I cried all over his perfect dress shirt. He gripped me too tight, held on too long and was far too understanding of the crazy woman who couldn't stop blubbering all over him. Even after I quieted to sniffles and silent sobs, he leaned my head to his chest, unashamed of the mess that was the best I could do.

"I can do better," he promised. "You're absolutely right. I haven't spent enough time with you to be able to send you off on a dangerous mission without giving you cause to feel this way. I do care for you. Give me time. I can learn if you're patient enough to teach me."

I couldn't believe he wasn't yelling back. He was gentle and kind as he held me, and I didn't understand any of it. I kept my mouth shut and simply held onto his shirt, scared of what might happen if I let go. "I'm sorry I'm being mean. I get that you're in a tough spot."

Ezra pulled a handkerchief out of his pocket. He didn't hand it to me, but dabbed at my cheeks, sweeping away my embarrassment as he kissed the top of my head. "How about we get you something to eat, yeah? Then you can tell me all about your time with Captain Finn in Silo. Not to strategize, but just to tell me about your trip to a new world. Would that be alright?"

"Really? You're not mad at me for yelling?"

"How about you and I stop being afraid of making each other angry. I'm in your life, October Grace. I'm marrying your mother, and I'm involved in your work life. I'm sure this won't be our last fight." He texted Lynna with one hand while the other remained around me. "Have a seat, darling. Take a breath and tell me everything."

2 2

JUST A LITTLE TASTE

I couldn't believe Ezra didn't once bring up work stuff regarding the stone while we ate dinner together in the conference room, just the two of us. Since he was making such an effort, I threw him a bone, letting him know where we'd dropped it, and the ensuing battle that had taken place.

I may have taken my participation in the battle completely out of the dressed-up PG version I told Ezra.

He had a great many clipped questions about the war, none of which I was all that eager to answer. I mean, sure, the zombies were dead. I'd killed a fair few of them. I still wasn't sure how that resonated with my conscience that felt tossed around inside of me. I couldn't feel with my moral compass which way was up, and which was very, very down. I was pretty evasive on the gory stuff and told him the story from a distance's vantage point.

"You know I'll just ask Captain Finn for an accurate retelling."

I finished the last bite of my carrots and put my fork down on the table of the conference room. "And I'll be very far away when you do. I'm not trying to hide anything important this time. I just don't know how to feel about it all. It's still fresh. I don't think I'm totally processing everything yet."

Ezra shifted the topic in a direction I was not anticipating. "Captain Finn is a good soldier. He's second in command of Dagat. There are a great many things I admire about him, but I don't let him near Mariang. He's not the guide I would've sent you to Silo with. His curse makes him obey King Banak, who doesn't put value on women's lives."

His hinting wasn't all that subtle. "Finn was fine. It was a bit of an adjustment, but we got used to each other. I think we hit the rank of friends toward the end."

Ezra sipped his tea. "I don't know if I should be relieved to hear that or far more worried."

"Jury's still out for me, too. I can handle myself around him, though. And for the most part, total professional."

I heard Von before I saw him. His I'll-talk-at-whatever-volume-I-feel-like voice reached me as he bolted through the mansion calling my name. My heart started beating faster, out of anticipation or dread, I wasn't sure. I'd missed him more than I could allow myself to admit to. The sound of his voice made me ache for the familiar back and forth I'd craved.

On the other hand, the last words we'd said to each other were horrible. I wasn't sure what to expect, and realized I'd started clawing at my hands again.

Ezra took in my trepidation and smirked, putting his teacup down. "I daresay I don't have to worry so much about you being swept away by Captain Finn. Go to him, darling."

I grimaced, knowing that teasing look, and wanting nothing to do with it. "Von's my friend."

"Your mother's my friend. I know the dance well." Ezra stood to open the door before Von reached us and kicked it in. "We're in the conference room, Son. Come on up."

Von's gold and blue eyes were wild when they fell on me after he bolted up the stairs. He braced himself with both hands on the doorjamb, as if holding himself back from a fight he couldn't wait for. "You!" he accused, and I heard the hurt, the elation and the longing that matched my own heart.

"I... I didn't mean... Um..." I had nothing but excuses that didn't hold water, and not a thing to hide behind. He was poised for attack, and I knew I didn't have a solid shield in defense.

His hair was more disheveled than usual. His black "You Thought You Knew" t-shirt was untucked, rumpled and had a coffee stain across the white lettering that matched the drip marks on his torn jeans. It was the same outfit he'd been wearing the last time I'd seen him, only dirtier. He was Von unplugged, and I couldn't look away. I was afraid of what he might do or say in his unhinged state with things so broken between us.

When he let go of the doorframe, I squeaked as he sprang forward, pulling me up into a bone-crushing hug I hadn't expected and knew I didn't deserve. "Never again! No matter what happens, we don't ditch each other. We don't throw it away." He kissed my cheek, and then seemed to rapidly grow addicted to the flavor, spreading affection all over my face. I broke down in his arms that lifted me slightly off the ground. Not Mason's hug nor Ezra's kindness made the tears unleash themselves like Von's crazed warmth did. He smelled like cigars, peppermint and home, and I'd missed the details of him with every fiber of my being. "I'm sorry. I'm so sorry."

"No, *I'm* sorry! I did it. I'm the one who ran."

"But I pushed you away!"

"*I* pushed *you* away! I thought you hated me."

Von tangled his dirty fingers in my hair, his eyes closed as he pressed his lips next to my ear. "I don't hate you," he admitted in a fierce whisper. "I love you, Peach. I'm just really bad at it. We've got the always kind of love, not the terrible kind you say and then regret later like dreadful Chinese food. You're my best girl. You'll never be old Chinese food to me."

I laughed through my tears at the sweetness that filled my heart to the bursting point. My arms wrapped around his shoulders so I could have him and keep him right where I wanted him. "Oh, Von. You're my best girl, too."

He laughed with relief into my skin. "You're home? You're safe? Where'd you go? What happened?" He inhaled in the crook of my neck with lust that made my eyes roll back and forget that Ezra was still in the room. "Oh, Peach. You cut yourself bad. You smell... Bollocks. You smell like I need a blood bag if I'm going to hear everything I missed, yeah?"

"I can remedy that. I'll give you two a moment," Ezra said as he exited the room, closing us in so we could be as weird as we were without an audience reminding us that our friendship was peculiar at a glance.

I exhaled with relief I didn't realize I desperately needed to feel. His shoulders were broader than I remembered, so I made quick work of memorizing his body, as though we'd been apart for a year. The four days felt like hundreds stacked up against me without the constant affection he bathed me with. Von's tongue laved over my stitches, and before I could stop myself, a quiet moan escaped my lips. "You don't want to do that," I reminded him, my eyes closed at the totally freaky seduction neither of us meant to have happen.

"You left," Von accused, still holding me as if I was precious to him, as if it didn't matter which world I landed in, so long as we were together.

"I'm sorry. I freaked out and ran."

"Then I freaked out and ran all over creation searching

for you. I took Ollie and went to every place he said you might be. Phoned all your friends while Mason started visiting the different countries to look for you in Terraway. Never again!" He gripped the back of my head, squeezing with too much force. "When I'm a wanker, just slap me upside the head to knock some sense back into me, yeah?" He shook his head, his cheek pressed to mine to warm it. "Scratch that. I won't be stupid like that ever again. Problem solved."

I could feel him gently pulling the waves of anxiety away from me, and I knew I'd been wrong to leave one of my greatest sources of comfort. "I do love you, Von."

"I know you do. You finally admit it when I'm inches away from tearing open this cut on your neck and sucking you dry." He brought my arms to his nose and drank in the scent of my blood beneath the bandages, his eyes rolling back as he moaned sumptuously. "If I tell you to run, only go downstairs until Ezra comes back with a blood bag. Don't actually run away again."

"Breathe through your mouth. Don't breathe through your nose; you have a harder time when you can smell the blood." I felt his jaw open as he took my advice, his minty cigar breath teasing my neck. I reached up and stroked his cheek, loving that, despite everything, we could be like this, that life could be like this. I did love Von, for better or far worse. "I love you," I whispered, partly in revelation to myself. "You don't want to hurt me."

He swallowed thickly before pulling back to press his

forehead to mine. "You're right. If I tore open your stitches and drank you until you collapsed in my arms like a dying flower, that would be bad."

"Very bad," I agreed, running my fingers through the hair at the nape of his neck.

He reached his hand between us and stroked my lower lip that was malleable to his touch. "If I bit you a little right here, it would be bad if I tasted your blood, yeah? I shouldn't do that." He was talking himself through, reminding his conscience to speak up.

"It would be very bad. It would get you one step closer to being rabid. Then I'd lose you forever," I reminded him.

"Just a little taste would be bad." His tone took on a note of begging. "Just a little taste?"

I held onto his face, making sure the only thing he saw were my eyes. "Love bug, you've got to get a grip on this. Breathe through it. Ezra's coming. When was the last time you had blood?"

He whined for a second when I mentioned his favorite food group. "We barely stopped for anything. I've been eating human food when I can, but I haven't even thought about blood since I lost you. Now it's the only thing I can think about. You smell like a glorious Christmas feast."

"Poor baby," I cooed, massaging his temples for him. I felt him take a wave of my worry and hissed in disapproval. "Pulling only makes you hungrier. Stop doing it until you get some blood in you."

"But I can feel your anxiety."

"I'll be more stressed if you try to eat me."

"Thanks for making a joke." Von snorted out a laugh and then kissed my cheek. "I love you so very much. It feels good to finally say it."

"Hold on, honey. It'll be okay. I'm right here."

Von's eyes closed, as if in prayer. "You're right here," he repeated, squeezing me tighter. "I've been replaying the awful things I said to you. I'm a horrible fake fifties sitcom husband. Just the worst."

"Oh, Mr. Brady," I teased, grateful I heard Ezra's footsteps running toward us. "Don't you know? I love you even when you're at your worst."

23

MY LETHAL KISS

Mason volunteered to patrol the mansion when it was time to turn in, rather than be in the same room as me. "I'll probably crash in one of the guest rooms," he said without looking in my direction. "Just call me if she needs extra pulling. Otherwise I'll see you guys in the morning." Without waiting for a response from the two of us, Finn, Ezra, Mariang or Danny, Mason stood abruptly and left the dining room.

"He's a wee bit frosty," Von commented as he downed his second nightcap. His arm looped around my waist so I was tucked tight to his side at the dining room table. It was like he was afraid I might run off again if I had an inch of breathing room. He eyed the rest of my burger with unconcealed lust. "You going to finish that, love?" Von asked, his chin on my shoulder.

"I am. You can have my fries, though."

Finn snorted derisively at us. "Give her some space, Von. I'm suffocating just watching you crowd her."

"Now, now. Don't be jealous, Finn. I've always got a place on my lap for you." Von had kept one arm affixed around me through our whole meal. Each time I'd leaned forward to take a drink or pass a dish, he'd scooted my chair an inch closer to his. Now we were practically sharing a seat, the outsides of our thighs glued together. He wolfed down my fries, my pickle, the second helping of steamed carrots I'd only made it halfway through, and still eyed my burger with too much interest.

"Oh, fine," I harrumphed, feeding him the last mouthful of beef. His lips closed around my fingers with a light moan at the sustenance he couldn't get enough of. When he drew back, he caught my wrist when he noticed a glob of ketchup on my thumb. Without hesitation, he popped my digit in his mouth and laved his tongue around it, sweeping the ketchup away and giving me the guilty shivers.

No, Von hadn't had germs in a long time. He was bathed in my love, so my OCD hiccups were forgotten all too often around him.

Mariang and Danny watched us with curious glances and an exchange of wary looks that I didn't have the energy to address. I had to whistle for my supper, which meant Finn and me taking turns regaling the others with our little adventure. I steered us around the battle, making Finn look like the hero, and me the battlefield nurse who only helped on the sidelines. We both left out any mention of our kiss and certainly didn't look at each other like we had participated in any kind of sensual foot rubbing. In fact, Finn and I tried not to look at each other at all.

When it was time to turn in, Von was reluctant to leave my side even to take a shower, but I insisted it was necessary. "I promise I won't leave. I can't." I held up my black leather bracelet.

No sooner had Von disappeared and turned on the shower did a quiet knock sound on the bedroom door. I opened it to find my favorite captain standing in the hallway. "Hey, Finn. What's up?"

Finn let himself in, moving past me to make sure we were alone in the bedroom that had been furnished in light green with gold accents. "I came to check your stitches before I went to sleep."

"Oh. Well, that's nice of you. I'm sure they're fine."

Finn pulled out the narrow chair for me that matched the blond wooden desk in the corner. "Sit down. And I'm not just here for that. Thanks for not mentioning what didn't happen in the tavern."

I lowered my voice. "It didn't happen, so we don't need to talk about it."

He moved my hair to the side after I sat down, poking at my wound like a layman. I'm pretty sure he was just stalling for time before he summoned up the courage to say his piece. He sighed irritably. "Von knows a certain side of me, so if he starts running his mouth, try not to listen. I was good to you some of the time in Silo. Remember that."

I was wary of his warning. "What's Von going to tell me about you? What kind of demons are you hiding? And nothing happened between us, so you don't have to feel the need to hide things from me. We're friends, Finn. I'm not your girlfriend or your mom."

"Thanks for the clarification," Finn simpered.

I lowered my voice yet further. "I know all about Von's time in Dagat, and that you signed him into the harem."

He cleared his throat a few times. "Yes, well, as soon as Ezra gives me enough of a punishment to where he trusts me again, I'm going home. I'll be back when it's time to move the stone again. Otherwise, I won't see you."

"I guess that makes sense." I don't know why I felt a slight bit bummed about that. I mean, we had only just started to get along, and now he was bolting. "Have a nice trip, then." His hand drifted from my wound to my shoulder, and I cupped his hand as it rested there. "Be good to the women you're in charge of. Don't order anyone into Banak's bed, Finn."

"You know I don't have control over that. I do as Banak orders."

"Be better than this. Dyesebel would want more from you than strategy and blind obedience."

"She's the one who used her Mer song on me to get me this way."

Fair point. "Well, *I* want more from you."

"See? I knew you'd go and make it all serious and dramatic like that. I knew you'd lay on the guilt. I should never have told you about Bel."

I didn't let go of his hand, but looped my fingers through his as I looked up at him. "Be a good man, Finn. Find a way to steal back your conscience. I know it's in you, otherwise you wouldn't be up here, hoping for a lecture and the serious and dramatic talks."

"Yes, well..." He frowned, and I knew he was grinding his teeth together to chew on his tart response. "I don't want to go home," he admitted.

"Where do you want to be?"

Finn's eyes fell to my lips, his hand migrating from mine to palming my chin in that possessive way I couldn't decide how I felt about. My heartrate picked up as I watched his tongue wet his full lips, and though we'd said we'd leave it all behind in Silo, a strong desire of feral want descended on us both. "Just one more kiss," he whispered more to himself than to me.

"Just one more kiss," I said, more to myself than to him. He drew me closer, his lips caressing mine gently, as if still holding himself back from me. As if I was the dangerous one. As if I might hurt him.

I let out a breathy "hmm" and sunk in to the kiss, letting the colors and the sounds dance around us. Finn wasted no time, introducing his tongue to tango with mine, which was new for us. His tongue tempted, and then claimed me, making me want only more as the green and silver swirled around us, looping us closer together.

A different sensation began to wind itself into our kiss, popping and sizzling like carbonation on our lips. The tingly effervescence travelled outward across my face, and I shivered in time with Finn, who let out a bleat of distress as he deepened the kiss.

Abruptly, Finn broke away and stumbled back a few paces before grabbing his chest like he was having a heart attack. He fell to his knees in alarm. "Something's wrong! Get Ezra!"

I blinked the colors away, but my body still felt the cool dance of the carbonation on my skin as I stumbled toward the door, too foggy to think more than a simple compliance of orders. "Zezra!" I slurred through the hallway. "Help!"

It was a thing of luck that Ezra had been down the hall in Mason's room to get his account of Silo when I called. I didn't have much more oomph in me. When I turned back to Finn, he'd collapsed face-down on the carpet.

Ezra charged in, calling for Danny, who bolted into the room with Mason two seconds later. "What happened to him?" Ezra asked, rolling Finn over and staring into his drooping eyelids. He roused, but not enough to assure us he was right as rain. Danny and Mason helped him to sit up, his limbs weighted and clumsy.

"I don't know!" I cried, wringing my hands. I dropped

to my knees and felt his pulse. "We were just... And then he grabbed his chest and collapsed!"

Just as quickly as Finn succumbed to gravity and whatever else, he seemed to snap out of it in the next few breaths, more confused than in pain. "What was that?" he asked, shaking his head to rid himself of the fog. He rubbed his chest like it was sore. "I felt a little of this creeping on before in the tavern, but I stopped it before it could... What happened?"

My eyes went wide in warning for him not to rat me out. I knew he was talking about our first kiss, and apparently something about it almost gave him a heart attack the first time. Whatever I almost did to him back in the tavern, I for sure did to him this time around. Was my kiss turning lethal or something?

Ezra's face was grim. "When was the last time you ate anything before dinner downstairs? Have you slept a full night at all?"

"I dunno. We got the stone delivered. That's all that matters." He shook his head. "I caught up on my sleep in the tavern. It's not that."

Ezra took a paternal shine to Finn, patting his back and helping him up, despite Finn's protests that he could stand on his own. "Come downstairs and get some more to eat. You know I keep *buhay* here for the council. Then you can stay in one of my rooms until you feel better."

"I feel fine," Finn lied, posturing. I could tell he hated

being fawned over. "I'm just going to port home. Sleep in my own bed."

Before any of us could insist he take some time to rest, Finn cast me a look of confusion mixed with silent alarm and then vanished.

Danny scratched the back of his head. "Well, I guess that's that."

Mason whirled on me, accusation in his face and tone. "What happened?"

"He was checking my stitches and stood up too fast, I guess. Then he collapsed and I called for Ezra first thing. That's all," I lied.

My mouth went dry and my palms were sweaty. I didn't need people knowing that now I apparently had the ability to send people to the hospital with a kiss.

24

A SISTER AND HER MISTER

I was relieved when the guys left shortly after that, and tried to push my encounter with Finn out of my mind. Mariang took out fresh pajamas with the tags still on from the drawers she'd stocked for me. I took my turn brushing her hair, holding her close through my sincere apology for worrying her as I'd done. All the clothes she'd selected were the correct size, and I don't know why this attention to detail struck me with just the right amount of sweetness. She fawned over me a few more minutes before she wished me sweet dreams, and I let her, basking in the glow of having a sister again.

The shower turned off a few seconds after she left. Von appeared in only a towel a minute later, standing in the bathroom doorway looking, well, exactly like Von would in a towel. His hair was dripping at the base of his neck, and he smelled like fresh soap and carefree guy, which it turns out, is a great combination. "Forgot my pajamas down-stairs in my bag," he explained of the towel.

"I'll go grab them for you." I had to get out of there. Finn scrambled my brains to where I was too attracted to Von to keep things platonic, as they had to be. *Stupid Finn.* I all but ran downstairs away from my beautiful BFF, barging in on a hushed conversation between Mariang and Danny in the kitchen. They sat close together on stools at the counter, and stopped talking as soon as I walked into the room. "Hey guys. You see Von's bag anywhere?"

Danny jerked his thumb toward the foyer by the front door. "Probably didn't even make it past the entrance."

Mariang caught my eye and motioned me to her. I expected another lecture on disappearing, but her sad eyes kept me from checking out before she opened her mouth. Her black hair was pulled back in a tight bun that made her look like the ballerina her body was suited to be. She held out her arms, and when I got near enough to grab at, she wrapped me in a warm hug, resting her head on my shoulder. "I'm so glad you're home safe," she said to me, and I could feel the relief in her embrace. "We're supposed to be sisters, but you left without saying goodbye."

"I guess that's true. I had a feeling your boyfriend wouldn't have let me go, so I bolted when I got the chance. I shouldn't have done it, though."

"We're supposed to be sisters first and coworkers second. I was worried about you. Don't make me worry."

The hurt in her tone matched mine when I'd

confronted Ezra about the exact same thing. Here I had a family member who treated me like one, and I'd kept her at a distance for no reason at all. "You're right. I should've told you." I wrapped my arms around her thinned frame and gently squeezed. I'd said as much upstairs when I'd been brushing her hair, but she seemed to need the extra reassurance. I found I had a hard time refusing Mariang anything, sweet as she was. "Can I make it up to you? Do something together that has nothing to do with work or anything serious?"

Mariang's smile filtered through her whole body, lifting her posture as she pulled away to look at me. "Yes! Tomorrow? Maybe we can go shopping or something. Anywhere you like."

Sweet girl didn't know I hated shopping. "Sure. Sounds great. You pick the place, and I'll be there. Let's leave around ten. I don't think Von will wake up any earlier."

Her aqua eyes grew serious. "I've never seen Von like that, and I've known him a while. He all but kidnapped Ollie and dragged him all over the place looking for you."

"Yeah. He was almost responsible. No wonder you barely recognized him," Danny groused, sipping his decaf. "Of course, he lost his charge in the first place, so there's that. Good old Von."

"Hey," I snapped. "I ditched quicker than any of you could find me. I'm tired of you always ragging on Von. He's trying to do the job right. He's actually making strides here, but you'll never see it with your nose stuck up in the air."

"Spoken like a girl in love who's only known him a few months. Give it time. That halo he wears is probably stolen."

"Shut up." I turned to Mariang, who looked distraught that her sister and her boyfriend were at odds. "Look, shopping with you sounds great, but your boy needs a leash or something if it's going to be anything other than a day of fighting. If he can lay off, I'm there. But if Danny's going to put Von through the ringer just for showing up, I won't make Von go through that. I would never let anyone talk about you the way Danny rags on Von. It's gone on long enough."

Mariang nodded, her chin lowered in sadness she didn't bother hiding. "That's fair."

I walked away and heard her say to Danny, "She's my sister, Danny. You have to try harder to get along with them. I need this. I need a sister. Please don't take that away from me."

"Whatever. Fine. I'll hang toward the back and keep my mouth shut tomorrow. But I hate him, love. I can't stand to look at him. All I see are all the times he pulled a Von and didn't show, didn't explain, didn't apologize, didn't think. He's going to wreck that girl, and I'm going to have to pick up the pieces."

"He's your brother, Danny."

"Don't remind me."

SEXY APPENDIX

I dropped Von's bag on the bed and took my turn in the shower. Though it wasn't my own bed in my own home, it was a bed, and not the hard ground of Silo. When I'd dressed for sleep, I was ready to forget all about the worries of the day and the detainee bracelet I couldn't get rid of. I'd forgotten about my incarceration when I suggested a day of shopping out with Mariang. I hoped she wouldn't be too put out that our girl date would have to be postponed.

Von was texting and smoking as he leaned against the headboard, the light green comforter covering his lap. His naked chest stared me in the face, and I knew his good looks would be a problem for me. He glanced up at me when I stood at the side of the bed but refused to get in. "What's up, buttercup?"

I addressed the ceiling as I spoke, too embarrassed to

look at him. My arms were crossed over my chest as I scratched at the bandages, wishing I could claw at the skin beneath. I shuffled my feet from where I stood on the other side of the bed from him, wearing my lavender tank top and matching cotton shorts. "Okay, this is... I don't know how to say this the right way, so try not to make a big deal out of it."

Von put his phone and cigar down on the nightstand and gave me his undivided attention. "Why do I get the sneaking suspicion the roof's about to cave in on us when you talk like that?"

"It's nothing dramatic as that. It's just... Could you put on a shirt? I've had a long week. I'm still catching up on my sleep, and things are going to start getting confused if you keep being half naked around me."

"Confused? How does me being without a shirt have anything to do with you not sleeping?" I heard him put the pieces together as amusement swept over him. I cringed and kept my eyes affixed on the ceiling. "Ah, I see. I'm too sexy for my shirt? So sexy it hurts?" He moved to the center of the bed and rubbed his chest seductively like a male stripper. "It was only a matter of time. I knew you wanted me from day one. All the good girls want me for my body. I think it's my appendix. I have a sexy appendix." He climbed out of the bed and started dancing suggestively next to me, shaking his butt and shimmying his shoulders to earn a laugh.

I batted at his body, my pink cheeks dimpling at his

antics that I couldn't help but find funny. "Yes, that's exactly it. Cover up your appendix before I faint from lust overload."

"You're blushing! You're actually blushing. You really do want me for my appendix! I didn't think you were capable of being attracted to a bloke unless he came with buckets of emotional baggage." He stopped his dance and scratched his head. "Hey, wait a minute. Is that what you want me for? My baggage, not my total package?"

I was so grateful he made a joke that I didn't fault him for his totally wrong assessment of my type. "Ha, ha. Laugh it up, clown."

He fished through his bag, slinking down to look through it like he was putting on a show for me, his stellar backside drawing my eyes away from the ceiling to gawk. I would not become one of his many adoring fans. I swore to myself I would not. He pulled a white t-shirt over his head with a dramatic frown. "Is that better? Am I Clark Kent enough for you now, or are you still dreaming of my Superman hot body?"

"I'm never gonna live this down."

"Nope. Made my day. Made my whole week, actually. The next time you disappear and scare the living daylights out of me, make sure to always tell me I'm too steamy to get into bed with. That'll solve everything."

"I never said that."

"Yes, you did. You said, and I quote, 'Von, you're a gorgeous specimen of the most perfect kind of man. I can't be too near you when my loins are burning like this. Either throw me down on the bed and have your filthy way with me or cover up the sexiness. I simply can't take it another second."

"I *cahn't*?" I said, mocking his accent. "Wow, I sure said a mouthful."

His proud grin nearly split his face as he sat back down in the bed and kicked his legs under the mint green comforter and matching sheet. I made to get in, but he stopped me. "Not so fast. Your turn."

"My turn to what?"

"If we're going to keep things platonic, you can't be flashing me your bare arms and legs like that. You know I have an elbow fetish. Come on, November. Be a professional."

"You have an elbow fetish?" I asked dubiously, my arms akimbo. "What is it about my elbow you find particularly appealing? That it's bony?"

"Tone down the rated-R language, baby. If it gets too hot in here, I'll have to take my shirt off again, and then where would we be?"

"I should never have said anything. You're enjoying this way too much."

He shrugged and made himself comfortable, leaning against the headboard as he resituated his pillow. "Who wouldn't enjoy a compliment from a beautiful woman? Tuck on in here, Peach. I was only teasing you." When I hesitated, he cocked his eyebrow at me. "You want I should fart on your pillow? Would that diffuse the sexual tension in here?"

"Pass." I slid into the bed after turning out the overhead lights. I was overthinking things, subconsciously scratching my arms as I laid down on my side, making sure not to touch him.

Von disregarded the tension and settled in next to me, draping his arm around my waist and drawing my back to his front so he could spoon me. He was quiet for a moment, and I could tell he was working up to saying something. "Peach?"

"Yeah, Von?"

"I know I said so before, but I'm truly sorry I unleashed on you. That's not me. I've replayed it over and over, and I don't know why I was such a wanker."

"Here's a tip from me to you. When you want me to forgive you, use plenty of those fancy British words. Makes you too cute to be mad at for long."

"Oh yeah? Bangers and mash, pip-pip, bloody brilliant. Did that help?"

"What were we fighting about?" I asked dreamily, pretending I was caught in a haze of mind-meld. "Are you James Bond? Where am I?"

"You're in my arms," he whispered, pressing a kiss to the back of my neck. "Right where you should be."

I shivered through my bashful smile I was glad he couldn't see. "Well, you went and made it all sweet." I snuggled my body into his. "I shouldn't have run."

His hand snuck under the hem of my tank top, his fingertips dragging up and down across my navel. The seduction was slowly driving me mad and sending goosebumps all over my body, pushing me into an unhurried writhe. "No, you shouldn't have. I had nothing but nightmares and walking daymares about Finn selling you off to the highest bidder."

I didn't know whether or not to tell Von that I'd developed a totally wrong crush on Finn. I knew Finn was trouble, but I still lost my brain and kissed him. No, I definitely wouldn't tell Von about the kissing. He didn't need to know.

"Do you remember that night where I told you all my stuff? That I'd sold myself for a few months to pay off Boston's gambling debts?"

I answered slowly, bracing myself for the bomb. "Yeah. I remember." I placed my fingers atop his under the blanket that were stroking my navel. "I don't like to think of you selling your body. I like your body." I closed my eyes, gripping his hand under the covers.

He paused, and I could feel him pulling some of my increasing worry from me. "King Banak's son Julius is a sick bastard, and Finn knew it. He knew it and he still gave me to him for three months. I was scared out of my mind, thinking of you out there with Finn. I kept picturing him taking you to Dagat and giving you to the king. I saw you doing all the depraved things I had to do to survive. Finn has no will when it comes to Banak. Banak controls him completely."

I turned in Von's arms and saw the scope of his agony painted on his handsome face. "Oh, baby. Nothing like that happened at all. Finn was just my guide through Silo. He knows not to mess with Ezra's daughters. And he was actually fine. Friendly, even."

"Finn's fear of Ezra was the only thing that kept me from going insane. That's when I knew."

"Knew what?" I stroked the side of his freshly shaved face, admiring his earnest eyes and the arches of his upper lip that always managed to arrest my attention.

"I knew that I loved you. I knew you were my best friend. That I'd search everywhere for you until you came home to me. That I couldn't relax unless you were safe."

My mouth fell open, his pledge leaving me breathless. He brushed his nose back and forth across mine as our legs tangled together in a messy web I knew we'd never get out of unscathed. "I'm safe," I promised him. "I'm right here, and I'm not going anywhere." I knew I was unbalanced, because I wanted to kiss him, to taste his tongue and suck on his lower lip. His mouth had never been so sweet to me, and I wanted what I shouldn't have. What I couldn't have.

Von saved us both by rolling me over so he could spoon me again. "Goodnight, Peach."

NIGHTMARES AND CONFESSIONS

*I*n the middle of the night, a frantic octopus swam through my dream, thrashing wildly against the Mermaids that were screaming for me to help them. The octopus was flailing, his tentacles tangling through my legs as he pulled me under. A noise of distress escaped my lips, jerking me from my underwater surroundings, and back into the bedroom I'd been assigned in Ezra's home.

The octopus faded from view and was replaced by Von, who was twisting in the covers due to a bad dream. He was sweating and fighting with the comforter for a freedom it wouldn't grant him. I leaned over to the nightstand and fumbled for the switch to turn the lamp on. The moment the light shone down on Von, he jerked three more times and cried out in what sounded like heartbreak and physical pain. I pressed my hand to his chest to anchor him before he started flailing around again. "Honey! Von, wake up. It's not real."

Von's eyes flew open, his shallow pants taking several additional breaths to calm as he examined his surroundings with a skeptical worry. "You? And then he... And I was... It was a dream?"

"Just a dream," I confirmed, brushing my fingers through his hair to unstick it from his sweaty forehead. "You're alright. Here, sit up. Let me get you a glass of water."

Von was trembling as he obeyed. I returned from the bathroom with a wet washcloth and a glass of water that I tipped to his lips. I watched his throat constrict and dabbed at the back of his neck with the washcloth to cool him down. "Thanks."

"You want to tell me about it?" I asked slowly, not caring that my hair was no doubt a tangled mess of curls.

He pulled his knees up to his chest like a little boy. "I was back in Prince Julius' chambers. Just reliving stuff, but you were there too. Same foul nightmare I've been having all week. Couldn't save myself. Couldn't save you." He shook his head, his eyes haunted. "It was dreadful."

"It wasn't real," I assured him. "We're both safe. Hey, we've got each other, right? I take care of you, you take care of me?"

He offered a hollow smile that didn't touch his eyes. "Something like that."

"Lay down, sweetie. I'm not going anywhere."

Von was lost, so I guided him down to lay his head on the pillow. "It was so real. I never want you to see me like I had to be back then. Talk about the gutter."

I laid next to him on my side, smiling with swelling affection when he rested his cheek to my breasts before I could settle myself properly in the sheets. I combed my fingers through his hair, listening to his breathing even out. "I don't know why you don't set Danny straight about what happened. He acts all smug when he talks about your escort days. If he knew you were trapped into it all and did that to save Boston, maybe he wouldn't use that to tear you down."

Von's arm draped around my hips. "I don't care what Danny thinks about me. He needs someone to hate, someone to blame for the things that go wrong in his life. If it's not me, it would be Mum, and I don't want that. She can't handle his anger like I can."

"What would he blame your mama for?"

"Mum told Dad to leave when he hit her, and he wouldn't. So I thrashed the lowlife and threw him out. The boys only know that Dad couldn't handle me anymore. They don't know he knocked Mum around, I hope. It's better Danny hates me. He needs Mum every now and then. I wouldn't want to cut him off from her."

My hand stilled in Von's hair. "Are you serious? You're taking too many bullets, Von."

"Better they're shot at one person than all of us. Danny made up his mind years ago. And all he'd hear in the truth would be the part where I let Boston get in over his head with gambling. That *I* let it get out of hand between Dad and Mum. Then I'd never hear the end of that. Plus, he'd lay into Boston, who can't handle it like I can." He nuzzled my breasts with the side of his face, making my heart flutter. "No, Danny hasn't earned the right to know me. I don't have it in me to hope he ever cares that he doesn't know me, and most likely never will. It's not his job to know me. I'm the eldest. It's my job to look after him."

I scraped my nails across Von's scalp, smiling softly as he melted in my arms. I prayed that Ollie didn't carry this same weight around, and was glad I'd made a point to touch base with him again on the phone before bed. "That's a sad story, sweetheart."

"I'll be cheery in the morning, but for now the sad kind's all I've got."

"That's alright." I ran the washcloth across his forehead to cool him down. "I love you when you're on top and I love you when you think you might crash." I set the washcloth on the nightstand and ran my knuckles over his cheek again. "But I'll never let you crash, Von. I'm right here, and if I've got you in my arms, nothing can touch you, not even Prince Julius."

Von's eyes squinched shut at mention of Banak's son's name. "Then promise you won't let go of me."

I reached across him and snatched his phone off the nightstand, careful not to loosen my other arm from the embrace. I flicked through his contacts and found Bishop's number, not caring what time it was in London. Bishop picked up on the second ring. "Did you find her?"

I softened, glancing down at Von's quizzical face, no doubt wondering what I was doing. "If you mean me, then yes, Von found me. Everything's good now."

I could hear the relief in Bishop's voice and felt a new pang of guilt. "Oh, good. Von was going mad trying to find you. I wasn't sure if I should hop on a flight to help out. You're alright, sis?"

I loved that I'd had just enough conversations with Bishop on the phone that he'd finally stopped calling me 'Lady October'. "I'm actually calling for Von. I think he's a little homesick. Could you tell him a joke or something?" I handed the phone to Von, who gazed up at me as if I was the sun and the moon. I couldn't believe anyone looked at me like that, and hoped I wouldn't do anything to screw it up.

Von didn't discuss serious things with Bishop, but the levity of talking to his younger brother made his shoulders relax. The phone call proved a great distraction from his demons. Bishop was with Boston, and Von laughed a few times when Boston took his turn to crack dirty jokes with his big brother. Von sat up, leaning against the headboard with me tucked tight to his side.

It was five minutes well spent, and five minutes Von had desperately needed. When he ended the call, he set the phone back on the nightstand and turned to me with an expression of pure wonder. "How did you know I needed that?"

I shrugged. "Ollie always calls me when he's lost. Danny may have written you off, but Bishop hasn't. He adores you. Seemed like you could use a little perspective on what a good guy you are."

He blinked at me, perplexed. "You love me."

"You say that like it's some revelation. Of course I love you. Now let's get some sleep. No offense, but if I'm going to have super lusty dreams about you, you're going to have to do something about those bags under your eyes."

The corner of Von's mouth pulled up as he laid down next to me. "I adore you," he confessed. He zerberted my armpit and kissed my face seven times before he closed his eyes.

I waited until his breathing evened out, and then I watched Von for another minute in the dim moonlight that filtered through the window across the room. I hoped that Von would sleep through the night, and that nothing would hurt him ever again.

STALKING VON

It was two long weeks before Ezra let me leave the house, removing his bracelet that had kept me stir-crazy. Ollie had been by a few times to update me on Bev's state and to check on me, but I assured him I was fine and didn't need him to worry. For obvious reasons, I couldn't bring myself to visit Bev yet. Since she was being released today, I was granted permission to move back home. Also, living under the same roof as the sagrado stone was proving problematic for Von, who was reaching his limit with how often I clawed open the cuts on my arms. The first call I made was to Ollie, who promised he would be sleeping at the house that night and couldn't wait to see me again.

Mason and I had reached a frosty stalemate in our frustrated status, choosing to be civil, but nothing more. He eventually came to bed with us, but was always in his wolf form. After the first week, the three of us woke up each morning wrapped around each other in various entanglements, but that was as friendly as Mason got, and it was only when he was unaware of what he was doing. He packed up my bag and Von's in the trunk, and caught a bus to my house to enforce security before we got there.

I drove Von, Danny and Mariang to the mall of Mariang's choosing for our delayed day of shopping. She'd been meticulously planning it since the idea was spoken aloud. I was uncomfortable using the bank account that paid me for Omen duties, but knew my own accounts were nothing to be thrilled with after a few months off the prison job. This would be my first time using the card for something other than bills, which made me not want to spend anything on instinct.

Mariang had no such hang-ups about spending her hard-earned money. She'd been carrying out Omen duties alone while Ezra took the time to decide if he could trust me not to bolt anymore. The mall was for fun, but we both knew I needed to start reaping again so we didn't fall behind. Now we only needed to reap five souls per day, which wasn't taxing on me, and was doable for Mariang. As we walked through the crowded upscale mall I'd heard of but had never been in, I paid close attention to my gut, letting it lead me to reap four people before Mariang could catch up.

"You're purposefully taking more of the workload

again," Mariang pointed out. "I'm much stronger now that you gave me that long break. I can do something."

"Yeah? Well, I don't mind. You've been carrying us for three weeks. It's time I gave you a little break."

"Good," Danny answered with his signature note of aggression. "We'll take it."

Mariang sighed with a compulsory 'thank you' and led us to a dress boutique. I couldn't believe she had room in her closets for one more outfit, but that didn't stop her from selecting three from the racks and taking them to the dressing room. Danny, Von and I hung back in our jeans and t-shirts that screamed how out of place we were.

"You're not having fun," Mariang pointed out.

"Says who? Go try something on. I bet the pink one looks great on you."

"You haven't tried a thing on all day."

I shrugged. "I don't really need a dress. I mean, I work and hang out with you guys. No real occasion for looking fancy."

Mariang frowned at my logic. "Well, what do you have at home? We can build on your wardrobe from there."

I scratched the back of my neck and uttered my scandalous confession. "I don't actually own any dresses."

Mariang gaped at me. "None?" She shook her head. "I'll set to rectifying that today."

Mariang was wearing leggings and a fitted top. She had a petite body that made her look like the model for anything she tried on. I had scars, and that's about it. I knew I looked like a kid trying on her mama's clothes when I was stuffed into a dress, so I didn't bother with the song and dance of it all.

Danny had the look of well-practiced patience about him as he stood near the dressing rooms, keeping his sighs to a minimum. Von was asked to leave because he brought his sloppy burrito into the store. It was his eighth mammoth bean and cheese masterpiece, and he couldn't eat it fast enough.

When we left the boutique, Mariang ran ahead with Von to sift through music together at the hipster store, trying to find something palatable for the ride home. I found myself strolling along next to Danny, my hands in my pockets as we kept a leisurely pace. I expected silence or some dull forced conversation, but Danny surprised me with, "Keep your eyes ahead. We're being watched."

"Huh?" Despite his instructions, I craned my neck up to look at him. "Are you serious?"

"I'm pretty sure an Aswang's on our heels. An Ekek."

I sighed. "You know, at some point I'd really appreciate some sort of glossary or something. Just when I start to wrap my mind around Terraway, more freaky creatures pop up. I know I'm going to regret this, but what's an Ekek Aswang?" I couldn't fend off the giggle brought on by the word that sounded dirty coming from my mouth. "Asswang. That's funny."

"Hear that sound?"

I listened, but heard nothing unusual. There was the

normal drum of voices and hum of the central air unit. "I don't hear anything."

"It's that whispering 'ekekekek' sound. Kind of like an air conditioner."

"Oh, well sure. I hear the air whirring. That's it?"

Danny gave a slight nod. "Langgam's people control bugs, right? Ekeks can control birds. They live in Lumipad with the Manananggals. Lumipad is Sylvia's country. You remember Sylvia from the council, right?"

"Sure, I remember the bat girl." Sylvia was a curvy woman with a half-moon shaped facial profile and black webbed bat wings jutting out of her back. The only thing I knew about her world was that it was so on the brink of a cannibalistic civil war that she couldn't hang out after the council meetings.

Danny wrapped his arm around me in a way that looked friendly, if not couplish, but I knew better. He was in guard mode, protecting me as we neared the store Mariang and Von were elbow deep in. "We call Manananggals 'Manas'. The Ekeks and the Manas need the souls we reap to fuel their country's suns, just like the rest of us." He clutched me tighter, his hand gripping my hip. "A few have started to migrate Topside. No one knows how they're doing it. Usually only royalty and high ranking officials have enough magic in them to make it to the surface, but this isn't the first one I've seen in the past week. It's why I didn't fight Ezra on keeping you locked up." He looked around for the exits as I tried to catch Von's eye. "This was a bad idea. We shouldn't have come. We should've stayed in the mansion."

"What's dangerous about them?" I asked, unsure if I wanted the answer or not.

"They don't eat only *buhay*, like most of Terraway. They can also live off raw meat. When that gets scarce, a few have started finding a way Topside to feed off of humans."

"Like blood drinking?"

"No, like cannibalism. The Ekeks are men who can shapeshift into birds when they're in Terraway's atmosphere, but not Topside. Even when they shift back to look like people, they have serious bird qualities to them. Long noses that kind of look like beaks, feathery hair, wiry legs."

"Whoa! Serious?"

Danny nodded, walking in step with me. "I don't think they know who you are, but they sure as anything know the three of us." He caught Mariang's eye and waved the two over. "They've got a particular taste for vampires. It's something about their skin that doesn't taste quite like a normal person's. Less decay in the meat or something. I don't know." He touched the knife I knew was tucked into his belt. "The Manas are women with bat wings. The more powerful ones, like Sylvia, can shapeshift into bats. They can also rip themselves in half."

"Come again?" I vaguely remembered Finn spotting a bat in Silo and telling me it was most likely a spy of

Sylvia's. However, I didn't see any sliced in half women roaming about.

Danny drew a line across his stomach. "Right at the waist. The top half turns invisible and flies around to search for food. The only way to kill them is to salt or burn the bottom half. Keeps the body from rejoining."

Something dinged in my brain. "If Sylvia's a Manas, shouldn't we call Ezra and tell him to get her up here to control her people?"

I was surprised that Danny took my advice. He pulled out his phone and explained the situation to Ezra, while making sure Mariang and Von overheard everything so he didn't have to lay it all out again. "We're closer to your house, kid. We should head there and wait things out while Sylvia sorts out her people." Danny pocketed his phone and switched with Von so Mariang was under his wing, and I was under Von's. I wished I was taller, so I could protect him from the monsters who wanted to eat my best friend.

One day I really hoped I wouldn't be able to say sentences like that.

HIT AND RUN

We walked steadily toward the parking structure, and I struggled to remember which floor I'd parked on. I heard footsteps and that same whirring whisper of "ekekekekek" behind us when we reached the correct level. By the time I saw Terence the Taurus, three pairs of boots were marching too close for comfort. Danny kept his voice uncharacteristically light. "When I say go, October unlocks the car and we all bolt. Get in and lock the doors."

I reached into my pocket, my finger on the button and my other hand in Von's. "Ready."

We were probably seven meters from the car, and the footsteps were about that far behind us. It would be close, but they were closing in on us, so it was now or never. My heart raced when Danny shouted, "Go!" and we all ran for the car.

I don't know how we managed to get inside and shut our doors before the three men banged their fists on our windows, but somehow we made it. I locked us in and shoved the keys into the ignition. Fear welled up in me as I took in the men's bird-like features that were paired with elongated yellowed teeth. Their sharp canines looked more weapon than anything else.

I didn't think about anything apart from getting Von out of there. I peeled out and ran one of them clean over with Terence, who'd never committed a violent crime in his life. A horror movie-style scream birthed out of me when the man with red hair and a sneer who I'd run over sat up and glared at me. His legs didn't work, but he was very much alive. I peeled forward, ignoring everyone calling out instructions to me, and ran over him again.

Hit and run: at least one year in lockup.

"I can't believe you just did that!" Von cried, fearful but exhilarated.

No sooner had the celebration of one enemy down lifted us up, did another Ekek jump onto the hood of my car, his boots denting my prized possession. Mariang shrieked over Danny's noise of surprise, flooding my ears with yet more apprehension. I got anxious when girlfriend tripped, so full-on screaming hit me like a bucket of ice.

The Ekek gripped the lip of the hood under the windshield wipers, gnashing his sharp yellowed teeth. They looked like too many had been jammed into his mouth, and then had been wiped with a brick of cheddar cheese.

He had a long beak-like nose and glassy eyes that seemed to see straight through to my soul, feeding on my fear. He hissed at me and started banging his fist on my windshield, hoping to shatter it.

I'd never responded well to being bullied. Try wearing the same dirty outfit to school for weeks on end and see who your real friends are. I barked at the Ekek like a rabid dog to show him I was the bigger animal, and shoved my foot to the gas. He hung on tight, never breaking eye contact. He tried to maintain his grip while I picked up speed.

A few yards before I reached the end of the row, I slammed on the brakes. The Ekek jackhole flew forward off my car, and I didn't miss my opportunity. I accelerated again and drove over him, so his crushed legs would match his buddy's.

Hit and run #2: at least another year in lockup.

I stopped short when something banged against Terence's rear.

"It's the third one!" Danny called. He was turned around in his seat behind Von. "Back up, quick!"

I obeyed, flattening the third guy without the hesitation I should've felt. It was getting too easy to kill.

"Good! Now stop the car and I'll finish them. Running Ekeks over won't kill them. I have to take their heads off, or they'll keep coming after us. Stay locked inside, you hear me?"

Mariang nodded, fearful and tearful. I watched Von

and Danny run to wrestle and try to slice off the heads of two of the three monsters. They'd broken through to my world to eat Von and who knows how many other humans. They were caught in their separate struggles, and Mariang screamed as she watched Danny absorb too many punches. The Ekeks were surprisingly quick healers, standing on crooked and janky legs with renewed determination. The Ekek on Von had a knee pointing the wrong way, but he didn't seem to mind the handicap.

The third Ekek was cracking his neck as he righted himself to sit up. I knew we wouldn't be safe for long in here. The Ekek who'd hissed at me and tried to bust out my windshield didn't look too pleased with my general existence. He turned and eyed Von with hungry lust that made my blood simultaneously boil and run cold.

"Stay inside," I instructed Mariang as I reached into the glovebox. I pulled out the closed balisong blade, unlatching the jade grip to reveal the curved and jagged nine-inch dagger Finn had given me to fend off the zombie apocalypse with. I'd stashed it there for safe keeping.

"What? Don't you dare leave!" she shouted, terrified.

I didn't listen, but fisted the handle when the Ekek jackhole pounded his anger down on the hood of my car, howling for me. "Come out and play!" he taunted, teeth bared as he stood in front of my car.

I changed my plan and stepped on the gas again. I pushed him forward, his legs skidding stubbornly along the concrete. I didn't stop until I'd successfully pinned his thin bird legs between my front bumper and the front of a poor unsuspecting brown sedan that looked like it had seen far better days a decade ago. The jackhole realized his predicament too late, and tried wrenching his mangled legs from the vice I'd stuck them in.

"Stop, October! Let Danny handle it!"

"Danny's busy," I said, getting out of the car. I couldn't get near enough to the monster's neck without getting snatched at, so I cast around for a better option. Revelation hit me, pushing me to climb up onto the roof of the brown sedan. I hopped down onto the rusted hood directly behind the problematic Ekek, where he couldn't reach me. I ignored Danny's cries of distress and sliced the throat of the monster who threatened to take Von away. I didn't have many people who would search through worlds for me for all the right reasons, and I wasn't about to give him up just because some birdman was jonesing for a vampire burger.

A crimson stream of fresh blood poured from the Ekek's neck like ribbons, but I knew my job wasn't finished. The head had to be removed, which was what was taking the guys so long. It wasn't a simple kill. It was a kill and a mutilation through bone and stubborn sinew. My blade was serrated on one side, just for such an occasion. I tried not to vomit while I sawed as quickly as I could through the birdman's neck. He choked and fought with weighted hands for freedom I sure as Sunday wouldn't grant him.

Danny ran at me with his Ekek's lifeless head under his

arm, his face vacillating between fuming and scared for me. "Get back in the car!"

"Not until he's good and dead," I argued, gritting my teeth when my blade met bone.

"Hold this," he instructed, handing me the prize of his attacker's severed head.

I don't know why this was the thing that terrified me. Something about holding a man's sawed-off head in your hands when his glassy eyes are still wide open tends to make a person freak out. I let out a short scream through my lips that were shut tight, and rested the head on the hood of the car. My fingers burned with the germs of the no doubt contaminated blood.

Danny put one hand on my guy's shoulder and gripped his chin with the other, the hilt of his knife resting in his teeth. Danny looked savage as he snapped the birdman's spine, giving my knife a clearer path to saw through. I made quick work of detaching the third Ekek's head, trembling and scared as my hands performed the dark duty on autopilot.

I pursed my lips through another choked noise of distress as Danny got into the car. He backed it out a few inches to release the very dead body of my Ekek. The headless birdman flopped to the concrete and bounced twice just to let me know I'd done something permanent and terrible.

Danny got out of the car and hefted the body up over his shoulder. He threw it in the trunk with no expression whatsoever on his face. He was Danny as he was meant to be, chopping down monsters and protecting the national treasures. There was something heartbreakingly sad about it all, and though I didn't like Danny one bit some days, I wanted more for him than this. I wanted him to actually be able to be bored in a mall while his girlfriend shopped to her heart's content.

Von dumped his monster's body into the trunk, and Danny grabbed the one he'd already chopped the head off of. Then the heads were rounded up and shoved into one of the overlarge shopping bags the weeping Mariang fed Danny through the window. Before Danny shut the trunk that was now stained in red smears, I snatched out my container of wipes to clean us up so my whole car didn't have to suffer. Poor Terence had been through enough.

Von was bleeding, the steady trickle running down his fingers from a bite that had torn into his hand between his thumb and pointer finger. Danny tossed Von a few napkins from the glovebox and motioned for us to get back in the car. "I'm driving," he ruled without room for arguing.

Danny wasn't going to get any pushback from me. My nerves were shot. I slid into the backseat with Mariang, letting Von stretch out in the passenger's seat as we all came down from the gore of the fight.

FINN'S BALISONG

I held Mariang in the backseat as she cried quietly while Danny drove us toward my home. It was ten whole minutes of quiet seething from the driver's seat before Danny tore into me. "Where did I go wrong? Asking you to stay put, or letting you drive in the first place? Or did I go wrong when I told Ezra I thought you were ready to leave the mansion? Where, October? Where did I go wrong?"

I didn't answer, but kept my attention on Mariang, who clung to me in her fragile state.

Danny's nerves were making his mouth shoot off unfortunate things I hoped he would regret later, but doubted it. I kept my mouth shut through his rigorous verbal assault, knowing there was nothing I could say that would quell the situation. When Danny couldn't engage me in a fight, his head swiveled to his brother. "Aren't you going to say anything? She's your charge, Von."

Von was quiet, staring ahead from his place in the passenger's seat as we whipped along on the freeway. "Where'd you get that knife?"

I cleared my throat. "I had it in my glovebox."

"Don't play games," Von snapped.

"I think what both of you mean to say is 'thank you. Thank you, October, for offing that bird guy before he crashed through the windshield and tore out your throat and Mariang's. Thank you, October, for having our backs.'"

"Where did you get that knife?!" Von shouted, making me jump. Von didn't yell at me usually, so I knew I'd crossed a line I'd have to answer for.

"It's Finn's," I admitted in a mousy voice, though I knew that was nothing to be ashamed about. "He gave it to me for protection when we were in Silo."

"That knife was given to him by King Banak himself. No way would he hand that over to you for no reason."

"We can talk about it later." I wasn't sure which secret would be worse – that I'd kissed the man who'd brokered his enslavement, or that I'd fought in a zombie apocalypse without telling them.

"We can talk about it now. That weapon is Finn's mark. If Finn wants one of his soldiers to broker a deal on his behalf, he sends them with that exact knife. It's sacred to him. Why did Finn give you his balisong blade?"

Danny was looking at Von in surprise that his brother

had caught a level of my treachery he'd missed. Danny cast me curious and furtive glances in the rearview mirror. "Finn doesn't give gifts to people for no reason. He's a man in it for himself and Banak alone. I could see him giving you a regular knife, but Von's right. I didn't even notice how off that is. Finn's balisong is special. Did you feel how easy it was to slice through that guy's throat? My knife's good, but my cut wasn't near as clean as yours, and I've been slicing through Ekeks for years."

I opted for the zombie confession because that seemed the lesser of two evils, if you can believe it. "He gave it to me because I may have fought with him, his men and Kabayo's men against Sama's army a little bit."

Danny nearly veered off the road, and Mariang squeaked her surprise as he corrected his trajectory. "You what? Finn and you both told Ezra you were behind the gate while the battle was being fought."

"I was, in the beginning. But Finn was losing, and there was a point where I could see him going down if I didn't do something. So I did something. It's not a big deal."

Danny had reached the point of fuming where he couldn't form coherent sentences, which I guess was the best I would get as far as a pardon.

Von had plenty of words, though, and thought them through so that each one had a clear point. "So you lied to us? You lied to me?"

I waited a few beats, hoping he wouldn't make me answer. Then I finally uttered a quiet, "Yeah. Because I knew you would freak out. Exactly like you're doing right now."

"I'm freaking out because you lied to me."

"Bull," I responded tartly. "You're pissed because I fought. Just like Danny's pissed I helped out just now. I get it. I have to stay safe for the good of the people of Terraway and all that. But I won't just sit back and let you die. And back in Silo? I wasn't about to do nothing and chew my nails like a sitting duck while Finn bit it. He was in Silo because I dragged him down to be my guide. He was *my* responsibility. So yeah, he gave me his fancy knife so I could defend myself if something happened to him."

"He didn't want it back after you both were safe and sound?" Von was hinting at something he had no business being near.

"He told me to keep it. That I saved his life or something, so that was my gift from him. Like I said, it's really not that big a deal. I'm safe, he's safe. We're all okay. Ezra made it clear I couldn't sneak off again with his little house arrest jewelry he made me wear, so whatever lecture you think I need to hear, skip it. I just beheaded somebody, and I'm not in the mood."

"You should've stayed in the car, like Danny told you to," Von grumbled, wanting to be right somehow.

I leaned forward so he could see me. "You're in this because you're my Reaper. If not for me, you'd be at home watching TV or guarding Ezra's home from errant flies or something. I'm the reason you were in danger today. I won't do nothing when three jaggoffs show up trying to eat my best friend. The fact that you think I'm even capable of that shows how little you know me."

I watched Von's expression vacillate between wanting to argue and being touched that my love for him went deep enough to awaken my dark places. "I love you, too," he said, reaching back to hold my hand. "And thanks for that. I was having a hard time getting the head off my guy. My knife's not as fancy as yours. But next time listen to Danny, yeah? Stay in the car."

"If you need me to lie to you and say okay, then okay. But I am who I am." My voice quieted even further. "I don't have many people in my life, and I won't give you up without a fight. I don't much care how bloody my hands get, so long as you're safe in the end."

Danny made a few grunts of protest when Von climbed over the console into the backseat. There wasn't enough space for him to sit in the middle comfortably, so Von pulled me onto his lap. He coiled his arm around me and pressed his forehead to mine. His hand cupped the underside of my knee and gathered my legs together so I was curled up on his lap, my back resting against the car door. "I love you," he whispered in my ear. "But you have to stop putting yourself in danger for the job. I matter to you? *You* matter to *me*."

"You're my treasure," I countered, "and I won't do nothing when someone's coming after you. A locked door does me no good unless you're locked inside with me."

Von kissed my cheek and checked my hands and arms for injury. "Are you alright, love? Did they hurt you?"

"I'm fine."

Von tsked me. "That's another dollar for the Denial Jar. When you use that money to buy me something pretty, I prefer my roller coasters without safety harnesses."

I rolled my eyes. "It's not *that* much money in the jar."

"Your denial runs deep. And I don't want just a trip to a carnival. I want a real, live roller coaster, named after me."

I smirked at him, making myself comfortable on Von's lap in a contented snuggle. "You got it."

I hadn't sat on all that many laps in my life. Every now and then when I was very little, Ollie would read a bedtime story and Allie would pull me onto her lap as we listened with rapt attention. He liked to do voices and sweeping gestures, making the stories come to life. Judge had read to me while I sat on his knee many afternoons, back when I was little, and trusted him without a blink. The only other time I can remember being on a man's lap was when Allie and Ollie took me to see Santa Claus once at a mall. We waited in a long line, and when I finally got to see the chubby old man in his red suit, I knew exactly what to ask for. I was a four-year-old on a mission. I wanted new clothes for Allie and for her to eat, for Ollie to stop getting into fights at school, and for Mama to like me.

The fake Santa didn't know what to do with me, the poor guy. I still remember his uncomfortable chuckle of

"Ho, ho, ho. Don't you want a new teddy bear? Maybe a new doll?"

Christmas morning came, and there were no presents under the tree. Well, there was no tree, so that was strike one. Allie kept wearing the same baggy sweatshirt that had stains on the elbows and a hole on the side. There wasn't any food at all. Ollie was nursing a black eye Christmas morning from who knows what fight he'd gotten into at school. Bev got stinking drunk on money that was supposed to be used for food for all of us. I don't remember what I did, but I set her off somehow. I spent Christmas morning being chased around the trailer while she wacked me over and over with the back of her hairbrush, until I found a safe place to hide in her hoard.

That was the year I stopped believing in Santa. Ever since then, I hadn't had the stomach for Christmas trappings, or sitting in men's laps who couldn't do a damn thing to help me.

Von hadn't promised me a teddy bear or a new doll, but he'd held my hand through Ollie's temper, Allie's distance and Bev's hatred. I didn't just need Von alive, I needed him unharmed, well rested and happy. He was so good at being happy, and I wanted to learn that skill.

I rested my head next to his on the seat, closing my eyes against the wary looks Danny was shooting me in the rearview mirror, and the hopeful ones Mariang cast in our direction.

30

CHINESE FOOD AND SANDWICH COOKIES

I called Ollie just to hear his voice when we got home, and the guys took turns washing up from the fight. My brother promised he would be home in an hour for dinner, and I breathed a little easier knowing we'd be reunited soon. I opted to go last in the bathroom so I could make sure everything was cleaned properly. Because, you know, boy germs.

Danny ordered too much Chinese food, but I knew we'd make our way through the smorgasbord by the end of the night. Mason had been waiting for us, and I could tell he was bummed that he'd missed a good monster fight. "I can't believe I've been sitting here, doing charm work like a chump while you all were out cutting off Ekek heads."

Von made himself comfortable on the couch with the bucket of chicken fried rice, since there wasn't room at the table for all of us. "Yeah? Well maybe you should get over your little squabble with November. Then you'll be around for the next attack, instead of sitting alone in an empty house, pretending to be useful."

Mason cast Von a look of deep displeasure. "October and I aren't fighting."

My head snapped in Mason's direction. "Hello, you can barely look at me. I don't care. I mean, you're welcome to feel as mad as you want, but call a spade a spade."

"Really?" Mason snapped. Ever since my disappearance, he'd vacillated from pissed to tolerating me. "I'm welcome to my feelings? Thanks, really. How generous of you."

"No, you're not mad," Von said, grinning over at Mason like he wanted to be slapped. Von oozed that particular kind of charm.

When Ollie got home, he nearly collapsed in my arms with mental, physical and no doubt emotional exhaustion. He was handed a plate of food and ushered to the couch where he unloaded all that I'd missed. "It's like Bev's a different person. I don't get it. I wouldn't have believed it if I hadn't been with her every waking hour. She's sincere now."

Of all the things he could've said, sincere seemed the most outlandish. I blew a disrespectful raspberry as I sat next to him with my sesame chicken. "Now you're just making things up."

"Honest. She's not proud, she's not in denial about everything, and she's not mean. She's done nothing but cry over every single thing she's messed up, then she apologizes as soon as she's coherent enough to speak." He bit into his eggroll as if it was the one thing missing from his life. "This tastes amazing. Thanks for getting food. I've had my hands full."

Danny grunted in response as he tore into his almond chicken.

"Do you think there's a possibility it's an act? I mean, it all came crashing down when Ezra saw her trailer, and that was the first time she was exposed."

Ollie shook his head swiftly, not breaking eye contact with the food he couldn't eat fast enough. "Nope. She broke off the engagement. Gave the giant diamond back and everything. Said she didn't deserve someone good like him."

That dropped my jaw. My mouth stayed open until Von scooted in next to me and closed it with his index finger. "You look like an adorable little guppy."

"Oh, hush." I batted Von's hand away and turned my focus back to Ollie. "I don't get it. I mean, Ezra explained to me about the sagrado stone's effects on humans, but it's not settling right with me. I mean, we lived with the stone, and we're not abusive hoarders."

Ollie gave me a look that told me he thought I was being stupid on purpose. "Maybe not hoarders, but Allie had her fair share of problems. Cutting, anorexia. I mean, did you see how much better she got when we moved out? She was like a different person. You, too! I always thought it was the therapy and the medication, which I know helped, but it was getting you away from that stone. It's poison to us, kid." He poked at the bandages on my arms that had been necessary when I was cooped up in Ezra's place. I knew I'd made life hard for Von, constantly smelling of scabbed-over wounds. "I can see you've had a rough time being in the same house with it. And it makes sense you never kicked your OCD. You visited Bev once a week. Got yourself a consistent unhealthy dose of the stone to keep things nice and unbalanced."

My welcome home toward my brother grew sour. I didn't like him calling out my metaphorical and literal wounds in front of people. "Kicked my OCD? Like how you kicked your anger issues, oh unscathed one?" I reached out and snapped the rubber band on his wrist. "Tell me, how exactly was growing up in a house like Bev's supposed to affect me? Am I supposed to just get over everything because the poison's not near me anymore?"

Ollie tapped his toe to mine. "Of course not. That's why I put you in therapy and why you're still on medication. It's why I kept up with Anger Management out in New York. But see? With the stone gone, we'll have a chance. Before that, we didn't have a prayer. Now we can someday be without all of it. Bev, too."

"I don't get you," I said honestly. "You hate Bev. You were mad I visited her once a week. Now, what? You're all about pushing it under the rug? Bygones? Family singa-longs and handholding? Legit Brady Bunch for Team

Reese? We're supposed to look the other way on all of it because Bev has a good reason?"

"I don't get you," Ollie echoed back onto me. "I was the one who wanted to write her off, but you insisted it was the right thing to do to try and look after her – that she was sick and couldn't help herself. Now that there's a reason she was so hard to love, a reason she couldn't help herself, you're willing to write her off?"

"I didn't say all that." I let out a heavy sigh just as the doorbell rang. I made to get up, but Von's weighted hand on my shoulder pushed me back down.

"I'll get it. We were just attacked. Your job's to relax. Mine's to get the door."

"You're not my butler, Von. You were the one who was attacked, if you'll remember correctly."

"And yet, I've got tons of energy for answering doors and entertaining beautiful women." Von stood in front of me as I sat with Ollie on the couch and started doing a sexy slow-motion shimmy, shaking his perfect backside in my face just to make me laugh. I swatted his butt, grinning at my mischievous daring and his playfulness. "I've got this, darling. You sit with your brother." He turned and pressed a closed-mouth kiss to my lips that could never get enough of his constant tease. My heart swelled at his random affection that always seemed to land on me. Von was the best kind of opiate, and I was growing wildly addicted to the flavor of him.

Von moved to the door while Ollie pointed his finger in my face. "I saw that."

"Really? You saw the butt that was popping and locking right in front of your face? Nothing gets by you."

"You did the cutesy girl smile-and-blush. Your cheeks are still pink!" Ollie whispered.

I touched my heated cheek with the back of my hand. "Whatever. I'm warm. Shut up about it."

"Careful, kiddo. I mean it. He's a nice guy, I'll admit, but his speed's far faster than yours."

"Is this you shutting up about it? Because it sounds like you're talking nonsense still. Eat your eggroll, Reese."

"Be careful, Reese," he cautioned me, watching Von with wary watchful brother eyes.

Von let in Gabby, who had two armloads of groceries. He grabbed one and called over his shoulder to us, "We got us some visitors, kids."

Mason and Danny wore matching frowns, displeased at the impromptu party Gabby always managed to figure the worst time to throw.

I donned a smile for Ollie's closest thing to a relationship. "Hey, Gabby. Is everyone coming over?"

"Of course! It's been too long since we've had both of my Reese's Pieces under one roof."

Rachel came in behind Gabby in her short red dress that "accidentally" showed off her underwear at least a dozen times whenever she wore it. She looked Mason up and down, sizing up the new addition she had once patted on the head when he was a wolf. "Who's this tall drink of too much water? Let's get this man a cocktail. I'm Rachel."

Ollie was already on his feet, taking out two-liters of pop and opening a bag of chips to toss into the overlarge popcorn bowl. "Hey, Rachel. You remember Danny, Von and Mariang. This is Mason, our newest addition. He's crashing here for a while." He raised a hand to wave in the others who were coming in behind the girls. Gabby turned on the music, giving her hips a warm-up swirl. Half the crew was filtering in, turning me introverted as I stood to greet my friends, offering Mariang a bland smile.

Mariang was grinning from ear to ear at the impromptu party. Her social life consisted of her father, her irritable boyfriend and magical Terraway creatures who, let's face it, were each terrible at making nice unless politics forced it out of them. "This is wonderful! So good to see you all."

"This is terrible," Danny countered, his eyebrows pushed together as he counted the growing number of people coming through the door. "Do you know all these people?"

"Yeah. Known them for years." I bumped fists with Jordan, Marcus, Amber and Katrina. "Ollie went to high school with most of them. They're fine, but they'll be here until one or two in the morning." I waved to the growing number of people and escaped to the kitchen to put some of the Chinese food away.

"Why didn't you tell me you were having a party?"

Danny groused, following me into the kitchen. "I don't like this many people milling about. I can't keep a proper eye on you two like this."

"A) I didn't plan this. Gabby likes to throw parties at our house because it's always clean and she knows I'm a giant pushover about this kind of stuff. B) You don't have to guard us against these guys. They're harmless civilians. You know, like you're supposed to be. So be a dear and put on your harmless civilian face."

"Forgive me if I don't trust your judgment on who's harmless. You asked Captain Finn to escort you through Silo." Danny said this like he was jealous, like the fact that I'd asked Finn and not him was an egregious jilt to his knife-wielding ego.

"You're seriously still mad about that? Finn's a rule breaker, and you're the king rule follower. Plus, I wasn't about to tear you away from your regular daily duties. What'd you expect me to do?"

Danny gave me a hard look before Jordan and Nick called to me from the living room. "Bait!" Nick made his way to the kitchen and clapped me twice on the shoulder. "Where've you been hiding, kid? We missed you. All work and no play, as usual?"

I looked up at him with a baleful expression. "You didn't miss me. You missed being able to drink yourself stupid and leave it all for me to clean up."

"You got any cookies?"

"No." When it dawned on me there was too much of a smile on his face, I held up my finger. "No, Nick."

It was no use. My friends had no boundaries, and no matter how much of a voice I wanted to have, it was always overlooked. "You know what I'm hungry for. I need an October sandwich cookie!" Then Nick yanked on my arm and tugged me into the living room, mashing me between himself and Jordan, where they hugged me and bumped me back and forth until I hit the floor to escape.

Nick was starting to get a beer gut to rival Jordan's – a thing I wished I hadn't figured out by it being bashed up against me.

It took only five minutes for fourteen of Ollie's friends to fill up my home. Mason was my constant shadow, making me jumpy, which meant he had to pull from me even more. It was a vicious cycle. Danny was glued to Mariang, horrified that Jordan and Nick might try to make a Mariang sandwich cookie or something.

Mariang was in her element. She chatted animatedly with Gabby, did shots with a few who'd congregated around the kitchen table to get to know the newcomers, and made plans with some of the girls to go shopping the next day.

It wasn't lost on me that she fit in far better with our friends in the first ten minutes than I ever had.

31

TO MAKE YOU HAPPY

We didn't have a story for how Mason got there, so I passed him off as a work friend. A friend who smiled only when social norms dictated it and stayed close to me, sniffing my water before I took a sip. "Where did Von drift off to?" he wondered aloud, searching the faces for a familiar one.

I stood near the back of the living room, leaning against the long taupe curtains I had drawn closed over the picture window. "Dunno. He's great in these social settings. He'll probably be elected King Von of the Beer-Chuggers or something."

Mason squinted as he scanned the room, his eyes landing on a space in the corner and widening in surprise. He coughed twice and wrapped his arm around my shoulders, corralling me into the kitchen. "I'm thirsty. Let's get something to drink over here."

"Okay." I was confused as to why Mason was being nice to me. Voluntarily touching me without pulling as a motive. "You alright?"

"Of course. You?" He asked with too much sincerity, too much concern. I wondered how haggard I looked if he thought an unwelcome impromptu party might turn me into a basket case.

"I'm getting used to your friends, I think. You know, I was thinking of making a swing by my home when we go camping next."

Camping was his clever code for mentioning Terraway, though he could've said Terraway, and no one would've been any the wiser. "Which home? The one you grew up in or the one you left to be here? Hayop or Sombi?"

Mason softened a degree and actually made eye contact with me that held no note of anger. I almost didn't recognize him. "The one I was born in. Hayop. I'm still recognized as royalty by my family and the people. I think you might like to see where I grew up. It's much different from here, but there's a charm to it. I actually haven't been back in years."

"Sure, we can do that. I mean, none of it's really up to me, but I think it's great you want to go home for a bit. Makes sense. You've been totally uprooted for months."

"Uprooted?" He bypassed the pop, the light-your-hair-on-fire punchbowl, and poured himself some water from the tap.

"Yeah. You've been in my world, sleeping on the couch, on the floor, sharing a bed with two other people. It's gotta be exhausting. You need a familiar place to rest your head every now and then. I'd love to see the lucky place that had you in it for a couple decades. I bet it's real nice."

He stared at me, confused, and then placed his cup on the counter without drinking a drop. "I don't get it. You're being sweet to me. Why?"

"Why wouldn't I be? I've always been decent to you. Just because you underwent a personality change doesn't mean I did. I get why you're crabby. You're frustrated, and nothing here's solely yours. I'd be crabby too if I felt constantly displaced. Why do you think I hate staying at Ezra's?"

"I guess I never gave it much thought. I'm doing the job. It's fine."

"But clearly it's not. You're unhappy." I crossed my arms over my chest. "How can we fix that?"

"Why do you care if I'm happy?"

I cocked my head to the side. "Seriously? Before it all hit the fan between us, we were starting to become friends. I care if my friends are happy, especially when they take it out on me when they're not." I blinked up at him, confused. "Did you really think I wanted you to suffer? I broke for you when Geon's men did what they did to you. I did everything I could to get us out of there, and I still failed you. I failed Von, too. I'd do just about anything to make you happy again – to give you back a little of yourself."

Mason scratched the top of his head. I could tell he was still unsettled by his short hair. "I guess I have been sort of mean to you. I'm not trying to take everything out on you, but maybe that's what I've been doing."

"I get it. You've been through a lot. You need a break, Mason. How about we order you a bed for the spare bedroom? Would that feel better? Give you some space that you could make your own? I mean, it's not like Allie's going to be using that room. I can move the desk out easy enough."

"You don't have to do that." Through his protest, I could see the light in his eyes at the prospect of not sharing a bed with two other people, one of whom he hadn't quite sorted out yet.

"If it would make you happy, I'll get out Allie's old bedframe and mattress in the morning. I might take me a trip to the store, too. Most of Allie's sheets were pink. Maybe you'd like to pick your own?" I rubbed the stress out of my forehead. "I'm sorry, Mason. I should've thought of that sooner. Totally self-involved of me. What else do you want? Maybe a dog bed, too, in case you want to wolf out."

He looked relieved, his hand on his toned stomach and a hint of a smile on his handsome face. "No, no. The regular bed's more than enough. Thank you. And on days we go reaping, I'll be sure to sleep with you two so we can do a double pulling while we're asleep."

"Are you kidding me? It's the least I can do. You're only in this mess because of me. It's my fault they cut your hair. It's because of me you're always looking over your shoulder." I shook my head at the unbidden emotion that threatened to choke my throat at the too public admission of all the things I loathed myself for.

"It's not because of you. It's just life."

I shook my head, ignoring the pulsing music blaring from the living room. "I took away your strength, your wife and your dream zombie-slaying home. You're the first Viking I ever met, and I broke your whole life. I can't think of a worse crime." And I'd done it all, hoping he'd kiss me, wishing I could be captivating enough that someone so wild would want me to fight and laugh next to him. "I'm sorry, Mason. For all of it."

Mason's eyes were unbearably sad as he studied my face, looking at me without the note of frustration in his eyes I'd grown accustomed to. I missed that look. "*Hani*, it's not your fault."

I shrugged. "We both know it is." We shared too many words through our connected gaze, so I turned away and headed for the living room to take a breather. I truly had wrecked Mason's life. He was a happy zombie killer before I'd met him. He was Bruce Campbell in action, and I'd ruined his whole world.

I broke my own personal Bruce Campbell.

Then I made Mason think about his dead wife, got him kidnapped, shaved and humiliated. I'd ruined what he'd loved about his life, and he had to stare me in the face every morning, protect me and give his freedom up for me. I was the worst kind of person. After the stone business was squared away, Mason would still be stuck with me in a normal, uneventful life. My idea of Heaven was the Brady Bunch, but he'd had his Heaven in Sombi, and had been forced to give it up for me. I'd unwittingly domesticated my favorite Viking. I couldn't think of a punishment severe enough for that.

"October? Wait!" Mason called, but I ignored him. I didn't want to be anywhere near him, for fear of breaking it all more. My eyes fell to the filled couch, scanning the room for a place to sit where I could disappear in the crowd, but still appear as if I was good at being social.

Von's relaxed and cocky smirk wasn't aimed at me, but was engaged with Katrina, who was sitting atop his lap on the couch. She was wearing her purple mini skirt and a gold shimmery halter top that was about two sizes too small, ensuring no man could look at her without being reminded she was a solid D-cup.

Von's smile didn't touch his eyes, but his hand was sure as Sunday touching the inside of her thigh. Her fingers were toying with his shirt collar, and she was laughing at something he said that had to have been hilarious, judging by the animated cackle of hers that shook her perky breasts in his face. She leaned down and whispered in his ear in a warmup-for-sex way that made me feel a slight bit sick to my stomach.

Now I knew what Mason had been trying to shield me from seeing.

32

PLAYING DIRTY

It was fine. Why wouldn't it be fine? Something childish started warring inside of me. I felt gross, horrified that I'd sat on Von's lap like a groupie in the car. I wasn't his girlfriend, and he certainly didn't belong to me. Von had every right to rest his hand on Katrina's thigh. They'd hooked up a few times already. Katrina was his age, and moved at the same fast pace he did.

I could feel my heartbeat in my cheeks. I had never felt more like the kid they all addressed me as. It was obvious, and I couldn't believe how much I didn't see it until that moment. I was twenty-two, and Von was almost thirty. My hands had scars and scabs from fighting too much. Katrina wore two gold rings and had her nails perfectly manicured. I was a kid sitting on Santa's lap, and Katrina was the sex kitten playing the game as an equal.

I knew all of this. *Didn't I?*

I felt hot all over, flushed from the inside out. I took a few steps back, looking for an easy exit. Mason's hand on my shoulder spooked me, but it was Beto's familiar voice that paused my flight. "Hey, kid. We were thinking of setting up," he motioned to the kitchen table that had an empty seat around it. "Want to play? I think it's time they lifted the ban on you."

Beto's hand was in Jessica's, and she smiled at me meekly, knowing good and well she'd started up with Beto long before we had ended things. I had every right to be pissed at the both of them, but the three of us all knew I didn't have it in me to nurse a grudge for very long. "Poker? Um, I don't know."

Ollie slung his arm around my shoulder, interrupting the awkward conversation to whisper in my ear, "I had a little talk with Von. Turns out you were right, he's not interested. Just a hopeless flirt. He'll tone it down around you."

The heat in my cheeks was washed out by the ice in my veins. I felt like someone had come up and dumped a bucket of cold, harsh reality over my head, drenching me with chagrin and regret. Of course Von didn't want me for anything other than someone to pal around with. I'd said from the beginning that we were just friends. He was starting to become my closest confidant, and I was pissed at Ollie for calling me out on my sore spots. I shrugged out of Ollie's half embrace and aimed him in Gabby's direction. "Go be overbearing elsewhere. Of course he's just flirting because I have boobs and a pulse. I never thought it was anything else."

"You game for a game?" Beto asked, immune to my nerves. Beto no doubt thought he was smoothing things over between us, forcing us to be friends to make Jessica happy and to put some sort of closure on it all. "I won't take no for an answer." He steered me toward the table and pulled out a chair.

Jordan groaned in defeat, pausing his shuffle before he dealt the cards. "Man! I thought Bait was banned from poker. We all know she counts cards. And cheats. She's a poker witch with magical witchy powers."

Beto's unwelcome hand on the small of my back spooked me forward, edging me toward the chair. I sat down, making sure I had a polite smile in place before I picked up the cards Jordan dealt me with his dramatic frown. We only ever played for quarters. I don't know what he was being such a sore pre-loser about.

Mason took the chair next to me, not touching his cards and looking around the cramped table at the five people he didn't know. "How do you play?" he asked.

Jordan's eyebrows rose at the prospect of possibly winning a few hands, now that there was a newbie in the mix. "You've never played poker before? You're Ollie's friend. How's that possible?"

"I'm October's friend," Mason corrected Jordan. "We work together."

A conspiratorial light dawned in Jordan's eyes. "Ah, I

see. We've never met a work friend of Bait's before. Welcome, welcome." He tossed me a grin filled with innuendo. "I knew it wouldn't take long for someone to snatch you up once you and Beto moved on from your non-relationship. Now look at the two of you, sitting around the table playing poker. You realize Beto's the only reason you're allowed to play tonight." He cast Mason a conspiratorial look. "She cheats."

I harrumphed, trying to scrub the image of Von and Katrina out of my mind. "Counting cards isn't cheating. Any of you are welcome to do the same."

Jordan waved off my protest. "Tell me – Mason, is it? Do you think Bait will let you call her your girlfriend?"

"She's not my girlfriend." Mason shifted in his seat, uncomfortable.

Jordan snapped his fingers, a wicked smile on his curved lips. "See? You've got him trained already. Well done, Bait." He turned to Mason. "You a medical guy, or one of the guards?"

"He's a guard," I answered succinctly before any lies had to be told. "You ready to lose?" I asked, sitting back in my chair. "I think I'm going to make myself a little pile right here of all your quarters, Jordan."

"Dream on, Bait. The last time you took us down better be a good memory. Tonight I take all your chips, kid. Now both your non-boyfriends get to watch you lose. Shame. Utter shame."

I wished I had the magical ability to melt into the floor,

but no such power came to me. "Shut up, Jordan. I know what you're doing."

Mason shifted next to me, frowning at Jordan. "I don't think *he* knows what he's doing."

I waved off Jordan's grin at getting my goat. "It's part of the game. He's trying to rile me up so I'm easier to read. Ignore him. Here. You've never played before, so watch my hand and learn the game. This is part of it. Just like me telling everyone Jordan's beer bottle's filled with pop. He likes to act like he's getting drunk a few hands in so we think he'll play poorly and we'll raise prematurely, but he's totally on his game." I smirked at Jordan's guffaw. "Not that he's got game."

"You suck, Bait."

Jordan turned to Beto, who was sitting on my other side. Jessica was rubbing her stellar boyfriend's shoulders as she stood behind him. "Hope Jessica's not as evil as your last girl, Beto."

Beto chuckled and kissed Jessica's palm. He cast over to Greg, who was frowning too dramatically at his cards. "You ready for Christmas, Greg? I'm sure you won't be expected to propose this year. I mean, if Carrie didn't get antsy your third Christmas together, why would she be expecting a ring on the fourth?"

Yes, the trash talk was in full swing. It was one of the rules of how we all played poker. Don't get in the game if you can't take your cage getting good and rattled.

Greg ducked behind his cards. His spiked brown hair

was too gelled and showed off his encroaching bald spot on the cap of his head. "Dude, keep your voice down with that kinda talk. She's been hinting since her birthday. You think I can get away with another cutesy gift?"

I fielded this one, discarding one castoff for an even better card. "Depends. What'd you get her last year? Oh, right. Wasn't it a stuffed monkey holding a heart that said... something. 'I'm bananas for you'? I can't remember what it said after she threw it in the trash. Maybe it was 'I'm smananas for poo'. That's probably it. Can't remember." I scratched my chin and looked up, recalling Carrie's hour-long rant at the following girl night about the stupid monkey gift she wanted to leave him over. "No, it couldn't have been that lame and generic. Was it when you got her a fake gemstone necklace in a gold-plated setting because the 24-Karat real gold was too expensive?" I laughed at the memory. "You even put it in a box that was similar to a ring box! Oh, Greg. It's going to be fun taking your money tonight. Maybe I'll buy Carrie a real Christmas present with all the money I'm gonna take from you. Poor girl deserves something pretty she can actually go smananas for."

When it was time to put our cards down, I knew I'd won. I wasn't much in the mood for foreplay. It was going to be a smooth takedown tonight. This was where I hoped to bury my confusion about why I couldn't shake the image of Katrina curled up on Von's lap like a cat.

Half an hour later, and Greg gave up after he ran out of

chips and pride. I'd hoped for a smaller pool to conquer, but Greg's abandoned chair was pulled out to host another player I hadn't expected. "Von?" I quirked my eyebrow across the table. "You don't want to play poker."

"Correction," he said as he eyed the cards Jordan dealt out, his cigar clutched between his teeth. "I don't want to *lose* at poker. It's been a while since I sat down with a bunch of blokes and was promised a good time." He tilted his head toward me. "Plus one lovely lady, of course."

"Call her lovely now. Wait until she takes your chips," Beto groused. Jessica had long since abandoned our trash talk, walking with Mason to the living room where she introduced him around when he tired of watching me play. Beto tapped my shoe under the table with a hint of a tease on his lips. "Just as cold as she was on a date."

"Ho!" Von laughed, taking in the tenor of the table. "So it's *that* kind of poker game. This'll be fun. Tell me, Beto is it? Just how unappealing does a bloke have to be to turn such a soft creature cold?"

"Get to know her a little better," Beto assured Von.

"I know her plenty well."

Beto's eyebrow rose at the innuendo that rested in the air between us. "Oh, you *know* her?"

Von rolled a chip between his fingers, sizing us all up before deciding which cards he wanted to keep and which he wanted to turn in. "Women are a constantly evolving mystery, but as much as a man can know a woman, I know our little November. I know she hates that I'm telling you all I know her. I know how she takes her breakfast after a long night." He cast me a cold, veiled smile. "I even know that she has a rainbow-shaped scar on the inside of her thigh. Succulent little thing."

I couldn't believe he went there. No one knew about that scar. Showing Von my glaring flaws had been a private moment that was precious to me, and he was flaunting it around like my body was fodder for gross guy jokes.

I gasped and pointed across the table at Von, all levity gone. "You shut up about that, or the only thing you're gonna know about me is how dirty I can fight. Trust me, you don't want to see that side. Go play with Katrina. You'll be much happier with someone who'll put out for your stupid jokes." I sat back when Von gave me an apologetic tilt. "Von has never seen me naked, for the record."

Jordan eyed us with a mixture of confusion and amusement. "Record noted. Wow. I've never seen Bait so riled up. We do our worst to rattle her, and she barely cares. I'm going to need some proof, kid. Take your pants off so we can put this whole thing to rest."

Jordan cast over at me the smile of a harmless cad who wanted a good scolding. I leaned across the table and patted his cheek, and then flicked his front tooth hard, sending a painful ring through his mouth. My fingers burned with his mouth germs, but it was worth it. "Enough about my thighs," I said over his exclamations of pain. "And shut up, Von. You're trying to hurt me, and I don't know why."

"Oh, kid. You know I love you. You and your delicious thighs."

The words rang hollow, and I could tell they tasted bad in his mouth by the slight grimace he wore after saying them. He looked at me across the table with a note of sincere regret, but then washed it off his face just as quickly as it came with the stupid bravado that had too much sleaze to it. He was putting on a show, but I couldn't understand why. What had I done to him? "No, you don't love me," I said, bringing down my gavel as I understood more fully all the things Danny warned me about.

Jordan stuck his finger in his mouth and held it up in the air as if to test the wind current inside my home. "Yup. Just what I thought. Too much sexual tension. Next time we let girls play, we make it strip poker instead."

I didn't like where this was headed, but knew as soon as I let them know they were tap dancing on a landmine, *I* would be the one exploding. I was seven hands away from taking Jordan out, if I could force him into raising his bet on this round. "Talk all you want, guys. So long as you've got cash to back up your chips, I can tune this out all night."

Beto cast me half a smile. "Save some sexy talk for later, kid."

"Why? Is Jessica also cold on dates? Yikes. Two in a row? Might not be the women, Beto," I jabbed. "I raise." I picked up two more chips and threw them into the pile.

Von watched me needle Jordan into raising even

higher, smiling with pride at my prowess when my royal flush killed the round and the rest of Jordan's sleazy jokes. I didn't much care if Von was pleased with my poker playing abilities. It was all about domination now, as far as I was concerned.

Jordan was in deep concentration mode for the next few rounds, not bothering to verbally assault any of us as his stack of chips dwindled down to a few measly ones without much promise.

"Von, did you want another drink?" Katrina asked, making her way back to him and placing a beer in his hand. She stood behind his chair, playing with the short hairs at the base of his neck. Of all the needling we did at the table, for no reason at all, Katrina's fingers in Von's hair poked at my sore spots the worst.

I lost count and track of what I was doing and bumbled the hand – badly. Jordan perked up while Von's smile grew sinister. "Not so amazing now, are you?" Jordan said as he dealt another round. I barely gathered my wits before I lost again.

I sifted my new hand into the proper order, averting my eyes as Von invited Katrina onto his lap, sharing his cigar with her. Sharing his germs with her. I hoped beyond a wish on a snowman in July that I hadn't looked like that when I'd sat on Von's lap. I vowed I would never sit on a man's lap again. It hadn't done me a lick of good with Santa. I only felt stupid for being so casual with Von, who was casual with everybody. "I think I'm good for the night, guys."

"Leaving so soon?" Von asked. "Something wrong, Peach? Sore loser, are we?"

"Nothing's wrong at all. I'll play another hand. You know, I'm glad you're fitting in so well. I was worried I'd always be your only friend." I sat back in my chair and pinched the bridge of my nose, feeling a mild tension headache coming on.

"You're hardly my only. I manage to make friends wherever I go. Some of them even know how to play poker. No one here, mind you, but in other parts of the world." Katrina whispered something in his ear that made him chuckle darkly. The smile didn't touch his eyes. He was forcing the laugh, though I couldn't figure out why. "I don't know, Katrina. Let me check with my brother." He shot over the table to me, "Do you think Danny will let me drive Katrina home? She needs someone to fix a few things around the house."

"I'll bet," I mumbled. I sat up straighter and faked a smile that was just as disingenuous as Von's. "I think Danny will be fine with it. It's your life. You don't owe Danny a thing. He knows you don't belong to him."

Von's gaze hardened as he stared at me. "Ollie gave me a hard time about it earlier. I wouldn't want to make Danny or Ollie or anyone else think I'm here for reasons that just wouldn't work for either of us."

"How noble of you. Do what you want, Von. I'm not

going to hold you back. If driving Katrina home makes you happy, then why are you checking with anybody? Just go do it. Do it as many times as it takes. Over and over. Why should I care?"

"It's perfectly acceptable to want to do things with other people who also want to do things." Von didn't break eye contact with me, even as Katrina stood to grab her coat and purse.

Jordan looked curiously between us, sensing something more complicated was going on than driving Katrina home. Jordan was a bright little bulb. "Are you two hooking up or something? The shifting wind just got real weird in here."

Beto had been engrossed in his hand. "Huh? Who's hooking up with who? You two?" he asked of me and Von.

I was about to answer with a resounding "no," but Von beat me to it. "Not in this lifetime." He let out a scoff at the idea that someone like him could ever be with someone like me. It made me feel on the outside of my own group of friends, and very, very small. "Bait's just a kid. Of course we're not hooking up. Can you imagine?" He let out another humorless laugh. "Ridiculous."

My friends called me Bait, and I hated it. Von was supposed to know how much I hated it, and not perpetuate the awful nickname. He'd called me Peach, which was a hefty step up from Bait. Now I was the kid. I'd just cut the head off a monster to save his life, but I was a useless kid. I was easy to throw away, as I'd always suspected. All it took was a party and a heated conversation with Ollie for Von to toss our friendship aside and treat me like I didn't matter. Von loved me behind closed doors when it was just us, which wasn't enough for me. He'd been my best friend, but now he was looking at me like he barely knew me, as if he had no clue how deeply his words cut me.

But he knew. He knew and he did it anyway.

I laid my cards down, winning the hand without apology or victory at taking Jordan clean out and diminishing Beto's hand to just a few chips.

Jordan was dying dramatically in his chair and swearing up and down he would never play poker with me again while we all started settling up. I patted Jordan's shoulder as I addressed Von without looking at him. "Go home with Katrina. Stay there as long as you like, Von. In fact, I think you should sleep there a few nights. Have all the fun you want. Enjoy her thighs that probably don't have any scars at all on them. You deserve to have exactly what you want out of life."

"Maybe I will. Mason can keep you proper company while I'm gone. Lord knows he's dying for the chance."

"Hush up with that talk. You know that doesn't help anything."

"I just want you to help yourself, kid. Play with the grownups a little. Maybe that'll get you to finally relax. Unclench so you can actually have some fun instead of being so uptight. Maybe Mason also gets off on perpetual handwashing. Who knows?"

I took a step back, as if his words had turned into an arrow and soared right into the heart I was swearing up and down I didn't have. I blinked at Von in shock, and I knew by the fumble on his face that he caught himself too late. "Screw you," I mumbled, embarrassed and hurt. My hands screamed at me to wash them, but I balled them into fists to keep my neurosis from calling the shots.

Beto clapped his hands in Mason's honor, though Mason was in the living room and out of earshot. He threw down a few bills. "Well done to Mason. Well done to you. I knew someone would come along for you, kid. The prison nurse and the prison guard. That's gotta be some sort of fairytale. I felt bad after what happened with us. But knowing you found someone? Good for you, kid. Good for you." Beto patted me on the shoulder, making me feel hollow inside before he left.

Katrina came back into the kitchen just to whisper something in Von's ear. When he grinned and responded with a, "Sure thing, Peach," to her, I nearly burst into tears at the gut punch.

It was *my* nickname. It belonged to me, and Von was passing it out like it was a party favor. I'd let the name become precious to me – let *Von* become precious to me. I felt stupid and small, staring at my best friend and seeing him for the stranger he now was. They strolled into the living room together, as if nothing catastrophic had just occurred.

My phone rang, and I answered without first checking

the caller ID, though pretty much everyone I would want to talk to with a cell phone was already at my house. "Yeah?"

Judge's low and smooth voice greeted me on the other end. "I didn't think you'd pick up."

"Is that how you're starting all your phone calls these days? I've always been a big fan of 'hello.'" I hung my head that these were the people who called me. "You couldn't have worse timing if you tried. What do you want?"

Judge cut right down to business. "I need you to do me a favor. Just a short visit to the prison to deliver a message to Fender for me. He's up for parole, and it won't look good if we're seen on the visitor's log for him."

I groaned as the table cleared, leaving me to my private conversation. "I can't do this game tonight, Judge. It's been a long day, and it's not nearly over yet."

He switched from business to friend-mode, and though we weren't friends anymore, I was too frustrated with the night to care. "What seems to be the problem, baby girl?"

"Nothing fixable, unfortunately."

"With enough money and influence, everything's fixable."

I looked down at my hands, my chin quivering with shame as I warred with the urge to wash them. "I'm not," I admitted.

"Tell me the problem, and I'll fix it." He spoke with the

same matter-of-fact tone he used when he'd taught me how to play *Monopoly* all those years ago.

"We don't play board games anymore," I whispered mournfully.

Judge paused, letting my words settle between us with all their weight. "It's been a long time since I've played anything at all." He cleared his throat, taking control of the conversation when I was content to flounder. "How about I pick up a board game and come over tomorrow. We can catch up without all the drama."

Tears pricked my eyes at the offer I didn't know I'd needed to hear. As much as a day spent rolling dice and putting aside age-old divides appealed to me, I knew I couldn't let anyone I loved near Terraway. Despite the abandonment that still burned my tender insides, I loved my Judge.

I closed my eyes to rein my emotions in. "What am I doing?" I whispered, hating the note of fear in my voice.

"You're telling me where you're at, so I can come pick you up. You sound scared. You're not in one of my neighborhoods, are you?"

I couldn't disguise the heartbreak in my voice. "How did I get here?"

The concern in Judge's swift response tugged at me. "Tell me where. I'm getting in the car."

"Not this place in the world, this place in my life. How did it come to this? What choices did I make to land myself here?"

He sighed, his voice velvety and tender. It was how he used to sound before he became important. I'd loved that guy. "You're a good person. I shouldn't have asked you to go see Fender. I'm a little desperate, and frankly, I've missed our back and forths. Everyone on my payroll is either a pushover or not trustworthy. Plus, it's the only way I can get you to have a conversation with me. But I shouldn't have bothered you with this. I won't ask again." The comfort he tried to offer me was sincere – I could always tell when Judge was lying. "Now tell me where you are. I'll come and get you."

I shook my head, feeling weighted and very, very old, but still far too young. "I'm at home. I'm fine. I'm working tomorrow, so I can't play board games with you. Thank you for the offer, though. I see that you're trying."

"Alright, baby girl. Stay in the house; I'll come get you out of there."

"Don't bother. I'm in it now. There's nothing else for me." I rubbed my temple, not sure if I could feel any lower. "Goodnight, Judge," I said as I turned off my phone.

I kept my eyes on my feet, wishing the floor would swallow me whole.

33

GETTING VONNED

I was still sitting at the table a few minutes later when Danny, of all people, came and sat down next to me. He set a shot down in front of my line of vision and chucked my shoulder. "You alright? I caught the tail end of that."

"You come to gloat? Because I get pretty violent when people slap me with an 'I told you so.'"

"I'm not gloating. Just sitting." He motioned to my face. "You've got that look. You just got Vonned, huh."

"Please don't make me a t-shirt that says that." I drank the shot in one painful gulp, not caring what was in it. "It's fine. I forgot that he and Katrina... It's fine. Why wouldn't it be?"

"Because you've got it bad for him. If he wasn't so stupid and immature, he'd realize he's got it bad for you, too."

"I don't think you're helping." I reached over and took his shot without looking up at him. I wasn't supposed to drink much on my medication. I rarely had more than half a glass of wine when I did indulge. It was depression that drove me to swallow the fiery liquid, and depression that shrugged at my brain when it told me that was a dumb move. *Shut up, Brain.* "It's not that. Von's my friend. I tell him stuff. I trust him with secrets none of these people know. I don't care that he's with Katrina. I care that he sold me up the river in front of the guys just for a laugh. It's like he wanted me to know for sure he wasn't into me, as if that wasn't clear already."

Danny eyed the empty glass in my hand. "That's rough. It's how Von is, though. You think you know who he is, and then he turns into something else." He lowered his voice. "Von's self-control won't last forever. One temptation could push him over the edge, and then he's gone. He knows he's temporary, and you've got permanence written all over your face."

"Is that supposed to be a compliment?"

"I think so."

I stacked the shot glasses, too despondent to respond. "I'm going to turn in. I'm tired."

"Want me to kick everyone out? This doesn't seem like your scene."

"Why would you say that?" I asked, my smile so forced, it could barely be classified as such. "It's almost like you're implying that my friends have no idea who I am and don't give a crap about me, so long as I let them play and drink as long as they like here."

I didn't expect sympathy from Danny, but I got it in the form of a softened expression and an awkward pat on the back that I'm guessing he thought meant, "I get it, kid." He took the glasses from me. "I'll take care of it, and send them all home."

"Don't bother. I'm going to bed. If I cared, I'd do something about it."

"No, you wouldn't. It's like you're afraid to take up space in your own life."

I stood, not wanting Danny to be the calm, wise one in the conversation. "Goodnight, Danny. Thanks for the drinks."

"Don't mention it, kid."

Kid.

I poured myself a cup of Gabby's punch that I usually didn't take more than a sip of. This time I added rum to my cup and downed the glass as quick as the harsh burn would allow.

I hadn't seen Von, and hoped he had already left with Katrina, who was also gone. I made my way to my bedroom, visible to my friends but somehow still invisible. I was miserable, and no one was a safe enough place for me to talk to about it, except maybe Ollie, who was dancing with Gabby in the living room. Her eighties hair band music blasted through the house, and she had a genuine smile on her face when she beamed up at my brother.

I was ready to discard a portion of my bad day and chalk it up to "things I should've known better", but a noise was coming from my bedroom.

My bedroom was off-limits. It was the universal rule. I had white carpet I didn't allow shoes on. I had a bed that was made perfectly, and I didn't want dirty coats thrown atop it. It was my safe place.

I slowly opened the door to my room and stumbled back in horror, my hand over my mouth to muffle my noise of distress. Von and Katrina hadn't made it home, but they'd made themselves at home in my room. Katrina's gold blouse was unbuttoned, and Von's hands were having a field day in the land of her comfortable D-cups. His shirt had been strewn on the floor in a fit of passion. He was sitting on my bed, as if it was the perfect place for a solid run to second base.

They looked up at my entrance, Katrina giggling and moving off of straddling Von's lap to button up her halter. "Sorry, Bait. We'll take it to my place. I know you don't like people in your room."

It was my one rule. I had one rule.

I looked at Von, who was doing his best to act like nothing was wrong at all with him making out with a woman on my bed. In my room. Her shoes on my white carpet. His drink on the nightstand. I didn't let food or drinks into my room. I don't care if that's weird, it's my room. It's my one safe place where I can be weird. It's allowed because it's *my* room. Everything in the world is messy, but knowing that there's one place that's clean and mine helps me get through all the times where I can't wash my hands three times, like I need to. The room tilted as the alcohol picked an inopportune time to hit me, but I held steady as I clutched the doorjamb.

"Get out," I whispered. "This is my room." It wasn't a statement; it was a plea for Von to break out of his jackhole mindset and care enough to realize how much this hurt me.

"Alright, alright. Come on, Von. We're going, Bait. Don't worry. You tired, kid?"

"Yeah. See ya." I kept my gaze fixed on my bed as Von stood with decidedly less bravado, zipping up his jeans. There were germs crawling all over the sheets now. I could feel them taking up space and crowding me out of my own room. They had to go. I moved to my bed and took off the top sheet, throwing it onto the white comforter with blue stitching they had kicked to the floor. Like, *onto the floor.* I started at the corner, untucking my blue fitted sheet from the mattress and balling it up with clumsy fingers to be washed.

"Give us a minute, Katrina. I'll meet you at your car." Von closed the door, shutting out the loud noise, Ollie's friends and his own BS with slumped shoulders. "That was out of line. I shouldn't have brought Katrina in here. It's your room. My fault."

I didn't say anything. Really, what was there to say? I took off the mattress pad and then picked up my pillow, but Von snatched it from me before I could remove the pillowcase.

"Would you stop a second? I said I was sorry. Out there at the poker game, I took it too far, yeah? You were all busting on each other, and I thought we were just joking around."

"My body is not a joke!" I yanked the pillow back and tried to pry off the pillowcase with fumbling hands that couldn't find the upside of anything at the moment. *Stupid Danny with his stupid shots.*

"You're right. I was a jerk. Complete wanker."

"Beto doesn't know what my thighs look like, and I didn't want him to ever know. I didn't trust him enough to show him the ugly parts of my body, but I trusted you! Like an idiot, I trusted you."

"Hey, I love your thighs," he said sweetly, his eyes going back to the compassionate ones that had shared secrets with me too many nights to count. "No part of your body is ugly."

I bashed him over the head with my pillow. "Shut up! You don't get to comment on my thighs or my scars or any of it. I don't care what you think. Go be with Katrina. She's perfect! I've seen her in a bikini, and she doesn't has a single smark on her. Enjoy." The alcohol had turned on me and jumbled my words, proving that neither Von nor rum were my friends.

Von's voice was even, which made me even more frustrated. "I have every right to go back to Katrina's place."

"Did I stutter? That's what I just said!"

"Then why are you acting like I'm cheating on you? Ollie scared the daylights out of me with his intentions speech. We're just friends, October. Nothing more."

I pretended to cry dramatically and then shouted, "Fine by me! And you know, I've got a whole roomful of friends out there who know next to nothing about me, except how much I love my bedroom and need it to be mine. You're s'posed to know me the best, and you did this?" The room tilted, but I was able to blink gravity back into its proper place. "You called her 'Peach'!" I shouted mournfully, hating myself for admitting to him that he'd sliced my vulnerable spot.

"I said I was sorry! Jeez! Overreact much?" He exhaled loudly at the fact that I was still wrestling with the same pillow, and jerked it out of my hands. "Let me do that. I wouldn't want you sleeping in germs. Who knows what kind of amoebas and STDs Katrina and I spread all over your precious sanctuary."

"You don't get to look down on me for this! I earned a clean room! I earned the right to go to sleep in a place I feel safe." My heart was pounding, and I could hear the rush of blood pumping in my ears. The alcohol was hitting me harder than I anticipated. "I bought this house with money *I* worked for! I lived in garbage before this! I don't have to sexplain myshelf to you," I slurred, stumbling over my words.

"Yes, you have the right to be crazy. Well spotted."

It was a well-aimed slap in the face from him, smarting where I was exposed. "I'm not crazy! Gimme that." I snatched the pillow back.

"I said I would do it!" Von grabbed the pillow and ripped it out of my stubborn hands, reeling backward as he fought to regain his balance.

It happened too quickly, but somehow I saw it all in slow motion. The pillow flung backward, Von's arm reaching back longer than either of us anticipated. The edge of the pillow brushed the glass of rum and coke Von had poured himself and brought into my room. The room he knew I didn't allow drinks in. The beverage started to tip, and I couldn't get there in time. My entire life crashed in time with the cup as it toppled off the stand and soaked my pure white carpet.

The world stopped spinning, and all I saw was the brown taking over my life. The garbage had found me, no matter how hard I tried to make myself clean.

34

I'M NOT CRAZY

*V*on's hand over his mouth and mumbled apology did nothing. It was ruined. My perfect room I'd waited and worked my whole life for was ruined. The brown splatter soaked into the pure white carpet, dying it permanently and murdering my safe place.

I rounded the bed and dropped to my knees in front of the stain. My tears broke loose and fell over my hand. I tried to stuff my sobs back into my body so I didn't have a meltdown in front of Von, who stood there like an oaf.

It was broken. It was all broken. All the walking through a world of mud, and then a country of dirt, and sleeping on the ground was okay because this room was untouched. I didn't have to worry about this one space in my world, and now it was gone. Everything solid would be forever shattered if I didn't have this one place to take me in, to make sense to me. Now it was gone, and I felt gone with it.

Von fell to his knees beside me and wrapped his arms around my body. He tried to still the rocking I hadn't realized I was doing. "I'll fix it. I'll get the stain out. It'll be alright, love. I'll make it better."

I couldn't hear him enough to understand his words. I could barely think, and as the panic set in and tightened my chest, I could hardly breathe. I felt him pulling stress off me in waves, but it was only a drop in the bucket.

He'd called me crazy, and I was.

I screamed through my hyperventilation and bashed my forehead to the wooden nightstand over and over, holding myself as I cried out my pain. Von promised me all the ways the world would be right again, but he was wrong. The world was broken and stained, and no matter how hard I tried, I didn't fit in anywhere. I had no safe place, no haven that would have me no matter what my mental state turned out to be.

I was crazy, and crazy people always ended up alone.

I don't know how Mason heard me through the music and the animated chatting, but he ran into the room amid Von's nervous cussing and my panicked gasps for air. My esophagus felt like it was collapsing in on itself, and I couldn't get a full breath. I frantically tried to tear off the bandages on my arms to rip at the skin that burned with an unquenchable itch beneath. Von kept switching between holding me tight to stop me from hurting myself, and releasing me to try to calm my breathing. "Get Ollie!" Von cried, frantic. "I can't calm her down!"

When Mason came back with Danny, Ollie followed in on his heels. "What happened?" Ollie demanded. Then he came closer and saw the horror on the carpet. "Oh, no. Shit. Oh, shit." He grabbed at his hair, his eyes darting around as he went into Superman mode. "Danny, Mason clear everyone out of here, but keep the music blasting until they're all gone. This second. Party's over. No one sees my sister like this. Not even Gabby." They were good soldiers and obeyed without hesitation or question. Ollie dropped to his knees, pushing Von out of the way so he could turn me to block my line of vision, shielding me from the stain. "October? Can you hear me?"

When my brother's face filled my scattered gaze, my panic finally had a place to put itself. I pawed at his shirt with desperation and fought through my hyperventilation to tell him the awful thing that happened to my perfect place. "The carpet! All of it... It's ruined!"

Ollie's face was stern and simultaneously kind. He was in control when I was spinning. "Who am I?"

I couldn't get in a breath to gather up an answer.

"I'm your brother. I can fix anything. You don't have to think about this at all, because I'm here. I'm right here, and it's going to be okay. Who's always taken care of you?"

I wanted to answer him, but my lips felt fuzzy and clumsy, and I couldn't find the oxygen to form words. I tore at my skin like a rabid animal as I sobbed incoherently.

"No, no," he scolded gently, wrapping his arms around me. "Don't hurt yourself." All the things I couldn't reconcile threw themselves at me, and I couldn't hold up my end of the fight anymore. I was lost, and didn't want to be found in the mess. "October!" Ollie shouted, and I realized he'd been talking to me for who knows how long, and I hadn't heard a word.

Danny came back, his eyes wide as he tried to keep up. "What can I do?"

"Hold her down so she doesn't hurt herself," Ollie instructed. "She's got medicine for when this happens, but I have to find it. It might take me a few minutes. Is everyone gone?"

"Mason's clearing out the last of them. How do I…"

"Like a strait jacket. Hold her from behind, or she'll break loose. She's a fighter, and she doesn't trust you."

I felt Danny slide onto the ground behind me, sandwiching me in with Ollie. I panicked at the claustrophobia and started to buck to break loose from the double hold. "What? Wait! No, Ollie! No! Don't get the medicine!" I begged, tears streaming down my face as I bucked in Danny's and Ollie's arms. I was on my knees, so I couldn't get much momentum. "No! I'm all better! I'm better! The doctor said I was better!"

"I know, sweetie, but you're not as better as you need to be. I love you. I'll be right back." Ollie stopped short before he let go of me, his forearms tightening. "Judge? Man, I don't know what you're doing here, but you've got to leave."

Hot tears of shame and panic raced down my face. Of all people, I didn't want my friendly arch-nemesis to see me like this. I didn't want Judge to see the mess I was. "No! No, no, no! Don't let Judge see the carpet!"

"What's wrong? She sounded strange on the phone, so I came over to make sure everything was alright." He rolled up his sleeves as he stood in the doorway of my bedroom. "What do you need?"

"I need you stay on the porch and make sure no one comes back inside. October's sick, and I need to handle it."

"I'm not sick! It's the carpet that's wrong! I'm fine! I'm fine!" I shouted, my face red as I struggled to free myself.

Ollie let go, and Danny secured his arms around me from behind, bending my arms so I had to hug myself. His knees enclosed around mine as he pulled my back tight to his chest, his chin positioned just above my shoulder. "No! No! Help! I'm not crazy! I'm not crazy! I can be normal! I can do better!" When I couldn't break free of Danny's grip, I let out a horrible scream that scared even me.

Danny was trying to keep his voice calm, but I couldn't make out a word of it through my gulping sobs. I was in a world unto myself, and not even Von kneeling in front of me where Ollie had been gave me any sort of peace. I couldn't stop the pain that roiled inside my helter-skelter brain. He cupped my face to keep my head from thrashing, and I felt his stream of pulling trying to force me to come down from the anxiety I knew I'd never escape. I felt the layers of stress leave me, but the only dent it made was that

I wasn't hyperventilating as much, so I had more air to scream with.

Mason ran into the room. "Bliss her out, Von! Move! I'll do it if you don't. What even happened?"

Von and Danny exchanged wary glances. Then Von finally looked into my unfocused eyes and nodded. "I'm going to pull a little harder this time, *hani*. It'll all be okay soon."

"It was perfect, but now it's broken," I choked out.

"Move, Von," Ollie ordered before more than a few waves of calm were shot through me. Ollie shoved Von out of the way and took the cap off the needle I dreaded.

"No, Ollie! I'm all better! I can do better! It's the carpet that's broken, not me! I don't want the medicine! I'm normal!" I sobbed, barely able to see him through my haze of tears that felt never ending. Judge came back into the room, following Ollie's lead. He knelt at my side and coiled his arms around me, helping Danny hold me still. I'd needed him so many times throughout the years. To have him come back right now felt like karmic payback for all my sins. "Don't do it! Don't do it!"

Judge's deep voice was the home I'd been ripped from, but never stopped needing. "I've got you, baby girl. I'm right here."

Before I could figure out a way to break free from Danny and Judge, Ollie shouted, "Hold her still!" and jammed the needle into the outer flesh of my thigh.

The drugs were quick, pushing an ocean of nothing

atop me. It wasn't panic. It wasn't peace. It was nothing. The stain on my carpet was nothing. Ollie shouting down at me as I was lowered to the ground like a limp noodle was nothing.

I finally wasn't crazy.

I was nothing.

35

SCARING PEOPLE WITH MY CRAZY

My dreams were choppy, moving in and out of focus like a broken record that was determined to get through an entire song. Philip's face finally found me in the chaos of the mishmash of scattered landscapes and stuttering colors. He centered me to the earth when he put his hands on my cheeks. "Why is everything like this?" he asked loudly to compensate for the vacillating reality that kept shedding light on us, only to take it away a few seconds later.

"It's the meds Ollie gave me. I had a bad night."

"What happened? Are you alright?"

"Not really," I admitted. I'm actually pretty crazy. 'Alright' is something I tell people I am so I don't have to admit that most days I freak myself out."

"I love you just the way you are."

I shook my head. "I don't. Being the way I am is hard,

and it hurts." I motioned around to the distorted reality we were in. "This isn't a normal person's dream."

He looked around at my bedroom that kept surfacing and disappearing at random. "Where are we?"

"It's my bedroom at my place."

Philip's eyes found mine with purpose. "I made it into your house?"

"Lucky you. Sorry my brain's freaking out. I would show you around."

His mouth found mine when the lights cut again, throwing us into darkness. The sensory overload made for more passion than I'd been anticipating, and we all but attacked each other, toppling onto my bed. The lights didn't come back on as Philip's shirt found its way to the floor. They didn't come back on when my shirt joined his moments later.

We were frantic to make good use of the time while we had it. I knew as soon as I woke up, my world would be bleak and all too real. "Make me forget it all," I begged Philip, tugging his lower lip between mine.

His hands moved up my body to stroke my cheek tenderly. "Oh, *hani*. I've been waiting for this for so long."

Philip and I discarded reality and the rest of our clothes as we made a mess of the sheets in the darkness of my broken dream.

I DIDN'T LIKE THE MEDICATION THAT WAS IN CASE OF emergencies only. I didn't like how it made me feel when I woke up however many infinite hours later from my broken, yet sexy dream. I didn't like what it said about me that there were times in my life when a little spilled milk had more of an effect on me than a simple childish cry. I felt like I was floating, and I prayed with everything in me that when I opened my eyes, Ollie wouldn't have checked me into a hospital for observation. I'd sworn to myself I would never let myself get so out of control again. My therapist had instructed me to make a safe place for myself so that when life got messy, I could draw solace from the fact that my one place was still clean and controlled. I needed that strength, that peace of mind. It allowed me to wade through mud, to treat bloody inmates and sleep in the dirt when I had to.

Now it was gone, and so was I.

"I could've blissed her out just fine. You didn't have to drug her like that. She's not a wild animal. Who knows when she'll wake up now?" Von's voice came to me from the living room, but I was all turned around, not even sure which room I was in.

Ollie's voice rallied and calmed me in the same breath. Things would be okay if Ollie was around; I just knew it. "She'll wake up when it wears off. And you've known October for less than a year. I raised her. I took care of her. I know when she's herself, when she's lost, and when she can't find her way back. Trust me, this is how I'm keeping her out of the hospital. She gets a mark on her record, and she won't be able to go back to work quite so easily."

"She has a job," Von countered. "Ezra doesn't care about her record."

"No offense, but you all suck at this. My sister's self-sufficient on most things. Since you all came into her life, she's lost weight, had a mental breakdown and lives with two men I'm not sure should ever be around anybody's sister. You have no idea how hard the three of us have to work to be normal, the mental stamina it takes to blend in."

"I don't get it. One minute she's killing Ekeks with no hesitation, no fear, and the next she's catatonic over a stain on her carpet. It's a steep learning curve, Ollie."

There was a pause, and when Ollie answered, I could tell he was thinking his answer through. "She can do those things because she can compartmentalize better than most. We're survivors, and we do what we have to. If it's pretending she's not scared when someone attacks her, she'll do it. If it's gritting her teeth and barreling through when life gets too messy, she'll do it. That bedroom is the one place she doesn't have to pretend. You wrecked her safe place, Von. Were you seriously getting to second base with Katrina on my sister's bed? For what purpose? Why? Everyone knows her room's off limits."

"Because of you! You got into my head with your fatherly talk about my intentions and what October deserved in a husband and whatnot. I saw that I'd let things get too familiar between us. I put some distance in there so she didn't get confused."

Danny's voice broke in. "So *she* didn't get confused. How altruistic. I suppose simply talking to her didn't cross your mind any more than actually going for it and doing something real with your life."

Von's anger rose in his shout that was aimed at Danny. "Something real? I'll give you real, little brother. I won't live long enough to give her anything real. You think I don't look at her every damned day and curse the vampire who bit me? You think I don't wish I could make her mine? I'm one paper cut away from losing myself forever. People like me shouldn't attach themselves to someone who deserves more. But by all means, tell me again how simple it all is. Tell me October doesn't deserve better than me, and how settling for a half-vamp is the best move for someone as amazing as her."

I could hear Danny's tart response seething through gritted teeth. "She deserves to get what she wants."

I opened my eyes and found that I was resting in Ollie's bed. The room started spinning, blending a blurred face with the color of streaked pink. There was a moving shape that was hard to place as the world kept tilting. "Oh!" I groaned aloud, grabbing for something to brace myself on.

I heard a woman shout, "Ollie, she's awake!" Then a reassuring pair of delicate hands gripped my flailing arms. I felt weighted, and still too erratic to make sense of the world.

"Allie?" I called, hopeful. "Allie! You came back!"

I heard a crash of footfall near the bed, and Ollie's arms were around me in the next breath. "Easy, kid," he said as he slowly lowered me back down to the mattress.

"She's back! I knew she'd come back for us!" I sobbed. I was confused and could barely see my brother, who was right in front of my face. The world kept tilting, moving too slowly, and then somehow too fast for me to comprehend everything I needed to make sense of it all. "Allie?" I called.

"Shh. Allie's not here, hun. It's just me."

I didn't know why Ollie was lying to me. Maybe he just couldn't see her. "I heard her! Right over there." I meant to move my arm to point, but ended up smacking myself in the face.

"That's Mariang. She hasn't left your side. Allie would be glad to see someone caring about you so much."

"Allie?" I called again, not ready to give up hope that my sister had come back for me. "Allie!"

A large hand swept mine up, and I felt a portion of my stress coming down. The hand was hairy, so I guessed Mason was there. I blinked over and over, but the world was still screwy, like an old TV you had to slap the picture straight in.

Ollie was shifting my pillow beneath me, his arm around me to keep my body from flailing. "How are you feeling?" Slowly the room started to come into focus. Mason, Von and Mariang stared at me with notes of fear in their faces. Ollie asked me a series of questions to test my lucidity, some of which I heard, and some I could not. "Let's slow things down, sis." Ollie shooed the guys out, kicking his feet up on the mattress as Mariang pulled the blanket up over me.

I looked down and noticed for the first time that my hands had gloves on them. Thin black gloves that looked like they were meant for driving. "Gloves?" I asked Ollie, who looked relieved I was speaking.

"Von got you some gloves to wear so you didn't scratch yourself. And this way you won't have to get your hands dirty."

"Oh." That was nice. I often felt the desire to wear my hospital gloves out and about, but knew that would be weird. This was a happy medium. I buried my arms under the covers and struggled to sit up. Ollie met me halfway and tugged me upright, while Mariang arranged my pillows so that I didn't have to put any effort into the arduous task of, you know, sitting. I cuddled into Ollie's side. "How bad was I?"

Ollie kissed my forehead and rested his cheek there. Mariang reclined in the chair next us. "Not terrible. You knew who I was. That's a step up from the last time. Who knows? Maybe with Mason and Von doing their pulling thing, I won't have to intervene again."

"I'm sorry, Ollie. I'm so sorry!"

"Shh. Don't worry about it. I think you're allowed one breakdown per year. You learned about a whole new world filled with freaky creatures, magic, Voldemort and who knows what else. I'm actually kind of glad the stain on the carpet forced you to take a break to deal with a little bit of all that's been changing around you."

"I can do better. I promise I can get myself under control."

"You're doing just fine, kid. Take a break. Watch some bad TV with your old brother."

"Did I hit you?"

"Nope. Didn't hurt me at all. You zonked clean out, which gave Von enough time to smarten up. So if you want a really good apology, you might be able to get it in song if you play your cards right."

Mariang's voice was quiet and gentle, which was probably how I confused it with Allie's in my befuddled state. "Von got the stain out, changed your bedding and vacuumed."

Ollie cut in with a sharp edge to his tone. "But if it's not how you want it, I'll have the carpet replaced, alright? Nothing to worry about. It's still your space. No one'll wreck it while I'm around."

"Von vacuumed?" I inquired, trying to visualize the oddity. "I can't picture that."

Mariang smiled and pulled her phone from her pocket. "I wanted proof, too, so I snapped a picture. See? Von with a vacuum. Lynna will faint when she sees this."

I saw my vacuum. I saw my room. I saw the side of

Von's face, his eyes haunted and expressionless. I'd scared him with my crazy, and now Von was vacuuming.

I scared Von into vacuuming.

No, no.

I threw the covers off me and tried in vain to get up, my arms flailing hopelessly while the rest of my body punked out on me.

"Lay back down, kid."

"I have to get out of bed. This isn't right. Von's vacuuming? I don't want that."

"You don't want Von to clean up his own mess?" Ollie clarified, leaning me against his shoulder when he could see I wouldn't be deterred. "Those are some low expectations you've got for him, there."

"I'm better. I can do better. I don't need people cleaning up after me."

"Alright, alright. Slow down. You can't walk yet. Remember the last time?" He kept me in his one-armed hug as he spoke to Mariang. "She stood up before she was ready, and her legs weren't working right. She smacked right down on the ground and conked her chin on the desk."

Mariang frowned. "Ouch. Would you feel better if you made a list? When I'm too weak for the day, I make lists of all the things I'd like to do, and plan to do once I'm on my feet again."

It dawned on me that I wasn't the weakest link. Mariang had many mornings where she woke up barely able to lift her head. No one looked down on her for that. Maybe I didn't have to be so angry with myself because I couldn't feel my legs yet. "I guess that would work. Yeah."

"I'll grab you a pen and paper." She scurried out of the room and returned a minute later. She sat on the edge of her seat, pen poised over the notepad I kept on the fridge. She looked like the most adorable secretary I'd ever seen, complete with her raven hair pulled back in a professional bun. "Here. What would you like to get done today?"

"Reaping. We need to keep on top of the quota, or we'll fall behind."

"No," Danny ruled from the doorway. "I let Mariang push herself, and it only hurt her. This isn't about being a hero. It's not a sprint. You need a day off, so take it. We're well ahead on the quota."

"I'm fine. Just a little setback last night. After I get feeling in my legs back, I can get to work."

"Talk all you want, the answer's no. We've got a good four days before either of you need to reap a single soul."

I grumbled, but as I couldn't get out of bed yet, I decided to let Danny win this one. "Fine. But tomorrow it's business as usual. We'll need to deliver the next bit of the stone soon, so we have to spend a few days stocking up on souls before we leave for Terraway."

"Fine. I made breakfast, but it's been sitting out for an hour. You want me to make you something else?" Danny's words, though very nice, had always the note of aggression to them.

"You made breakfast?" I asked, looking up at him in confusion.

"Yeah. No one felt like leaving the house this morning, and none of us were all that hungry, so I made some scrambled eggs. You want?"

I nodded, unable to look up at him. "Thanks. That's real decent of you."

Danny didn't know what to do with a sincere compliment from me, so he ignored it and went out to the kitchen.

"He was worried sick last night. We all were. Dad stopped by," Mariang said, updating me on the events of the night. "Left a bit ago to sit with Mother."

"Why?" I asked, my nose scrunched. "She gave back the ring."

Mariang frowned. "Yes, and he gave it right back to her. She said she won't accept it until she has her life together. She said she's going to give herself a few months to try to sort things out. Figure out who she even is, since she doesn't really know anymore. She's been living near the stone for so long. She's a bit lost."

"Understatement," Ollie agreed. "I'm supposed to go in to see her, but Ezra took my place so I could be here."

"Taking care of yet another crazy person," I said, stating bluntly the thing we were all thinking. "Lucky you."

"What are you talking about? I'm here because I want to hang out with my sister. We've barely spent any actual time together since I moved back, what with the Terraway crap tornado that keeps sweeping through the trailer park. I believe when I came into town a few months ago, you promised me a *Nightmare on Elm Street* marathon you never delivered on. Or was it *Evil Dead*?"

"Hello, you were with Gabby that whole weekend. You don't want to watch stupid movies with me. You're only here because I freaked out. You're being nice to me because I'm pathetic."

Ollie's mouth dropped open. "Okay, I didn't think you were crazy before, but I do now. You just called *Evil Dead* stupid! Heresy!" He felt my forehead to check for a fever.

Mariang giggled at our playful fight as Ollie got up to turn on the TV. "I very much wished I had siblings growing up. You're so close. It's nice to watch."

"Yeah? You're next, little sister," Ollie grinned, jerking his head to the other spot on the bed next to him. "Best seat in the house right here. Tuck on in, kids. We're skipping work and watching movies for the day. We're so rebellious. I say we go full-on pirate tomorrow and steal a boat or something."

Mariang and I looked at each other, smiles breaking out on our faces as I tried to scoot over to make room for her. Ollie pulled me to lean against the headboard on his left, and Mariang slid in on his right, barely taking up any space at all. Ollie grabbed his remotes and clicked through the movies we owned to locate the first *Evil Dead*, or as it could also be called, the Greatest Movie of All Time, which Mariang had never seen.

Ollie opened the door and called out into the house, "Come on in, guys. We're having a movie day. Whoever brings up work or last night or anything serious has to make the first beer run."

Mason and Von meandered in curiously. Then Danny came in with a plate of scrambled eggs for me he'd nuked in the microwave. "Thanks, Danny. They look great."

Ollie sized up how many people were in the bedroom and shook his head. "On second thought, movie marathon in the living room. I don't think we'll all be comfortable. We can't watch Ash get attacked by the hand of death in here."

Mariang took my plate for me, and I tried not to let anyone know that I still couldn't feel my legs. Ollie was already in the living room turning on the TV and finding the first movie for our marathon; I didn't want to ruin the fun by reminding him that I wasn't my best self yet. I picked up one leg and flopped it over the side of the bed like a dead fish. No, this was definitely not ideal.

"Wait a second. You're not supposed to be walking." Danny crouched down in front of me and looked up into my face. I was horribly embarrassed, so I turned away, wishing I wasn't pathetic. "Can I carry you?"

I leaned forward, my head in my hands while the others set up in their seats of choice in the living room. "Ugh. Could this whole thing get any worse? Please don't carry me. It's so humiliating."

He turned my chin to face him so I had no choice but

to look into his eyes that were earnest, and without their usual loathing. "Hey, it's one bad night, yeah? That's all this is. Ollie's right; we all need some time to just be normal. No stone, no monsters, no Terraway, no family drama."

"You've clearly never seen *Evil Dead* if you think today will be devoid of monsters and drama."

Danny managed a small smile at my joke. "I've actually never seen it before."

My mouth fell open. "You're not serious."

Danny shrugged. "Mariang likes the romantic 'I hope he falls in love with me because I've got three months to live' sort of rubbish. I'm actually kind of excited to see something new."

"Oh, well stick with Ollie and me. This is going to be totally different than what you're used to."

"So I'm to carry you, yeah? And when you're strong enough, you can carry me around, if it makes you feel better."

I blinked at him, shocked. "You just made a joke. I didn't think you knew how."

He ran his hand over his face, leaning back to rest his butt on his heels. "You scared me last night, kid. Ollie's right. We need a little balance. I saw what happens when you're pushed too hard for so long. Today we make jokes and watch movies and remember the good things about the life we're supposed to be living in between saving other worlds." He shook his head, touching his heart. "You scared me. I don't do well with scared."

I blinked at him, shocked. "I honestly didn't know you cared."

"Why does everyone say that?"

"Because you're mean."

His eyebrows pulled together, giving him that monster of Frankenstein look. "I don't have any sisters, but somehow you became mine. I don't like seeing my only sister so out of her mind. Today we do nothing responsible. We do nothing at all." Danny rose slightly and picked up my arm to loop it around his neck, tilting my body so I rested against his chest. One arm slid beneath my thighs, and in a fluid motion I couldn't help but be impressed by, Danny lifted me off the bed. He was gentle with me and shot the others glares of warning not to say anything about me not being able to feel my legs yet. He carefully set me on the couch between Ollie and Mason, and then took his seat on the recliner. He invited Mariang onto his lap after she handed me my plate of eggs.

The movie started, bringing me back to a thousand memories of watching this movie too many times to count, but still never enough. The familiar credits and the feel of wasting time with my brother brought a smile to my face. No one except for Von had ever seen the *Evil Dead* movies, and Von had only seen the first one, which as we all know, is the gateway drug for awesome cult horror flicks.

Von sat on the floor at my feet, not ready to look up at my face, but also unwilling to be parted from me. I took a chance, leaned down and put my gloved hand in his hair, exhaling when his shoulders drooped. He leaned his head to my knee and looped his arm around my calf, holding it like a teddy bear.

I didn't understand all that had gone down between us yesterday, but I clung to hope as Von clung to my leg, that somehow we would find a way to make things right again.

36

PINK CARNATIONS

The polite knock on the door was answered by Danny, who checked the peephole before letting Ezra inside. Ollie had long since fallen asleep next to me, so I shared the blanket Mason had draped across my lap with my brother, making sure he didn't get chilly as he snored softly on the couch.

Ezra had an armload of flowers and kept his voice quiet when he saw Ollie asleep. He quirked his eyebrow at Mariang's horrified expression as she watched the bloody mutilation that was unfolding onscreen. "Darling, how are you feeling?" he asked me, making sure not to block the TV.

"I'm fine."

"Might I have a word?"

"Sure." I made to stand, but Von shot up and backed me down onto the couch. "I can feel my legs now, Von. I'm fine."

"Then you'll humor me. Easy now." Von moved slowly and with deliberate purpose as he lifted me off the couch to stand, taking care not to wake Ollie. "To the kitchen?" he inquired, offering up a humble downward tilt to his head when I nodded. He kept one arm curled around my back and used the other as a crutch for me to lean on. My feet plodded forward unsteadily, like they'd fallen asleep.

Things were tense between us. I hoped that if I kept not looking at him, we wouldn't have to have the awkward conversation where he told me I was a sweet kid, but I wasn't his flavor of tall, leggy blonde. I already knew as much, and didn't need it spelled out for me.

Von lowered my limp and weakened body to the chair at the kitchen table, holding onto my hand as he took the seat next to me. I dropped his grip, not out of anger, but because it felt wrong to touch him so intimately.

Ezra sat down across from us, setting the bouquet of long stemmed pink carnations down across the table. "Do you have an extra vase?" Ezra asked me, taking off his suit jacket and folding it over the back of his chair.

Extra? I didn't even have one vase. "No, but I'm sure they'll be alright until you get them home."

A curious expression fell over Ezra. "I won't be taking these home, darling. They're for you."

"What are?"

"The flowers. I confess I don't know your favorite

flower, or even your favorite color, but it's a start. How are you feeling?"

"I'll run out and fetch you a vase," Von offered quietly, looking grateful he had a reason to be helpful.

I shook my head and pointed at the top cupboard with a weighted arm. "There's a tall stein up there for Ollie. It'll work fine. Thanks, Ezra. You really brought me flowers? Like, you went to a store and bought them for me?"

"That's typically how the process works, yes."

Von got the beer stein down and cut the tips of the flowers so they didn't stand super tall and fall over in the glass. I picked a stem out to examine the oddity once they were slid to the center of the kitchen table. The blooms brightened my bleak world with their unapologetic shock of pink. "No one's ever bought me flowers before."

"I'm sure that can't be true. I noticed a vase filled with lovely flowers in your bedroom when I arrived."

"Huh?"

Von filled in the blanks with a closed expression. "Judge sent you flowers this morning, along with a board game. Monopoly, I think. I put them in your room."

"Seriously?" I frowned. "I bet there was a card asking me to do him a favor or something."

"There was a card, but it was just him wishing you a speedy recovery. Nothing more." He cleared his throat. "Not that I read it."

Ezra watched me study the pink carnation in my hand,

smelling it and turning it over to see it from every angle. "Do you like them?"

I nodded, transfixed by the gesture. "Did you do this because I had a breakdown?"

"No, dear. Mariang, Lynna and your mother also got bouquets today, if that makes you feel less suspicious of my intentions. I merely wished to brighten your day, to show you that I do care for you, and that I'm trying."

I smelled the flower again, amazed at how beautiful my kitchen looked with the shock of pink lightening the room. "They're amazing. Thank you, Ezra. That was right decent of you."

"You're most welcome." He folded his hands over his stomach as he leaned back in his chair, looking tired, though it was barely noon. "I have something else to deliver. It's a message from your mother. She wanted me to tell you that when you're ready to see her, she would like very much to speak with you."

The true reason for Ezra's visit became apparent, and my shoulders drooped. These were bargaining flowers. "Sure. Probably not today, but when she gets out, I'll come by to see her. You can bring back the message that I'll still come by to take her out once a week when she's ready. But I don't want to go to the psychiatric ward." I held up my hand. "It's the best I can do."

"It's more than generous. Thank you. She's positively distraught over what she's done to you over the years. She's been writing everything down that she can remember because she wants to go over each point to tell you how sorry she is."

"Yeah, I can't really wrap my mind around that right now, so I'll just say 'cool,' and you'll say 'smashing' or something British that means we can drop it."

"Sounds smashing," Ezra smiled, relieved we were finding our own language to discuss the hard things. "I admit, I anticipated a bigger fight from you."

"Best time to coerce me into something I don't want to do is when I'm still in my pajamas at noon. Apparently I have no pride anymore, so sure. Why not let Bev say her piece? If it helps her be more functional, great. She's my mama, and I've never turned my back on her. I'm not about to start now."

"I'm proud of your mature stance on things. I know your mother will be happy to hear it, too." He crossed his right ankle over his left knee. "Now for some work talk. A few members of the council would like to set a date for you taking the stone to the next country. Lumipad would be next, and they're in desperate need. Their drought started only a month after Silo's, and things are quite bleak there. Not to mention the problems in the other countries."

I was about to answer, but Von chimed in first. "No work's happening today, Ezra. Ollie was firm on that. You and Danny can drum up a plan that makes sense for everyone, but today October's taking a day off. That means no conversations about work." He sat back in his chair, staring down the boss man who was basically his surrogate father.

"It matters if the Omens collapse. She only just got feeling back in her legs. Today's for rest. Tomorrow we can reap to get the numbers back up *if* she feels up to it."

Ezra looked out of sorts at the mild chastisement, so I met his gesture of flowers with one of my own. "Do you want to stay and take a day off with us? Something tells me you don't get many of those. We just started the second *Evil Dead* movie. I'm not sure Mariang has the stomach for it, though."

"Nor I, though it has been a long week." He leaned forward and rested his face in his hands, sighing out too many decades of wear. "It's been a long few weeks."

I took my time standing and used the table for support, making my way to his side of the table to place my hand on his back. Slowly I rubbed his spine, hopefully showing him that my house was a safe place for him, even if it wasn't a haven for me anymore. "Looks like it's been a long life. I've never seen someone with so much on their plate. I don't know how you're juggling it all." My eyes rested on the pink declarations of love and happiness on the counter in the stein. "And yet you still find the time to bring me flowers? You're taking care of Bev when you have no idea who she'll turn out to be by the end of it all. If there's anyone who needs a movie night with his family, it's you." I reached down and held his hand without the note of hesitation, due to my awesome gloves. "Three of your kids are having a movie day. Come be irresponsible with us."

Ezra looked up at my face, his eyes searching mine for

the solace I was promising. "How could any father say no to such an offer? Thank you, dear. That sounds like just the right amount of good medicine."

I took a chance and ruffled his hair, gasping through my giggle at the scandal of Ezra with his perfect blond Ken doll hair out of place. He laughed, and the sound was melodious. He stood and offered me his elbow, leaving his hair disheveled just to entertain me. "Shall we?"

"Thanks. I can mostly walk, but it's not so graceful."

"Von?" Ezra glanced over his shoulder to the messy-haired boy who didn't follow us.

Von took out his cigar apologetically. "I'll be back. Gotta make a run to the store in town. You want anything, October?"

The lack of a nickname wasn't lost on me. We were polite now, which perhaps was better than fighting, but it sure as Sunday wasn't us. We'd lost our fun, forfeiting it to reality, which was nothing short of sad. I loved our child-ishness, but now it was broken, and there we stood – two adults. "No, thank you. But I know Mason's hungry. Would you mind picking him up something? Danny's probably hungry too."

"Of course. Is there anything you want for *you*?"

"I've got flowers. What else could there possibly be?"

Von begged me with his eyes. "Please. Please let me do something."

"You've done enough." I wasn't being cold, though I'm sure I could've sounded harsh if I'd wanted to. But it was true. Von had done enough to snap me out of the idiotic crush I knew I couldn't have on him. He'd done enough to remind me of just how stupid my hang-ups were. Try as I might, no part of anyone's life could be allowed to be perfect. People were messy, and you had to take them as such. My world wasn't safe, and I'd been pretending that playing with monsters wouldn't come back to bite me. That white carpet would never dare to stain.

Von left, dejected. I tried to put our fight out of my mind as Mason helped me to sit back down on the couch. He took Von's spot on the floor so Ezra could sit next to me on the cushion.

I felt someone watching me, but I didn't see anyone. The eerie feeling came from behind me, but when I turned, no one was there.

Ezra adjusted his shirt, as if the absence of his suit jacket made him feel out of sorts. He squinted at the screen. "So is there a plot I've missed, or is it just going to be... Oh, I see. Oh, my. That's unfortunate. Oh, how dreadful."

I tried not to giggle too loudly at Ezra's British mannerisms and conservative assessments of the over the top gore that only ever entertained me. It wasn't quite the Brady Bunch, but I was home, and for now, that helped erase enough of the bad things for me to find a portion of my smile again.

37

SEXY AND STILL INNOCENT

on was gone a few hours, but I sure as Sunday wasn't going to be the one to voice my concern. When he walked through the door, I breathed a sigh of relief. He gave me a nod toward the kitchen, so I got up off my place on the couch between Ezra and Ollie. My brother had woken when Ezra shouted, "Oh, goodness!" at a particularly violent scene. Totally precious.

I followed Von into the kitchen and helped him unpack the groceries no one had asked him to pick up. "I didn't know you were going grocery shopping. I would've given you money."

"Please, I'm almost as rich as you are now, and I haven't had any time to spend a dime. Least I could do was deal with Deli Frank so you didn't have to." He pinched the bridge of his nose. "That's not true. The least I could've done was not be such a wanker to you yesterday. And this is the first time I've picked up the bill for groceries. You're always footing the cost for Mason and me. That's not proper." He shook his head as he pulled out a jar of peanut butter and placed it in my cupboard on the wrong shelf. "I don't know why I was like that yesterday to you. Ollie gave me a speech that terrified me to my very soul. And I saw your face when Katrina was with me. You looked... I dunno. I just know I made you look like that, and it dawned on me that we were already married. I guess I freaked out a little."

"A little?"

"I'm trying to apologize here, October."

I hated it when he called me by my regular name. There was no tease, no flirt, no familiarity. I slowly put groceries away as I thought on my response. "You told the guys about the scar on my thigh. That was private. You made them think we were hooking up, and I've worked hard to make sure I was never that girl for them. Everyone's always changing partners and hooking up. I don't want to be in that rotation. It's hard to be taken seriously or even feel like you have a true friend in the mix when everyone calls you 'Bait'." I paused, waiting for my courage to rally to make it through the rest of my speech. "You were different. You were supposed to know all that, but you used me for a laugh. Now they all know I have ugly thighs. And the hot foreign guy was the one to tell them." I recalled the feel of Von's lips on the inside of my thigh and shivered. "That moment? That time when you saw my scar and still looked at me like I wasn't a beauty pageant failure? I felt beautiful for that whole moment, like the ugliest parts of me weren't so bad that I'd always be alone. I don't know why you took that moment away. It was precious to me, and now it's garbage."

Von swallowed thickly, not looking at me as he took a bunch of bananas out of a bag. "I suppose if I told you that moment meant a lot to me too, you wouldn't want to hear it."

I kept my voice quiet, without any hint of biting anger. I tried to be matter-of-fact, so we wouldn't devolve into a full-on fight. "I don't need you to lie to make me feel better, no. If it meant so much, you wouldn't have used it to sell me out. You don't throw away the things that matter, and you threw me away without a blink."

Von nodded, looking down at the counter while he gripped the edge of it, as if hoping the Formica would tell him what to say. "I don't want to get married. I'm a vampire. Everyone tries to skate around that, but one day I *will* turn. I'll leave everyone I love behind and not recall any of the people who were dear to me." He pursed his lips as he kept his eyes trained on the counter. "Even if I did want to be married, that's not in the cards for someone like me."

I blinked at his swift left field topic shift. "O-kay," I said slowly. "I don't actually think Katrina's ready to settle down just yet. So it won't be as big of a letdown as you're thinking for her."

Von looked up at the ceiling in exasperation and then whirled around to face me. "You don't get it. I wanted to have sex with Katrina because I knew I couldn't be with you. The last time I went to Katrina's I couldn't... we didn't..." He motioned to his lap, embarrassed. "It wouldn't..." He cleared his throat. "I came back here because I wanted to be with you. I knew I couldn't fall asleep in Katrina's bed. I only went there in the first place so I wouldn't accidentally blurt out that you and I belong together, and that I only ever want to be naked with you."

My eyes widened as the graphic image danced in my vision. "I didn't know you felt that way."

"Are you joking? Do you think it's every woman I take into the bath?"

"That was because I over-reaped."

Von shook his head in exasperation. "Oh, love. You're daft if you think what drove me to get into that tub with you wasn't the kind of lust you should slap me for." He squinted at me. "You really didn't think that was something special?"

I was flustered at his direct questions, and tried to scratch my hands, but the gloves kept me from cutting my skin. I wasn't sure how I felt about that. "Of course it was a big deal to me, but you're more experienced at that kind of thing."

"I've never had a bath with a woman, but I think about it now when I should be out being young and stupid with Katrina or Rachel or any number of women I don't have to care about. I should be taking advantage of what little time I have left! *You* did this to me!"

My mouth fell open. "Are you having a stroke or something? If you're trying to say something to me, just say it. Don't pick a fight with me so you don't have to grow up."

He cleared his throat, recalling the trail of his argument. "When you were gone with Finn... Finn!" he accused, his temper flaring. "When you were gone with *Finn*, nights were the worst. I'm not a full vampire. I still sleep! And I had to sleep without you. I hate that I'm getting to the point where I need you, that I need *us*." He turned back to the bag of groceries that was only halfway unpacked. "The look on your face when Katrina was on my lap? I saw the same thing there. That somehow we already belonged to each other, that you're bloody Mrs. Brady, and I'm reading the paper at the table, watching you be sexy in a housedress while our six kids play and dream up mischief! I can't give you that, but that's exactly where we are!"

I held up my hands in surrender, eyes wide. "Whoa. Maybe you need some of my meds. That's what made you be so mean?"

"Obviously!"

"You realize you made all that up in your own head, right?"

Von looked over his shoulder and glowered at me. "I saw your face. You can't deny that."

"Okay, yes. I'll own up to my face. I wasn't expecting you to jump back in with Katrina so quickly."

"You looked like I'd just shot your puppy! I don't want that on my conscience. I'm not going to stay me forever. I have to enjoy life while I can still call it mine. I can sleep with whoever I want!"

I crossed my arms over my chest. "Who's stopping you?"

"You are!" Von shouted. "With your looks and your face that keeps asking me why I'm not at the party with you instead of Katrina. Every time I give you just a little nip of a kiss, my whole body's screaming for more. You're a dangerous one, and you know it. You know exactly what you do to me, and you just keep doing it!"

"Doing what?"

He waved his hand toward my form, as if he was afraid to look directly at my body. "Being all sexy and still inno-cent. You know you're driving me mad! Stop drawing me in. I can sleep with Katrina or whoever I want!"

"You're cracked. Totally gone. You can go off with Katrina or any other of my friends. What's it to you if it makes me unhappy? I'll get over it, which is why I didn't say anything to you about it. You didn't have to be so mean to me. I know you're not really Mr. Brady." I don't know why my voice sounded so sad on that last note. We both knew we were just friends. I wanted a Mr. Brady who was passionate about me, who loved my scars and didn't throw me under the bus when he had an insecure moment. Von wasn't that guy. I wanted him to be, but he just plain wasn't.

"Yeah? Well, apparently *I* don't know that I'm not Mr. Brady!" His eyes were wild as he dipped his hand into a grocery bag and pulled out a curvy vase wrapped in tissue paper. "I don't buy rubbish like this! But I know you deserve flowers in a real vase, not a beer stein. I'm at the store, stocking your fridge with things I know you like – almond milk instead of regular milk, whole wheat bread that's got so many seeds and nuts, there's hardly any bread to it – and I just put this into my cart. I put it into my cart! You know who does cracked things like that? Married men! Mr. Brady, that's who!"

I didn't care what kind of meltdown he was having. I arrested the vase from his hands before he dropped it by talking too animatedly. "You bought me a vase?" I took the tissue paper off and saw it was clear glass with a row of teal circles lining the bottom. It had a feminine, curvy shape to it, and I couldn't stop staring as I turned it over in my hands. Without a word, I filled it with water and set it on the table, transferring my beautiful pink carnations from the stein to the vase in the middle of the round cream-topped kitchen table.

The whole room was transformed. I wasn't a kid in a grownup's house. I was a woman in her home. I turned the flowers and played with the petals, shifting them so there were no bald spots in the bouquet. "So pretty."

Von's voice was softer this time. "See? And I knew you

would like it. There was a pink vase at the store, but I knew you'd do that face!" He pointed at my grimace.

"You bought me a vase," I repeated, finally meeting his gaze. "Thank you. It's so beautiful."

After a few beats, he broke eye contact, his palm rubbing his forehead as he looked down at his feet. "I'm so sorry about last night. I was trying to push you away by bringing Katrina into your bedroom. I didn't mean to ruin your carpet. I got the stain out by the way, but I completely broke your world last night. I shouldn't have done that. Everyone takes away from you. I shouldn't have been that guy."

My voice came out barely above a whisper. "Why were you that guy?"

"I was afraid you were getting confused, but it was me. *I* got confused. I forgot that you're my best friend, and I treated you dreadfully. I'm utterly sick about it."

I didn't know what to say to that. I didn't want to hold a grudge, but shrugging it all off seemed insincere. So I went with a nod, which as it turns out, was on the furthest reach of all I was capable of saying.

"How are you feeling?" Von asked. Before I could open my mouth to answer, he spouted, "And don't say 'I'm fine.' I truly can't take that rubbish today."

"Well, you took my answer, so now I have to actually think about it."

Von glowered at me. "That's the whole point of me asking in the first place."

I wasn't sure what to say, now that my tried and true response had been taken from me. Ever since I'd come into the living room, I'd felt someone watching me. Some odd presence I didn't know how to equivocate. I did my best to ignore the feeling that I was crazier than even medication could fix.

I fiddled with the carnations, pulling a few up an inch so the whole thing stood taller. "The medication messes me up, so I sorta feel like I'm outside of my skin, but it'll wear off. I'm sorry for scaring you. I didn't mean to let you see that. My room's important to me. Probably more important than it should be. It's stupid for me to love something that much."

"No, it was stupid of me to wreck something you love that much."

I shrugged in response.

When Von didn't get a fight from me, he pushed on with all that had been brewing in his mind. "You went through a lot to get that room. I knew you didn't like food or drinks in there, so I did it to make you mad. I didn't know... But I should've. I know it doesn't look like it, but I care about you, Peach. I understand you enough to know how to push your buttons. That's all I meant to do – to push your buttons in hopes I'd push you away, not push you clear over the edge. I want you to find someone who can actually stay human long enough to give you a good life. With everything in me, I want to be Mr. Brady for you, but I don't have that option. I'm temporary."

I looked up at him, my voice thick with emotion that threatened to make itself known. "You called me 'Peach'."

Von's hands jammed into the pockets of his worn jeans. "I always call you 'Peach'."

"No, you called me 'October' today, and you called Katrina 'Peach'."

"You know I only did that to push you away."

"Well done. Worked like a charm. Broke my heart a little bit," I admitted quietly.

"I didn't want that."

"Yes, you did. I liked when you called me cute names, but it's ruined now. *We're* ruined."

"If 'Peach' is tarnished, let me think up a new nickname." A hint of the smile I loved toyed with the corners of Von's mouth, making him look handsome instead of haunted. "What if I started calling you sweet-ums?"

"I wouldn't answer."

"How about love muffin?"

"I'd think you were hungry. I wouldn't even know you were talking about me."

"What about honey lips?"

"What about shut up?" I countered, my face breaking into the sliver of a smile I'd needed. We stared at each other for a long minute before my smile fell into disrepair. "None of it matters. If you wanted to put distance between us, just spill something on my carpet. Apparently I'll go insane, and any confusion will be cleared right up. Katrina never looked more appealing than when compared against this cold mess." I'd meant to play it off as a joke to make light of the situation, but the truth of it all hit me over the head harder than I was ready for. "She's the peach now. I've got to... See you in there," I said as I made to leave the kitchen for the living room. I wanted to lose myself in a good screamfest where the problems were simple. "Who's going to cut my arm off with a chainsaw?" is a far sight smaller problem than the too many issues Von and I had stacking up between us.

Bruce Campbell can fix this. Bruce Campbell can fix anything.

Von caught my arm as I passed him. He pulled me closer and moved his hands to my hips, surprising me when he lifted me up to sit on the counter so we were eye to eye. Only I couldn't look at him. I could barely look at myself.

Von tapped his finger under my chin until I had no choice but to soak in the concern on his face. "There's no comparison. You know I'm madly in love with you. You're always my peach, soft and sweet. I should never have called her that."

My words choked out of me in a whisper that made my eyes fog over. "You hurt me on purpose. Your love hurt me. It wasn't supposed to do that."

Von tangled our fingers together, holding them between us as he leaned his forehead to mine. "Don't let me push you away," he begged in a whisper so quiet, I had to press my cheek to his so I could hear him. "It's you. It's only ever been you. Give me time to get there."

I hesitated, and then nodded, knowing that he would have to be far more patient with me in the long run. My issues ran deep, and I knew that even though he'd been childish, Von was worth being patient for. He smelled like mint with a hint of cologne and cigars.

"You're wearing cologne," I observed quietly. "That's new. It smells nice."

Von swallowed hard, meeting my eyes with an uncharacteristic note of insecurity. "I thought it was the Mr. Brady thing to do. You're the kind of woman who should be with a man who wears cologne."

"I am?" I brushed my nose to the side of his neck to inhale the scent I'd been worried I'd have to live off the memory of. The smell of Von's skin was there beneath the faintly sweet note of his cologne, and the mixture was utterly bewitching.

"You're confusing me again," he admitted. His eyes closed as he tilted his chin back, inviting me to be a perfect glutton and smell him as much as I wanted. His arms snaked around my hips, my legs parting as he drew us closer. He was standing in my body space, taking up residence in a place I didn't allow trespassers. He looped my legs around his waist. "I need you, Peach." His eyes closed, his eyebrows knitted together as if being so close to me was physically painful.

I knew the feeling well.

His words came out a pained whisper. "Don't let me do this. Don't let me kiss you."

My eyes widened, taking in his desperation with confusion. "Von?"

He reached up and thumbed my lower lip, studying it with a longing that drove a man to do dangerous things. "Don't let me wreck us."

Von's perfect lips were soft, insistent and everything I hadn't been expecting in that moment when they closed the breath of a gap between us and caressed mine. I squeaked my surprise and then lost myself in the kiss that took my senses and set them on hyper drive.

The hairs on the back of my neck stood as the colors in the room began to melt like dripping candles. The pink of the carnations blurred into a brush of paint across my closed eyelids as my lips parted to finally let Von in.

FIRST KISS, WEDDING, AND HONEYMOON

It was stupid, and I knew it from the first time I'd labeled my feelings for Von as a crush. He would crush me with his roguish smile and blasé attitude about relationships. He would steal my heart, step on it and then somehow get me to apologize.

I tried to hold onto the kitchen as the room started tilting at Von's sensual gasp into my mouth. He had one arm around me, pressing me tight to him, and the other cupping the underside of my thigh that was hooked around his hip.

"Oh, what is this?" he groaned.

I tugged on his hair, anchoring myself to him as my house started lifting into the air. We were spinning at odd angles, tilting and shifting through space as our kiss grew frantic, our tongues tangling and our teeth nipping while we lost our hold on reality. That familiar carbonation feeling toppled over me, starting from my lips and working its way down to my toes. Part of me was afraid I might give Von a heart attack when his head pulled back to let out a quiet bleat of distress, as Finn had done before he collapsed, but like a magnet, Von's lips found mine again. The carbonation faded, but the kiss did not.

Though my eyes were closed, I could see us. I could see myself kissing Von, wrapped around him like he was a stripper pole between my eager thighs. I glanced down and realized I wasn't wearing my pajamas anymore. The kitchen blurred with brushes of blue and glittery gold, and suddenly I was wearing a white dress with too many layers of decadence. There were folds of satin with pearls sewn into the stitching. It was strapless, but when Von caressed my shoulder, I could still feel the material of my regular shirt I was wearing in real life.

My hair was stunning in my vision, no doubt fixed up by someone who actually knew how hair should be pinned on the most special day of your life. My naked leg that wrapped around him revealed that I was barefoot. Beneath his tux that was half on him and half off, he was barefoot too. His hair was a mess of black spikes that I would never dream of taming. I didn't want to tame Von. I wanted him to be young and bold. I just didn't want him to hurt me in the process.

"So beautiful," he murmured as he gripped my back, pressing into me so we could get our fill of each other. Only we both knew we'd never be full. There would always be that desire for more that would turn into a desperate need if we were parted for too long.

Streaks of blue were paired with the glitter of gold as Von kissed me. I heard bells – chiming, tinkling bells, each one adding to the magic that felt blessed by fairies or garden gnomes or whatever else Terraway had up its sleeve.

I saw too many things while we made out on my counter. I saw us in bed, my white dress a pile of expensive material on the floor next to his tux. I gazed up at him as he caged me in with his toned body, his expectant and modestly diffident smirk shining down on me. He warmed my cold spots and made me soft and pliable where I'd been unyielding. I saw him in all of his glory and captured his lips again, relishing his intense moans that tasted like gold. I'd never tasted gold before, but in bed in that moment, I knew gold had the flavor of Von to it. We tangled in the sheets, eventually kicking them off to add to the growing pile of discarded material on the floor.

Von had been eager, but then he was hesitant, silently asking if I was ready. If he could be my first, and if I would please, please be his last. "Please?" I heard him whisper, and I couldn't tell if he was speaking in my vision, or if we were in the kitchen.

"Please," I answered, accepting everything he was, and all the things he was not. I welcomed everything he gave me, shouting to the ceiling when I couldn't bite my lip through the ecstasy any longer.

39

IT MEANT NOTHING

Von's lips left mine in a blur, and seconds later, the house stopped rotating and planted itself firmly on the grass on Lenoy Avenue. I was panting as I came down from... whatever that was. Von ripped himself away, lust flaring in his eyes as he looked at me like I had three heads.

"What the crap was that?! Why... Huh?" I asked as I came out of my haze. My hand found my forehead as the room made one final tilt.

Von was in similar disarray, his shirt pulled up at the edge, his hair sticking out more stubbornly than usual, and his lips slightly swollen with the best kiss of my life. I was grateful we both had clothes on. We stared at each other as shock gave way to revelation. If I was seeing visions when we kissed, that would mean I was... that I was in love with Von. "I didn't see anything!" we both shouted in unison.

Von backed toward the door with the same look of chilling fear that painted my face as I hopped down from the counter. My legs weren't quite as sturdy as I'd been counting on, and I collapsed like a newborn deer testing out its ability to walk unsuccessfully. "Oh!" I cried as my knees smacked to the floor.

Von darted to my side, helping me to the chair at the kitchen table with shaky hands. "You alright? You okay?" His voice lowered as his eyes darted guiltily down my form. "Did I... Did I hurt you?"

I wasn't sure if he meant our fight, the fall, or the fake honeymoon. "It was only a little painful," I admitted, and then shook my head as the deepest blush in the universe took over my body, turning me nearly purple. "Was it real? Are we real?"

Von stared at my mouth, biting his lower lip until the separation of a few inches proved too much a temptation to resist. He cupped my face and brought me in for another kiss, dipping me back into the hallucination as if we hadn't missed a beat. His tongue danced with mine as we rolled around in the metaphysical sheets that served as our only clothing. We wore passion. We wore unfettered love. We wore blue.

We were gold.

Carbonation popped and fizzed on my lips again, jolting from my tongue to his the second they started to dance together. I wanted to stay with Von like this forever. No fighting. No confusion. No running.

Then we were suddenly back in the kitchen again when Von yanked himself away from me with a choked shout of distress. He rubbed his chest as if something had slashed him there, looking up at me in shock. "What did you do? What was that?" He shook his head, clearing away the vision as best he could.

I touched my lips, feeling a current buzzing through them, as if I was electric.

As if *we* were electric.

Von dropped to his knees and bent over on all fours, breathing like a beast in pain through his gritted teeth. "Something's happening!" he eked out, reaching for my hand to squeeze it so he could get through whatever was happening to him.

I was barely myself, but tried to be in the kitchen with Von, instead of in the sheets with Mr. Von Brady. I lowered myself next to him and held his hand while his body tensed and released, tensed and released. Sweat started beading on his forehead until finally he let loose one last grunt of relief, signifying that finally whatever tore at his innards had passed. His head lolled, drooping to press his forehead to the floor, exhausted and befuddled. "Sorry. I don't know what that was. Did you feel something shredding at your insides just now?"

"No, but I'm not kissing an Omen. Maybe something

knocked loose. I don't know! Are you alright? My kiss hurt you? Like, my love actually hurt your body?"

Von shook his head. "I don't understand it. I feel different. Something's different. Was it like that with... Never mind." He sat back on his heels, steadying his breath. When I moved in to wrap my arms around him, he shook his head. Still mildly breathless, he tried to sit up straighter and hold onto some measure of bravado. "Nothing happened. Just a kiss, right? We're friends who sometimes kiss. That's not a big deal." He patted his pocket. "I need a cigar. And some air. I don't know what just happened. But nothing happened, yeah?" Von let out a nervous laugh. "I mean, something, of course, but it was nothing." He cast me a troubled look as he stood, extending his hand to help me up. "Right?"

I rubbed my forehead, not sure what to make of any of it. I felt like I'd undergone some sort of rite of passage, a physical change, though it couldn't have been. I was still fully clothed in my pajamas. "I can't really even see straight yet, so conversation and me? Not so much."

Mason meandered into the kitchen, sifting through the fridge for anything he could eat. "You guys coming in to watch the movie?"

"I said I need a cigar! Jeez!" Von shouted out of nowhere. Then he looked at us both like we'd accused him of something. "I didn't see anything!" Then he ran – actually ran out the front door, started up the car and peeled out.

"Did I walk in on something? Are you two fighting still?"

I sank into the chair at the table and gazed up at Mason, my vision still cloudy around the edges. "Huh? I said I didn't see anything! Like he's the only one allowed to not see something? Man!"

Mason's nose crinkled. "What did I ask?"

Danny came into the kitchen, making me wish for the good old days when I lived alone. "Are there any beers left-over from last night?"

"I don't know!" My volume was beyond my control. "Would everyone stop giving me the third degree? Give a girl a minute to think!"

Danny raised an eyebrow at me. "It's getting a little moody in here. Should I open a window to air out the crazy?"

"A window? Yeah. Okay."

Danny and Mason exchanged curious looks before Danny knelt down in front of me. "Look at me, kid. Let me see your eyes."

"I'm fine. Yeah. Maybe the window. It's getting hot in here."

Danny felt my forehead as he checked my pupils. He looked up at Mason with a stern expression. "I thought I told you that you weren't allowed to kiss her for a while. Then you go and pull something like this when I'm in the next room?"

"Calm down, Danny."

"Calm down? What'd you expect? You messed her up the first time. You really think you're so past it now that it's okay? We've got a job to do, Mason. Mess around after the mission. After the stone's in place you can think about it again."

Mason held up his hands. "I wasn't the one kissing her."

Danny whipped his head to me like a caricature. "October Grace, don't tell me. Don't say it. Don't tell me you kissed him. You're one of the few people I actually respect. Don't make me lose it." He stared me down until the thing I wouldn't admit to became undeniable in my eyes. Danny stood and swore with too much vigor. "Daft girl! What were you thinking? You know he's a waste! You know he's beneath you! You're a hard worker. You're smart! Tell me you didn't see a vision."

I looked up at him, scared and so very, very lost. "I didn't see anything!"

Danny swore again, seeing through my lie. "This is exactly how the smart girls go down." He pinched the bridge of his nose and squinched his eyes shut, taking in a deep breath. "Where is he?"

"He didn't see anything either. Neither of us saw anything, Danny. It was nothing. He told me it meant nothing. Just a little nothing we don't need a conversation about."

Von's words bashed me over the head with their utter dismissal. The best kiss of my life meant nothing to Von.

BUSTING BEV OUT

*N*ight fell, and for all the blow it off excuses I made for Von to the others about why he wasn't home yet, deep down I was nervous. It had been the most intense kiss of my life, and the guy was nowhere to be found. Mason changed into pajamas and made himself at home in my bedroom, making it clear I would have to face the room again.

I took my time changing into my pajamas in the bathroom, and found myself checking out the front window more often then I should've if I wanted to keep up appearances that I wasn't worried.

"He's not home yet," Danny stated, his arms crossed in disapproval at my obvious pining.

"I know."

His shoulders deflated. "But he should be. I called him

an hour ago, but nothing. He might think he can avoid you, but everyone should know they can't avoid me. He's probably at the pub in town, the pisser. I'll go see if I can't wrangle him up and bring him home."

"No. If he wants to stay out, he can stay out. No big deal. He's an adult. I just thought he would've called by now. I'm starting to worry."

Ezra had left after the third *Evil Dead* movie. I didn't want to bother him with something stupid, but it didn't sit right that Von was still gone. "I'll be back in twenty." Danny grabbed Ollie's keys off the hook, calling over his shoulder to Ollie that he was borrowing the car.

"Hey, Danny?"

"What's up, kid?"

I met his eyes as he stood with his hand on the knob, ready to go out into the night to bring Von home. "Thanks for not listening to me."

"Anytime, sis." His flicker of a smile wasn't lost, but any remnants faded when he opened the front door and found a note stuck to it with silver duct tape. He swore, his body tensed all of a sudden as if readying to spring into action. He slammed the door shut and locked it, backing up with his eyebrows raised in alarm. "Get away from the windows! Everyone pack a bag! Wake up, Mariang! Hurry!" He shoved the note to my chest and ran to Mariang, who'd been given Ollie's bed for the night so she could share it with Danny.

I read the words on the note, but scarcely comprehended them. "What is this? Is this some sort of a joke?"

"Does it look like I'm joking? Stay right here in the living room. Mason! Pack October a bag now!"

Ollie snatched the note out of my hand and read aloud as my brain began to fog over. "Bring Lumipad the stone, or your half-vamp dies. We've lost too many to wait. You have three days until we unleash the Ekeks Topside to feed." My brother looked up at me, his eyebrows tenting in the middle. "What is this?"

"The Ekeks. There must've been more of them than the ones we killed at the mall." I ran into my bedroom, not caring about the stain or that Mason was in the room as I ripped off my pajamas and pulled on jeans and a t-shirt. Mason was dressed and packed in seconds, shoving things in my backpack he guessed I might need. An endless stream of planning and fear ran through me as I whipped around my room, and then grabbed what I needed from the kitchen.

"Let's go!" Danny barked, clapping his hands at the side door for us to all get moving.

"I'm driving," Ollie ruled, snatching his keys from Danny and grabbing Mariang's bag up off the floor. We ran to the car, piling in at random as Ollie and Danny shoved our things into his trunk. Ollie peeled out of the driveway, letting the stars see exactly where we were going. "Explain," Ollie demanded after phone calls from Danny to Ezra didn't shed any more light on the subject.

Danny leaned forward in the passenger's seat. "The Ekeks and Manas are from Lumipad. They're not supposed to be Topside. They're cannibals who live off meat and *buhay* shoots. Usually the meat of animals, but as those get scarcer because of the draught and famine in Lumipad, they occasionally feed on travelers. Only royalty's powerful enough to port Topside, but somehow a few of the lessers found a way here. The three Ekeks we killed at the mall? I thought that was it. I mean, Ezra called a meeting with Sylvia to warn her to get her people in line. I'm guessing that was a wasted effort. I don't know why I just assumed those three were the only Ekeks Topside, but Von's a prize piece for them. He's only half-vamp, so he'll taste amazing to them, but he's still got his soul, so he'll feel it all. He'll put up a good fight, and the more twisted ones love that sort of thing. I'm guessing since there's a ransom note, we're dealing with the more twisted ones."

"Hurry, Ollie! Go faster!" I cried. I was sitting in the back with Mariang. Mason was wedged between us, holding both our hands so he could pull a trickle of the stress away. "This is all my fault! I didn't chase after him. I thought he needed some space, but he was kidnapped! Hurry, Ollie!"

"I'm going, hun. Hold on. We'll find him."

Danny shook his head. "The only thing we're going to find is the sagrado stone. We're taking that sucker to Lumipad and chucking it in their well. That's the only way we'll get Von back. I know the Ekeks. I know the

Manas. They don't pull punches. If they say this is what has to happen, then our best bet is to get that stone moving." Danny was sweating, rubbing his palms on his jeans as his eyes scanned the road for signs of Von's struggle.

Ollie was resolute. "I'm coming with you this time. Not out of my sight, October."

"No. Not even a question, Ollie. I mean it. Terraway's no picnic. It's dangerous. And Lumipad? We're walking into a land full of cannibals, parading around in our meat suits. You get to be home base. Make sure Von has a place to come back to."

Mason gripped my hand. "They chose Von to get to you. You're the one they want to control. That means me and probably Ollie are also targets, since we're close to you. There really isn't a safe place for Ollie." Mason cast me an apologetic look. "That means he's safest with us or in the mansion."

"In the mansion," I ruled.

Danny let out a string of swear words before he spoke coherently. "Ollie, we're busting your mum out of the facility before we go to Ezra's. Mason's right. They snatched Von because they know he's important to October."

"But Bev and I aren't close."

"You are on paper. She needs the protection of the mansion."

Now it was my turn to swear like a sailor. I punched the door of the car. "Fine. Yeah. Let's pick up Bev first." It wasn't how I'd wanted to see her. I wasn't ready for the mess, but here it was.

Ten minutes later, Ollie was pulling up to a psychiatric facility I didn't want to glance at. Sure, Bev was here now, but I knew if I didn't get myself under control, I was a couple stained rugs away from landing myself here. I leaned forward and gripped Ollie's shoulder before he and Danny left to retrieve Bev. "Ollie? Don't let me end up here."

He placed his hand over mine, firm in his conviction and in the solidarity between us that nothing had been able to shake. "Never. I'm here. I'm always looking out for you."

Then Danny and Ollie ran into the facility, taking twenty minutes too long to retrieve Bev. Mason slid me onto his lap and scooted us to the center of the backseat when the three came out to us, making room for Bev where we could.

I swear, I'm really not a person prone to sitting on men's laps.

I wasn't used to seeing Bev without buckets of hairspray and makeup. She actually looked nice without the hot pink smears across her eyelids and the clumpy mascara that fooled no one. Her hair was cut short now in a blonde pixie 'do that looked... nice on her. Her eyes weren't painted to appear perpetually wide, so she looked a little sleepy. Though it was nighttime, so she could actually have been tired.

Ollie shoved her suitcase in the trunk. Once Danny was buckled in, he drove out of the parking lot toward the freeway.

My heart pounded for several reasons, and one of those reasons was staring at me with equal amounts of longing and dread. "October Grace? I didn't think you'd come to see me, much less break me out."

I didn't have the heart to tell her I wasn't doing this for her, but for a guy who had the emotional IQ of a potato. "Of course I would. I used to come see you once a week, didn't I? Why would that change? I've just been busy with the Terraway stuff. Ezra explained all of it to you, right?"

She nodded. "Yes. It doesn't make a whole lotta sense, but I suppose that's okay. Nothing's made sense to me for a while." Bev wasn't brash. She was humble, and a little lost. I barely recognized her.

Danny turned around in his seat and asked loudly, "Did you sleep with Von?"

"What?" I stared at him like he'd just started speaking in another language. He knew the three of us had slept in the same bed. He couldn't mean...

"Sex, October! Have you and Von had sex?"

"What? No! Why would you even ask that? We only just kissed for the first time tonight."

"You're sure?"

I raised an eyebrow at him. "Pretty sure on who I've slept with, since it's a big whopping zero people on my list of conquests. You want to tone down the weirdness? Why would you even ask me that? And in front of my mama and my brother, no less."

Danny turned back around to face the front again. "Never mind. I thought you'd be able to reach him psychically, but I guess not."

"You know, there's not a thing about what you said that I don't need explained."

Danny let out a labored sigh, and gestured with his hand while he spoke. "When an Omen has sex with someone she's in love with, they can visit each other while they sleep. It's called dreamwalking. Mariang and I do it all the time."

I put my head in my hand. "I really hope this is the weirdest conversation I'll ever have. No, Von and I aren't having sex. Thanks for making me say 'sex' in front of Ollie and Bev. Really. Super swell."

"I'm just trying to find Von."

Ollie managed a small smile back at me in the rearview mirror at my admission that I was a virgin. "We'll find him, hun."

I didn't answer, and the silence draped around the car and grew uncomfortable until Bev broke it with a polite nod at Mason. "I've met you before. You were with me in the emergency room when I stepped on that glass."

Mason reached around me and shook Bev's hand. "Mason. I'm your daughter's Puller. Do you know what that is?"

Bev looked around the car in confusion. "Not really. I

probably should. How could I not know what's going on in my own daughter's life? To miss a whole world is one thing, but to miss my own daughter?" Tears welled up in Bev's eyes, and if I hadn't seen it for myself, I would've thought it impossible. Bev wept into her hands. "Tell me what a P-Puller is."

My mouth dropped open, and I was incapable of speech. Mason fielded the question for me. "Your daughter and Mariang are special. They can take the souls from people who are about to die, and it gives the person a peaceful death. After they take the souls, they give them to us. I pull the corroded souls from her. Von and I."

"Von? I remember him. The funny young man. Ezra's gardener? Guard? I don't remember. I'm sorry." She touched her forehead through her tears. "I'm not m-myself lately."

Mason reached out and picked up her hand to calm her, and I knew he was pulling to soothe her palpable ache. "It's alright. It's our fault. We dragged you out of bed. You're not supposed to be on top of everything at this hour."

"Why are we going to Ezra's? I've been trying to send him away. I think it gives the wrong message for me to show up on his doorstep like this." She motioned down to her white hospital scrubs. "He's an incredible man. He should be with someone who's good." She shook her head. "I'm a terrible person. The things I've done? I don't deserve to be in his house."

Danny answered when I was still stone cold mute. "One of the creatures from Terraway, called an Ekek, abducted Von. He's my brother, and October's other Puller. The Ekeks are targeting people October loves, so you're in danger. We're taking you to Ezra's to keep you safe."

Bev looked up at Danny and then at me, her eyes glassy with tears. "You couldn't p-possibly love me after everything I put you through."

"I... I..." I didn't know what to say. Did I love my mama? I'd never had to answer that before. The woman crying next to me sure as Sunday didn't look like my mama. Bev, I couldn't love. It hurt too much to feel anything for her, to give her that kind of power over me. But this woman? She was a completely different being, and I didn't know her well enough to decide if I could love her, if I could trust her or ever let myself need a mama again. "Ezra's," I repeated. "You have to stay with Ezra. It's the only safe place for you and Ollie."

Ollie scoffed, shaking his head as he kept his eyes on the road. "Oh, no. Nice try, kid. I'm going with you."

"Bev clearly needs you more right now." I could feel Mason pulling waves of anxiety off me. I leaned back against his solid chest to get a handle on all that loomed before me, while Mariang rubbed my back like the amazing sister she was.

"It's out of the question. You're my responsibility. If you're going straight into the lion's den, I'm not letting you go there without me."

"I went just fine without you the other times. I'm not a kid anymore, Ollie. I can handle myself."

I could hear the small smile in his voice. "That's exactly what you said your first day of junior high, but I still walked you to school every morning. You said it when you were sick that one Christmas when you were little, but I didn't leave your side until you were better. You said it your first day of work at the prison, and I still drove you to work and talked with the warden and the guards, making sure you were safe. Say what you want, but I'm far more stubborn than you are. I'm going, and you'll be an adult about it."

"But I love you," I said, wishing I could make him understand.

"And I love you." Ollie reached behind and grabbed my hand, bringing it up to rest on his chest in a hug that wasn't comfortable, but was very necessary. "It's settled. I'll always be the one who looks out for you."

I squeezed him before sitting back so he could drive more easily. Bev watched our exchange and asked for a tissue. "I don't even remember your first day of junior high. And I don't remember you being sick on Christmas. Was it nice after you got better? Did I at least get you a good present?"

"No," I answered, my tone clipped. I could feel it all bubbling under my skin like poisonous lava – the things I'd never said to confront her, but absorbed the sting and bit my tongue through. "You spent all your money getting more of your special things, so there was no food in the house."

"October," Ollie warned.

I ignored his insistence on caution. "They shut off the water the week before, so Ollie had to ask Mrs. Kitsa if we could shower in their trailer one morning before school. I went to school with wet hair and caught a cold. Then the power in the trailer got shut off, so my cold turned to pneumonia. Ollie took me to the doctor while Allie babysat after school to earn enough money to pay the heat bill so I could get better! You got me nothing for Christmas, but you got yourself a few hundred dollars' worth of crap! Total crap that you bought instead of spending anything on me. Christmas morning was spent trying not to die of pneumonia while you tried on your new clothes!" Once I started, it all spilled out. Years of pent-up fury poured out that I'd not given voice to, since I knew she couldn't have cared less if I'd confronted her.

Now she cared. She was capable of actual tears, so I let the dam break and unleashed on my mama, ignoring the emotion that streamed down her face. "You know what you said to me when I lost one of the stupid beauty pageants you made me do?"

I waited for her meek "No" that came over her hiccupped sobs.

"You said next time I'd have to try harder to be prettier.

You told me we lost because my hips were too wide and my face wasn't right. Who says that to a four-year-old girl? You got drunk that night and told me I was the second worst mistake you ever made, and that Allie was your first. Allie was my mama! You're not my mama! You were never my mama! You're the woman who threw me away, and I won't let you do that to Mariang!" Mason's arms wrapped around me, pulling harder than usual.

"October!" Ollie shouted with all the finality of a parent. "Knock it off. This isn't the time for that. Bev's fragile, so best not push her too hard. She's not the person we grew up with. She doesn't even recognize her actions! Punish her later when a therapist is there to moderate."

I looked down at my lap, trying to get ahold of myself as I seethed. "Yeah. Okay. Sorry everyone."

"Apologize to Bev."

My head snapped up at Ollie's orders, anger burning through me. "Are you joking right now?"

"That right there sitting next to you? It's not Bev. Not the one we knew. She was being poisoned, October. Her mind was warped. You haven't been here through her coming out of it. She didn't know what she was doing. She wasn't in control. Be mad all you want, but you can't treat her like she's the same person. She's not. She's just as shocked at all the stories as other people are."

Mason rubbed the nape of my neck and slid my legs to the other side so I was facing Mariang, my back to Bev. He cradled me to his chest, stroking the side of my face and resting his cheek to my forehead. "Take a break, *hani*. It's alright. It's all coming at you at once. We'll get the stone and give it to the Ekeks quick as we can. Then we'll get Von back."

"Von's gone," I whispered, my eyes locking on Mariang's. I was scared to my very soul that someone had taken him. He wasn't meant for torture, and certainly not from cannibals.

Mariang gripped my fingers with one hand and wrapped her other arm around my hip, bringing her face close to mine. She loved Von like a brother, but was trying to be strong while I freaked out. "We'll get him back. Danny and I won't stop looking. I won't reap until the day the count runs out. We'll find him, sister. We'll find Von and bring him home to you." She squeezed me. "I know how much you love him. We'll find him."

I gulped down as much of my dread as I could. Von was gone because of me. I'd kissed him, and now he would pay. If the appearance of visions was an indicator that I was in love, I knew I would take it all back in an instant if it meant Von was at home with me. I would watch him take up with Katrina and who knows who else if it would mean that he was safe.

But he wasn't safe. I didn't have any real assurances that he was even alive.

Mason tucked my head under his chin, making sure my back was to Bev so I could pretend there was one less thing that clawed at my insides and tore me into uneven pieces. I closed my eyes and pictured Von's adoring gaze in my mind, hoping with everything in me that he wasn't in pain, and that we would find each other before it was too late.

Love the book? Leave a review. Otherwise, you know, Von dies.

41

TREAT

Enjoy a free preview from *Treat*,
book five in the *Terraway* series.

The world seemed to be moving in slow motion, taking far too long for the simplest things. The drive from my side of town to Ezra's should have taken only an hour, but the universe bent itself so that the hour felt like seven hundred hours all hooked together, stretching out longer than they should.

Von was gone. We'd had the best kiss of my life, and when we both ran from the intensity of a life neither of us were anticipating, he'd been snatched up by Ekeks – a cannibalistic people from Terraway whose favorite snack was fresh vampire meat.

I tried not to think about all the body parts they might take that could still leave Von alive. I loved every part of Von, even the childish, selfish ones, and wanted him intact.

When we reached Ezra's, Danny had already apprised him of the situation over the phone on the drive. "Where's the stone?" I asked in lieu of a greeting as I marched into the house on a mission.

"It's in a lead-lined safe so it doesn't poison the minds of any humans in my home." When this answer wasn't specific enough for me, he pointed to the basement. "Downstairs, but we're waiting on Sylvia. You remember she's the Queen of Lumipad, and she can port us down and lead us to the main well with less interference from civilians. If all goes without interruption, the whole thing could be done by tomorrow night."

"That's not soon enough!" I was irate, worried that no one was taking this as seriously as they should. "Every minute that ticks by is another that Von's life is in danger. I'm not waiting around for Sylvia to manage her people. Can Lang take us? Finn? Give me a map, and I'll go by myself. No one else has to get hurt."

Ezra wasn't listening. He had Bev swept up in a hug that looked like it hurt them both with the raw emotion they couldn't suppress. "I'm so sorry you were brought in on this. I don't want you worried."

"My children. They're going to do something danger-ous? This is the country filled with cannibals, isn't it?" Her voice was barely recognizable. She wasn't brash or bossy.

She sounded afraid. Actually concerned for Ollie and me. Her southern lilt came off as a delicate Belle, and not a brash, demanding woman on the prowl to manipulate men with money. I didn't know who she was, but Ollie was right, this wasn't the Bev I knew.

"I'll be with them. I'll make sure our children come home safe. I won't leave their side." He kissed her lips, and for some reason this made me very squeamish.

"She's so small," Bev whispered. "They'll take her, and I'll never see my daughter again! Then they'll take Ollie and you. I can't sit back while that happens! I'm just starting to see my family for the first time. I can't let you all just go walking straight into danger! We're talking actual cannibals, Ezra!"

I had to get out of there. Bev never referred to me as her daughter unless there was something in it for her. The look on her face was raw, unmakeuped and earnest, and I had no idea what to make of it. I'd never seen her sincere before, and didn't know whether to be overjoyed or very, very afraid.

Ollie had the same reaction, though he'd spent more time with the new Bev. "It's alright, Bev. I'll watch October. I'll make sure we all come home. Like Ezra said, it'll probably be a day of traveling, and then we'll be right back. Easy as that." When Bev made to argue, Ollie held up his hand. "When have I ever not kept October safe?"

Bev left Ezra's embrace to wrap her arms around Ollie, squeezing him tight and shaking in his arms. I'd never seen them hug before. My mouth went dry, and I heard everything as if my ears were stuffed with cotton. Bev shook like a leaf battered by the wind in Ollie's embrace. "I remember the day you were born. I was so scared I would screw you up. Now that you're perfect and I had nothing to do with it? I can't let you die like this. You're my only boy!"

This choked Ollie and I simultaneously, and I knew I had to leave. I ran to the conference room down the hall and shut myself inside to escape land of the body snatchers, lest they come for me next. It was a complete personality change. In passing, I'd heard Bev's old school friends mention that she'd been a real sweetheart, but I never believed it. As soon as she'd run into them, they'd run straight out of our lives when they caught wind of Bev's new deranged personality. This version must've been the one they were expecting to see. The kind of woman who hugs her son and cares if her daughter gets eaten by cannibals.

I barely recognized her.

I waited out the waves of getting everything in order, holing myself up in the conference room, since I knew this was where we would all end up when things were ready to be set in motion. I heard Mason escort Bev toward the stairs to settle her in, but they stopped just outside the conference room door. "Mason, please. You have to see how dangerous this is. A land of starving cannibals? Am I the only person who cares about my children?"

Mason's voice was calm, and I could picture his kind

eyes as he remained patient with Bev. "Ezra cares about your children, and he cares about thousands of people's children in Terraway. And all this *is* for October. An Omen needs her Pullers, or she won't live very long. Getting the stone to Lumipad is the only way to keep October safe in the long run. It's a risk, sure, but it's riskier not sending her."

"But why does it have to be her?"

"Because only your family is immune to the stone's magic. Only you, October, Ollie and I suppose Allie can touch it without turning to stone. The tradeoff is that it warps your minds. That's why you were the way you were, and why October is the way she is." Mason was matter of fact about there being something wrong with me, and it made me clench my fists. I was fine. I didn't need Bev knowing my business. It was one of the many reasons I told her next to nothing about my life. That, and she never asked.

Bev's voice was small. "What way is she? I don't know the first thing about her. I'm still sorting things out. For the past who knows however many years, I remember her picking me up and taking me out for the day to make sure I had food, but I don't know anything about her."

"Maybe you should ask her."

"Have you seen the way she looks at me? She won't talk to me. I've lost my chance to know my daughter, and it's killing me! Ollie's giving me a second chance, but I know that look. October Grace won't let me in. Please, Mason. Tell me about my daughter. She trusts you."

"Well, then you already know your daughter has terrible judgment when it comes to trust and that sort of stuff."

"Please. Tell me anything."

"I'm not sure I want to get in the middle of…"

Then Bev cut him off, her voice raising hysterically. "Please, Mason! Tell me about my daughter!"

The sound of her plea shook me up and rattled around the parts of me I assumed were untouchable. I sunk to the carpet, kneeling at the door with my ear pressed to it. I didn't want to see or talk to Bev, but I'd never heard her want to know more about me – or anything about me, really. My fingertips hesitantly fluttered over the door as I let myself consider the painful, confusing and hopeful thought that maybe Bev actually did want me around.

"Okay, alright. Calm down. What do you want to know?"

"Is she happy?"

Mason let out a long and low sigh. "I don't know. She's funny, and she smiles a lot. She's the kind of girl who finds a way to get the things out of life that she wants, and I don't think that kind of person tolerates being unhappy for very long. She'll be glad when this whole mission is over. I know we all will."

"Does she have good friends?"

"No," Mason ruled. "She hides from just about everyone. Made the job so hard in the beginning. Won't let people she doesn't trust help her, so she ends up doing everything herself. Von and I do our best, but she guards herself even from us, not that I can blame her. It was harder in the beginning, but I think we're finding our way."

"Tell me more. I hate that this is all new to me."

"She's kind. Too unselfish sometimes. Not to be disrespectful, but she should've stopped going to see you years ago. She kept it up because she's a good person. The flipside of that coin is that she doesn't care about her own life. A beautiful woman like that working around inmates?"

"Has she ever been attacked by any of them?"

"Do you really think she'd admit that to me? She doesn't work there anymore, so at least that nightmare's over." He paused, and I wondered what his eyes were saying in that moment. If part of him still hated me, if any part of him was capable of forgiving me for all we'd put each other through. "You want to know about your daughter? She's incredible. That's pretty much the sum of it."

I couldn't believe Mason had such lovely things to say about me. He didn't bring up my OCD or how impossible I sometimes made things for him. He was generous with my good parts and politely covered over my ugly ones. He was turning out to be a good friend, despite all we'd been through. A layer of hurt crumbled away, and I felt one degree closer to my constant protector.

"You love her," Bev pointed out.

Mason was thoughtful as he mulled this over. "I do. I love her enough to know that I'm not good for her. Not in the way I want to be, anyway. I was married before, and I think I tried to jump back in too soon. You should know I hurt her in ways I'm too ashamed to mention to her mother."

Bev was quiet, and I feared they'd hear my heart pounding.

Just then, I heard a commanding voice coming from the foyer, calling out for me.

Read *Treat* and continue with
the next book in the *Terraway* series.

ABOUT THE AUTHOR

USA Today bestselling author Mary E. Twomey lives in Michigan with her three adorable children. She enjoys reading, writing, vegetarian cooking, and telling her children fantastic stories about wombats.

While she loves writing fantasy, dystopian, and paranormal tales for her readers, Mary also writes romance under the name Tuesday Embers, and cozy mysteries under the name Molly Maple.

Visit her online at www.maryetwomey.com, and sign up for her newsletter, so you never miss a new release.